Breathing
UNDER WATER

contents

This novel is entirely a work of fiction. The names, characters, and incidents portrayed in it are the work of the author's imagination, and any resemblance to actual persons living or dead is entirely coincidental.

Nicole J Kimzey

Website: https://www.authornjk.com

Newsletter: https://www.authornjk.com/newsletter

Instagram: https://www.instagram.com/authornicolejkimzey

Cover design: Hannah Howell, https://www.instagram.com/the.footybandit

Editing: Kaylee Mason, kaylee.j.mason@gmail.com

Dedicated to Boyfriend (my husband)

You truly are my sunshine.
This book breathes because of you.

Water is the essence of life; make your life
an essence of positivity and joy.
-unknown

CHAPTER 1

Samantha

"SO THIS IS YOUR two weeks' notice?" The shock on my boss's face is the most movement I've seen on it in weeks. Maybe months. Her too-frequent Botox injections, paired with the yearly facelifts, have made it harder and harder for her face to move, so it's always surprising when her face actually registers an emotion. The skin on her face is pulled as tight as her personality.

Before I respond, I subtly check my watch. Five more minutes. "For the third time, Clarice, I'm not quitting. I'm taking an extended leave of absence. I'm stepping back and taking a break. Trying to find a life outside the walls of this office." In my profession, remaining calm under stressful situations is essential. But this isn't stressful. It's ridiculous. Everything is with Clarice.

She's the kind of person who, with a to-do list of 100 things, would claim that all 100 are a "top priority." It's exhausting, and today I don't feel any obligation to cater to her dramatics. So I throw some dramatics right back at her.

"Clarice, I can understand why my decision might take you by surprise. I've only sent weekly emails the last two months about this very thing." Is my voice laced with sarcasm as I speak? Yes. But I don't care anymore. "All of my emails explained that I would not be available during my leave of absence and provided my expected departure date, progress on all my cases, and information about whether they would be wrapping up or getting reassigned to any of the other—very capable—attorneys in the firm." It's the least professional I've ever sounded inside this office. And while it feels completely foreign to me, I don't change my tone when I go on. "But I recognize that I probably should have given you more information. Or maybe I should have had more than three conversations with you directly going over the information in the emails." I say all of this while never breaking eye contact with her.

My words, not shockingly, don't register with Clarice. I look at my watch again, trying not to draw attention to the action. The phone call will be coming in less than two minutes, which means I have less than two minutes left in this office that has come to feel more like a cage. Just the thought of leaving for a few months makes my shoulders think about relaxing for the first time in what feels like years. I can't wait until they actually relax.

I remain unruffled and professional as I stand in front of her overly large, polished desk, with posture that makes me appear five foot eight instead of my actual five foot five in a perfectly starched, white button-up shirt and dark-gray pencil skirt that is neither too tight nor too loose. It's all about balance in this profession, especially as a woman. Balancing everything so that the scales tip in my favor is second nature to me now. I've spent the last eight years at this office, and most of law school, perfecting the skill.

Clarice shifts in her oversized leather chair and reaches up to touch her excessively processed, platinum-blonde hair that belongs on someone half her age. "Where can we get ahold of you while you're gone?" Why am I not surprised that Clarice asks this? It's one step forward—because for the first time since I entered her office today, or even the last several weeks, she has finally acknowledged that I will actually be gone—but then immediately two steps back—because she obviously hasn't grasped that my leave of absence will not include any contact with the firm. At all. In any capacity.

"When I am better situated in my new location, I will let you know." It's a lie. I'm not sure I've ever told one of those to my boss before. I'm expecting my heart rate to soar, or guilt to set in, but neither occurs. I simply grow even more impatient for the feeling of the sun on my face and the sand in my toes.

"Samantha, you are invaluable to this firm. Since hiring you right out of law school eight years ago, you quickly rose through the ranks to become the highest-billing lawyer out of over fifty attorneys in our beloved firm . . ." I tune out her words because it's the same speech she's used to manipulate me ever since I was hired. I used to beam under the praise of this speech; I would soak it up like it was water for my sun-parched soul; it's a speech I can recite in my sleep. But now I can't stand it. Clarice hasn't seen that beam from me in years, and she's never noticed.

I glance at my watch again, this time not caring if she sees me do it. Any second now . . .

Somewhere my brain processes that Clarice is going off script. ". . . and that's why I'm pleased to let you know that at our Board of Directors meeting last week, we all decided to make you a partner. You'll be receiving the formal offer within the week. The firm would become Parker, Jenkins, Snow, and . . . Turner." She adds my last name with a voice that drips like a thick, sticky sap, creating an uncomfortable sensation somewhere inside me. Again, she doesn't notice that her words don't thrill me. She thinks she's offering me a golden chalice.

I can't blame her. The thing is, she knows that since my first semester of law school, my version of the golden chalice was making full partner. It's what I've been working so hard for. And I didn't want just any partnership—I wanted one at this firm. Parker, Jenkins, and Snow is the most prestigious law firm in Boston, and it was the only one I applied to coming out of law school. I was top of my class and specialized in mergers and acquisitions specifically to be an asset to this firm. I knew what I wanted, and I went after it. It's been my plan since day one.

But the last year has taken a toll on me. I need to breathe. Why can't I breathe? I know my body is breathing, but my soul, most definitely, is not. I didn't even know souls could breathe until I noticed mine had stopped. Maybe that sounds too dramatic?

Put in simpler terms, I need to remind myself why I love my job. I need to become reacquainted with myself and figure out a balance that hasn't existed for a long time. Somewhere along the way, I learned to despise Sam Turner, the fun-loving girl who sings off-key karaoke loud and proud and would do anything on a dare, and embrace Samantha Turner, the lawyer other firms come to dread and clients come to hire. The money is good. More than good. But that was never what interested me when I chose this profession. At least, that's what I think I remember.

I focus back on Clarice's offer and form the best reply I can right now. "Clarice, the Board's confidence in me is flattering, and it would be an honor for anyone to receive an offer for a full partnership at such a prestigious firm. I will look it over when I get back." I'm sure my words stun Clarice; she most likely expected me to drop to my knees weeping and thanking her for the position I have wanted for so long.

But if she's stunned, I can't tell. I guess the Botox only lets one emotion show on her face per fiscal calendar.

Then my phone rings. Right on time.

When I answer, I am back to my usual tone of voice: all business. "This is Samantha Turner. What can I do for you?" I pause while I listen. "Yes, thank you for getting back to me on that. What's the timeline for getting you that documentation?" I point to my phone and mouth to Clarice as I leave her office, "I need to take this call, but thank you for the offer."

I head straight for the elevators, all while being very engaged in my phone call, adding the occasional "I understand" accompanied by sympathetic nods. I push the down button, and when an elevator door opens, I get on and select the button for the ground floor. Once the doors close and I'm alone, I give a small sigh and keep talking into the phone, "Thanks, Steph. I owe you one. You're the best."

From the other end of the call, Steph rattles off a reply with her usual flare. "Sure, Sweetie Cakes." She has a new name for me every time we talk. Her next three sentences come out as one word.

"You're-welcome-You-owe-me-nothing-And-you're-right-I-am-the-best." I can hear both the smile on her face and the sincerity in her voice, and it pulls at my heart a little to know I won't see her for a couple of months while I'm gone.

Stephanie has been my roommate for the last two years; she's my complete opposite, but I love that about her. I knew exactly how the conversation with Clarice would go today, and I planned my exit strategy accordingly. I didn't care what Steph said, only what time she called: 3:45. Steph may act like a free spirit with no sense of direction, but I knew exactly when my phone would ring.

The elevator doors open to the lobby, and I step out as I give Steph the same speech I give her every morning, "While I'm gone, don't have too much fun!"

She laughs as she dishes out her standard reply. "And while you're gone, please TRY to have fun!" And then she hangs up. She really is the best. She's been trying to get me to loosen up ever since she moved in. Unfortunately her efforts have been in vain. Until now.

I walk through the lobby, heading straight for the front door, my stiletto heels clicking on the Italian marble. As Randy, the doorman, opens the door, I give him a smile and exit the building. I step outside, take a deep breath, and inhale something I haven't in years.

Freedom.

CHAPTER 2

Samantha

I HEAD TO MY car, where my bags are already packed and waiting for me, and drive straight to the airport. I hired a service that will take my car back to the parking garage at my apartment building sometime later today.

Both my flights—one commercial to a larger island and the other via puddle jumper to my final destination—are uneventful, which is how I like it.

I land, grab my luggage, find my rental car, and start driving to where I will be spending the next six weeks.

I've rented one side of a beachfront duplex on a small Caribbean island. The island isn't considered a tourist destination, so it won't be crawling with people. Since I'm craving a quiet life, that's an added bonus. The condo is on the other side of the island from the airport, but since the island is so small, it only takes a quick twenty minutes to get there.

I pull up, step out into the sun, and get my first in-person look at the condo. The exterior is a soft Caribbean pink with white shutters and trim, and there is a turquoise front door for each side of the duplex. As I pull my luggage up the stone pathway, I can tell that the palm trees and large floral bushes are trimmed and taken care of, and I'm impressed with how clean and well kept the house looks.

I feel like I'm standing on the threshold of something new. At least I hope I am. So, I open the front door and step into my new, albeit temporary, home. It could not be more different than what I am accustomed to.

I'm used to polished, cherrywood desks; overly large and ostentatious conference-room tables surrounded by perfectly aged, leather-bound armchairs, all built to create the embodiment and smell of money; and rooms with fixtures made of antique, polished brass designed to showcase stability and power. The clients we entertain in those areas wear William Fioravanti suits or haute couture fashion at its highest level.

The type of people who come here, on the other hand, are most likely wearing flip-flops and sunscreen. I take in the space: it has high, vaulted ceilings; clean, white cabinets; soft-gray walls; and decor that puts off a distinctly beachy, Caribbean vibe. I have no idea what to make of it. Even the couch, looking so soft and comfortable, makes me feel decidedly *uncomfortable*. It's so different from what I'm used to. But I guess I'm here to make some changes, so different is okay.

I pull my luggage through the main area, which includes a family room, kitchen, and dining area, and down a small hallway off the dining room, where I find the owner's suite. It has a king-size bed with a clean, white comforter; nightstands; and a large wicker chair in the corner.

Once I unpack and look at the rest of the condo, which consists of two more bedrooms and a bathroom down a hall off the kitchen, I open the back door and walk onto the deck.

The deck is completely picturesque. The table and chairs in the center promise comfort—not only for mealtimes but also for late, lazy conversations after the food is long gone. Two lounge chairs holding island-colored pillows are against the rail, looking out at the ocean and begging to be sprawled out on. I walk to where a hammock is hanging in the corner, gently swaying in the warm island breeze, and turn to look at the back of the house. I see two sets of French doors, each leading into one side of the duplex. Between the French doors sits a BBQ grill, looking ready to conjure up some fresh fish, shrimp, or steaks for those wanting to embrace the pace of island life. Everything here speaks of recreation and relaxation—two things I may have forgotten how to do entirely.

If I wanted to, I could walk down a set of four stairs and enjoy the duplex's private beach, which stretches for about fifty feet until it meets the clear, blue waters of the Caribbean ocean. But I simply admire the dazzling sunset from where I stand, watching the water transform to sparkling crystals as the low sun kisses the surface with its light.

The beauty is almost too much for my senses to digest, so I close my eyes and inhale deeply. Would I ever get used to these new sights and smells?

As I exhale and take another deep breath, my phone rings—the new phone I bought about four weeks ago in preparation for my self-imposed exile. It's a cheap flip phone with no internet and a new number that only two people have: Steph and the property management company I'm renting this condo from. Yes, that's how desperate I was to get away from the office, Clarice's nonstop calling, and the unthinkable number of daily email notifications I would have been facing otherwise.

Having a new number will really only affect the law firm's ability to get ahold of me. With how little I talk to my mother, I'm sure she will never even realize I've left the city. I have no siblings to miss me. My friendships with everyone but Steph have fallen by the wayside due to my work schedule, and my relationship with Trevor ended over nine ugly months ago.

I take one more deep breath, open my eyes, and walk inside to answer the call.

"This is Samantha Turner. What can I do for you?" I hate that I still sound like I'm in the office.

"My Sweet Little Samantha! This is Cheryl from Beach Front Properties." This is how she has greeted me on all of the five or six phone calls we've had to set up my rental contract. The smile in her voice always takes me by surprise and soothes me. We've never met in person, so I don't know what she looks like and I honestly have a hard time imagining a single thing about her. She sounds sweet enough to be a sixty-year-old grandma but talks with the style and speed of a twenty-year-old. Oh, and then there is her use of old-fashioned phrases, like "my sweet little Samantha," that make me think she's ninety-nine. I actually love it all. Thinking back, she's probably the main reason I rented from Beach Front Properties. In my profession, every phone call is tense and analytical and lacks any warmth. Cheryl is different, and it makes me want to draw out our conversations so that I can hear her talk longer. "I just wanted to reach out and make sure you got to the condo and everything is to your liking." Cheryl doesn't even know what a balm she is to the emptiness I've been feeling.

"I appreciate your call. I do need some clarification about the property." Why do I have to sound so cold and businesslike? I've been talking like this for so long, maybe I don't know how to be different. "I'm concerned that there are no dead bolts on the doors, and I can't find the washer and dryer."

"Darling!" There it is again, the adorable way she addresses me. She says "darling" like I'm her four-year-old daughter who has just asked a silly, yet adorable, question. I look up and see myself in the mirror across the room. I'm smiling. Smiling! She continues, "There isn't a need for dead bolts on the island. We don't get many unwanted house guests, and even then, most are pretty harmless."

"Most are pretty harmless?" Something about that is unsettling.

"Sweetie, it's nothing you need to worry about. But if it will make you feel safe, I can get dead bolts installed right away."

My profession has trained me to dig until I receive answers. Cheryl didn't answer my last question, but before I press for more information, she goes on.

"As for a washer and dryer, you share them with the adjacent condo. They are in a small room that you both access from the back deck." That must be the single door I saw next to the BBQ grill.

"Who lives in the adjacent condo?"

"Oh my word!" Cheryl suddenly has extra pep in her voice. "The nicest people. You're going to *adore* them!" She really hangs on the word "adore," and I become quite certain that my new neighbors are old grandmas that will be baking me cookies all the time. "Now, I will get those dead bolts installed for you right away—I'm hoping by tomorrow—but you better let me know if you need anything else."

"Actually, I don't have any food yet, and it's getting close to dinner time. Where can I go to get a bite to eat?"

"Sam's."

"Wait . . . what? Did you say *Sam's*?"

"Yep. Best food and best drinks on the island. But there's not a lot of competition for that title—so take that for what it's worth. If you drive down the shoreline about two miles, you couldn't miss it if you tried." She laughs a little at what I assume is the idea that someone could miss Sam's. "On another topic, I've been so excited for you to get to the island in the hopes that . . . well, . . . would you want to have lunch with me someday?"

"You want to go to lunch with me?" This feels as foreign to me as everything else on this island has so far. "Do you need some legal advice?"

"Oh, heavens no! I adore you and thought we could go on a lunch date and have some girl talk." She says the last two words like they are a closely guarded government secret that has to be slightly whispered in order to be uttered.

I'm stunned for so many reasons. First, since I turned twenty-four, I have only had lunch dates with those interested in Samantha the Lawyer, not Samantha the Person. My lunch dates consist of contracts on mergers, strategizing the hostile takeover of a lesser-than company, or other completely non-personal topics. Second, Cheryl adores me? What have I ever said to make her adore me? I am usually praised as being efficient or punctual—but I'm never adored.

Now, after only two hours on the island, someone adores me and wants to go on a lunch date just to have some girl talk?

"Cheryl, I would actually really love that." This time I don't even have to look in the mirror to know I have a smile on my face.

"Oh my word, I'm so happy! We will keep in touch about that. For now I'll start working on getting those dead bolts on. Until then, ta-ta."

I don't remember the last time I heard "ta-ta" as a farewell greeting, and I find myself wondering—again—how old Cheryl is.

I'll be processing that phone call for a while.

And *Sam's*? Really? I should have asked what my other choices were. I feel . . . I don't know how I feel, but I don't think I'm ready to face a place called Sam's. That's the name I've been running from for years.

My stomach picks right then to growl at me. I guess Sam's will do for tonight. And I guess it's also time for me to change into something more casual.

CHAPTER 3

Deacon

As I WALK INTO Sam's, I find the usual scene. Boisterous people talking over one another, telling fish stories and slapping backs in the way friends do, the jukebox in the corner blaring a song, and Marco at the bar, making everyone feel welcome. Sam's is many things, but quiet is not one of them.

The large areas to my left and right are filled with people sitting at tables, eating, drinking, and relaxing, but I walk straight ahead to where the bar is. As I do, everyone greets me in the customary way. "Deeeeeeek!" I swear every time they call my name, it gets a little longer. After living on the island for eighteen months, I should be used to it, but I'm not. It still makes me chuckle a little. A loud "EEEEEEEK!" comes from somewhere over in the corner by the jukebox, but it sounds slow and slurred and nobody seems concerned, so I am going to assume that no one is in trouble.

"What's on the menu tonight?" I call to Marco, who is the bartender, cook, and my best friend on the island. He's about six foot three and 240 pounds of pure muscle. When I met him, I made the mistake of thinking he would be tough as nails, but he's actually a big softie. He also has a laugh that can be heard around the world.

"What are you in the mood for?" Marco yells over the noise.

"I'll eat anything good!" I yell back at Marco as I make my way to my favorite table in the back. Sam's is directly on the beach, and its back walls are only table height, offering patrons the feel of the fresh-island breeze and a view of the crystal-clear Caribbean ocean. I've always loved the water. It soothes me. Comforts me. It's one of the reasons I moved here. Mix the smell of the ocean with the odor of spices from Marco's cooking, and Sam's is the kind of place that movie studios try to recreate for those beach-n-bar scenes. But nothing compares to the real deal.

Well, until right now. Right now, I need some noise-canceling headphones because "Shadow Dancing" by Andy Gibb is blaring from the jukebox, and I can't listen to that song. Something about the way that man sings makes my skin feel wrong and my ears itchy. I've gotta stop it.

I walk to the jukebox with a quarter in my hand, ready to select almost anything else, when a hand slaps down on top of mine. It's not a violent slap, though maybe it was meant that way. I look up to see intense green eyes staring me down, certain to do me bodily harm if my quarter goes any closer to that jukebox.

Unfortunately for the green eyes, they are attached to a five-foot-five frame that looks about as threatening as a wet noodle in a sword fight. Yeah, that bodily harm isn't going to happen. The stare down I'm getting doesn't deter me at all from trying to liberate my burning ears, so I keep moving my quarter toward the slot.

"NO!" It's all the woman says, but it makes my eyes snap back to hers. And now I can't look away. Not in a *she's so attractive I can't keep my eyes off her* way—though she is incredibly attractive. I'm simply so curious. She's obviously incredibly drunk, and this level of intoxication can provide entertainment for friends and strangers alike. So I decide to play for a little bit. Nothing mean or cruel, but enough to entertain myself.

"I'm sorry, but are you trying to stop me from saving everyone's ears from bleeding?"

"You're bleeding?" The woman's voice gets breathy and concerned as she grabs the hand she originally slapped and guides me onto a chair. She has the strength of a small snail, so I could stop her at any time, but again, my curiosity is getting the best of me, so I allow it. "Where's your bleed?" At this point, she is lifting my arms up, moving my head from side to side, and doing what she can to find evidence of this "bleed" she thinks I have.

I take this time to really look at her. Based on her attire, she's definitely new here. She's wearing a short-sleeve, white, button-up blouse that is starched to perfection, very neatly pressed khaki shorts that go all the way to her knees, and clean, white, Maui-brand shoes. I've never seen anyone on the island dressed so formally—and I attended a few weddings here last year.

Her hair is pulled into a neat little doodad of some kind at the base of her neck, so I don't know how long her hair is, but it's a deep, rich red that is perfection when paired with her green eyes. Her skin looks golden brown, but I can't tell if it's because of genetics or the sun. And the way she's lifting my arms around without any help from me? I mean, I'm not the biggest guy on the island—that would be Marco—but I'm not a slouch either. I've got enough muscle on my arms that most people her size would struggle at least a *little bit* to lift them like she is, but she doesn't seem to be exerting too much. She obviously spends some time working out. But, it's her emerald eyes that steal the show. I can tell they are intense and focused and . . . trapped inside a drunk woman's body. I don't want to laugh at her, but it's actually kind of funny and charming the way her wide eyes are combing over every inch of me, looking for my "*bleed.*"

"Oh no!" She looks so sad and concerned all of a sudden as she pats the logo on my front chest pocket. "You do have a little bleed!" The logo is a lobster. A red lobster. And she thinks it's a small wound on my body. I can't hold back a little chuckle.

"I can help. I know things on bleeds." She picks up a napkin and starts to rub the lobster like it's a spot she can get out. Then she gets a contemplative look on her face, stops rubbing the lobster, and starts poking it with her finger instead. She stands there and pokes my left pec about ten times. "Is that you?"

"I honestly don't know what you're talking about, but if you are asking if the lobster is mine, it is. At least, it's a design on my shirt." This woman is adorable.

"Not that. This." And she pokes my pec a little harder. "Look." Poke, poke, poke. "My finger stays there and doesn't go inside." Poke, poke, poke. "Trevor's made my finger go inside like it was a pillow, but this," she places the entire palm of her hand on my pec. "This is very firm. You must exercise a lot." All of a sudden, I'm embarrassed because I think this woman is appreciating that my left pec is very firm, and apparently Trevor's—whoever he is—is soft like a pillow. I don't want this woman to embarrass herself, so I remove her hand, show her to an empty chair at my table, and sit across from her—where she can't reach me.

As Marco walks over with my food, an amazing plate of shrimp nachos, I stare him down a bit. "What did you give this woman?" Marco is a great guy and a responsible bartender. He doesn't over serve alcohol to anyone, so I need to know what is going on.

Marco looks sheepish, and I can tell something is wrong. "Marco's Island Sampler . . ."

"WHAT?!" I jump to my feet, and I'm loud enough that several heads turn my way. I lower my voice and pull Marco to the side. "You gave this very small person your version of an island sampler? What were you thinking?" An island sampler is a decently potent drink, but Marco's Island Sampler is basically the most toxic drink on the planet. If an alcohol could be 250 proof, this drink would be. Marco only gives it to the big boys on the island that can hold their liquor well, with very few exceptions, and then he makes sure it's the only drink he gives them all night.

"Marco," I draw his name out a little bit as I run my hand through my hair. "Why on earth would you do that?"

"She walked in very confidently and asked what the most colorful drink was. I told her it was my sampler. She asked what was in it, and I told her. I promise! I told her everything, so when she still asked for one, I figured she knew how well she could hold her own. I mean, I told her all of the things I put in it! *Twice!* When I saw how drunk she was, I felt terrible and put her in the corner. I've been keeping an eye on her ever since." Marco looks like he is pleading for his life in front of a jury. This is Marco. I know he would never intentionally give someone, especially a small person, a drink that would make them pass out drunk.

"It's okay, Marco," I say with a deep breath. "But I think she's going to need some help tonight." I turn toward the green-eyed girl then look back at Marco with curiosity. "She really just wanted a colorful drink?" When Marco nods his head, I smile. Who orders a drink based on color preference? "Alright, do you know who she is or where she's staying?"

"I don't know anything. But she's gotta be new on the island. Look at her shoes!" Marco points to her clean, white shoes and shrugs.

I let out a deep sigh because this was not how I was planning on spending my evening. "Let me call Cheryl. She knows everyone." As I take out my phone, I look over at the mystery woman. She is standing again and swaying back and forth. Her arms are over her head, making her look like some kind of graceful tree blowing in the wind. Her eyes are closed and she is completely immersed in the music, singing along with passion and conviction.

I'm mesmerized.

As long as I live, I will never hear another person sing this way. She's singing so loudly and so . . . badly. She's terrible. She's so off-key that she's almost back on key—but in a *comin' around the other side* kind of way. I can't let her do this to herself. I mean, at this point I would be less uncomfortable and embarrassed letting her poke my chest for the rest of the evening.

I walk over to her and gently place my hands on her upper arms to guide her back to her seat, but she takes this to mean I want to dance. She slides her arms around my neck and nuzzles into me. I'm tall enough that her cheek is now resting very close to the lobster she thought was a blood stain earlier.

I'm frozen because I don't know what to do at this point. The woman is drunk and still singing—though thankfully it's more like a whisper now—and she's throwing all of her body weight into getting me to sway with her. I finally give up and start to sway.

I've seen rejected drunk women in bars before, and it's never a pretty sight. There are always so many tears and so much loud crying. I don't want her dissolving into that if I don't dance with her, because in the morning—on the off chance she remembers any of this—I don't want her to remember that she humiliated herself. Well, . . . humiliated herself beyond reason.

After a few awkward moments of what feels like the junior-high two-step, Harry walks into the room and gets the accustomed greeting. "HAAAAARRY!"

The woman, my dance partner, abruptly stops and yells, "AAAAAARRY!" Okay. Now that "EEEEK" from earlier makes more sense. Can this woman get any more entertaining? And where on earth did she come from?

She must sense I'm thinking about her, because she looks up at me, her arms still around my neck, and tries to make me sway even more. "I think I own this place. Is it nice? I can't tell."

"Why do you think you own this place?" I try to sound genuinely curious, which, I guess, is easy, because I am.

"It's named after half of me!! It's called Sam's." She hangs onto the last sound a little long, so it sounds more like Samzzzz. "My other name is Masamtha. No, wait. Masamtha." She looks off into the distance with a look of complete concentration before blurting out, "Samantha! Yeah, that's it. My other name is Samantha, but they used to call me Sam." She says the last part like it's a swear word that's left a bad taste on her tongue. "I don't want Sam. I want my name . . . be called the Samantha." She says Samantha like she's a superhero with a cape announcing her presence.

"What's wrong with Sam? I like Sam."

"You like me?" Her eyes go warm and gooey and her soft smile glows as her body melts against me a little bit. Her arms feel heavier now, pulling me down instead of side to side. "That makes two in one day," she murmurs as her eyes gloss over for a moment. I'm terrified she is going to start crying.

"Sure. I like you just fine." I'll say almost anything at this point to help this woman not draw attention from others while she's acting like this. I start guiding her back to the table where my nachos are waiting. "Let's get some food in you." I sit her down and hand her a nacho.

"You say you like me," she uses the nacho to point aggressively at me, and a shrimp flies off the chip and into the sand on the other side of the half wall, "but no one takes Sam seriously." Again, there is bitterness in her voice. "That's why Masamtha is better! She gets more respects and stuffs like thats." Her words are starting to slur more and more. "But

Sam is funnerer." At the admission, her whole body sags a little bit. "Sam is fun and adventure-er-ish, and she laughs strongly," her words die off a little as her eyelids droop and seem to get heavier. "But Samantha is smarts and . . ."

"Barracuda" by Heart starts on the jukebox, and before I can stop her, this woman named Sam—or Samantha, I'm not sure which to refer to her as—pops up, jumps on top of her chair, and starts playing the air guitar to the long instrumental introduction.

I take this moment to call Cheryl as quickly as I can. "Cheryl! Hey!" I yell over the top of the music. "There is a woman at Sam's who is drunk. She's going to need some help home tonight, but we don't know who she is." As I listen to Cheryl, I look up and see Sam, or Samantha, still as engaged as ever with her air guitar. I've gotta give it to her: it's much better than her singing. "All I know is she's referred to herself as both Samantha," a sign with the bar's name is on the wall above her head and I smile, "and—ironically—Sam. But . . . Oh, you do? . . . Great. So where does she live? . . . You've got to be kidding me!" As I hang up, she starts singing again.

"So this ain't the end, I saw you again, today,
I had to turn my heart away,
Smile like the sun, kisses for everyone."

And just like that, she stops singing and feels the need to kiss everyone around her.

She grabs Tony, who is seated to her right side, and kisses his cheek. He doesn't even react as he eats his tacos. I reach out to stop her from continuing around the room, and as she sees me coming, she wraps her arms around my waist and eyes the lobster logo on my shirt.

"Hello, little lobster," she whispers before pressing a long, lingering kiss to my left pec, right over the lobster.

Then she passes out.

CHAPTER 4

Samantha

I WAKE UP WITH ringing in my ears.

I remember ordering a drink that was colorful, a car ride home, and
. . . that's about all in my sleepy, hangover-induced daze.

I'm one of those rare adults that has avoided drinking alcohol since my
one-and-only drinking experience at age twenty-one. During business
lunches, I order my clients their preferred drink but something nonal-
coholic for myself. Although I've ordered hundreds of client drinks over
the years, I never took the time to learn what went in any of the drinks—a
decision I am deeply regretting this morning.

Last night the bartender rattled off all sorts of ingredients I'd heard of
but admittedly didn't know much about. I can remember not only the
look on his face when I told him it all sounded great but also the skeptical
tone his voice took as he repeated the ingredients to me. Why hadn't I
listened to the screaming voice of reason in my head? Now said-head is
pounding, and I'm wondering what on earth possessed me to act so out
of character.

And interestingly enough, I now associate colorful drinks with pain,
dancing, and . . . lobsters? Which is a weird combination, because I've
always liked lobster.

My mouth feels like cotton, my head feels like stone, my body feels like it's been violently run over by something large and powerful, and there is still a ringing in my ears.

I carefully sit up, only to realize the ringing in my ears is my phone. It's been ringing this whole time.

I know it's either Steph or Cheryl, but I don't know which one, so I try and muster up Professional Samantha in case it's Cheryl. Ugh. I can't do it, and I answer with the best I've got.

"What?" I say with no delicacy or tact; my own voice is like a jack-hammer in my head. It's now obvious to either Steph or Cheryl that last night I was not at my best.

There is a slight pause, and maybe a small gasp, from the other line.

"YEEEEEEES!!" is followed by high-pitched squealing, and I want to throw my phone against the wall. But I don't, because I can't muster the strength to do it. "I'm so proud of you!"

I can tell by Steph's tone of voice that she is doing a celebratory dance around whatever room she's in. If her room had security cameras and I looked at the footage, I feel confident she'd look like she was either dancing at a nightclub, doing lunges, or prancing like a baby deer.

"Stephanie," I only use her full name when I'm grumpy or serious, and right now I'm seriously grumpy. "For the love of all the tea in China, lower your voice. I've done nothing to make you proud since I've been here. And I say that honestly, because I can't remember much after about six o'clock last night." A low moan escapes me as I stand up, and my head throbs even more.

"That's the point!!" Steph screams into the phone, having no respect for my brain. "I've told you every morning for the last two years to go out there and have fun—AND YOU FINALLY DID!"

"Wait!" a sense of dread fills me. "How do you know what I did?! Steph, I ordered a colorful drink, and then everything went fuzzy." Something churns in my stomach.

"First," she states matter-of-factly, and I can tell she has stopped her celebratory dancing, though her voice still drips with glee. I'm in no mood for this. "I knew something was up because of your voice when you answered the phone. YOU HAVE A HANGOVER!" My head hates her so much right now. "THEN, as if I wasn't already happy enough about that, you told me most of last night is *fuzzy*," she really draws out the word fuzzy, and I cringe everywhere. "Which is even better!"

"You think accidentally getting that drunk is better?"

"You know that's not what I mean. You broke out of your carefully constructed box last night and did something unexpected. That's huge for you! And even if it means you have a huge hangover today, I'm still happy for you." I can tell she's dancing again.

"How are we even friends?" I say with no energy, combating the wave of *stampeding buffalo level* energy she is sending over the phone line.

"Darling," but she says it all drawn out and in some ridiculous accent, so it sounds more like *Daaaahhh-ling*. It reminds me a little of how Cheryl said it the other day. Was that just yesterday? "We are friends because you loooove me." On the last two words, she copies the tone of voice Sandra Bullock uses in *Miss Congeniality*. "And more than that, you neeeed me." The tone again. "Cuz I'm the only thing that's been keeping you afloat the last two years."

"It's only been the last nine months," I argue.

"Psh, no! I was trying to save you long before your breakup with Sweater."

I sit back down on my bed and pinch my nose with my fingers. "First off, his name is Trevor, not Sweater, and you know it." Grumpy Samantha may never leave.

"Po-ta-to, po-tah-to. He only wore sweaters. Who does that? The name works! Sooo . . . ," I hate her tone of voice because I already know what's coming, "here's my question: Did you wake up alone this morning? Or with something warm to cuddle?" She makes the wagging of eyebrows have a tone of voice.

"Yes, I did wake up with something warm to cuddle. My *pillow*. And as for Trevor . . ." I look down at my pillow and scrunch my face; there is something significant I need to remember about a pillow and Trevor.

"Boooring. No more Sweater. He's such an expired coupon." She makes a sound like a cat coughing up a furball. "Let's talk about . . ."

"NOOOO!" A wave of nausea crashes over me that has nothing to do with a hangover and more to do with a hazy memory that is starting to become a little more clear. "I think I did do something last night. Something bad."

"Finally, some details!" Steph's voice is full of delight. If I had to guess, she's now on her bed lying on her stomach, propped up on her elbows with her chin in her hands and feet in the air. This is Steph's *tell me something dirty and juicy* pose. The only time she's used it on me was the night things ended with Trevor, because she was so excited about it. I mostly see it when she's talking to her sisters, nieces, or mom. (I don't even want to know why she has those *tell me something dirty and juicy* conversations with her mom, of all people, but this is Steph. I don't think anyone is off-limits to her.)

"I can vaguely remember poking a man's pec." I hold my breath, because this is big news coming from me.

"Aaaand?" Steph prods.

"What do you mean 'aaaand'? I poked a random man's chest. And I am pretty sure I groped it at least once!"

The hysterical laughter coming from the other end of the line pains not only my head but also my pride. She understands that this is not the behavior I want to be known for. I've spent the last ten years curating a persona of professionalism that, under no circumstances, includes the groping of *any* body part on *any* man.

It doesn't include getting drunk either, but we've already established that I have major regrets about my decision-making abilities last night.

Steph calms down the laughter and actually sounds sympathetic, which is rare for her. "Sammy-Sam-Sam . . ."

"Please don't call me that," my voice droops with my shoulders.

"Fine. My Little Hottie, I don't mean to laugh at your expense. You know I love you, but what you have described is not scandalous. Maybe not the best thing to do at a dinner party with royalty, but you won't be arrested for this behavior." She has adopted a tenderness in her voice that I appreciate. "And, without wanting to sound inappropriate but knowing I will anyway—*but not caring*," she says the last three words like she's at a club yelling for the DJ to drop her a beat, "may I ask whom this man you groped is and what his reaction to said groping was?"

Why can she eke a small chuckle out of me despite the fact that last night was the most humiliating experience I've had in a long time? "I honestly don't know. My mind is still too fuzzy to recall his face. I just remember a very strong pec. I think somehow a lobster was involved, but I can't figure out how. Maybe I had one for dinner?"

"Look, just relax today and let the hangover go away."

"How do I do that?" This is only my second-ever hangover. I've always felt the need to be in control, and—especially since my previous hangover—being drunk has always been one of my greatest fears. In fact, a couple mornings after that hangover was when I stuffed Sam inside a box and made sure Samantha was given total control of my life. Last night was a gargantuan lapse in judgment.

"Maybe lay off the colorful drinks for a while. But please don't stuff all your fun back in a box again. Last night might have been the best way for you to break out of your shell! Look, Chase is calling and he's on the road, so I need to take it. Remember I love ya, Pookie Bear." I can hear her laughing as she switches to the other call. Chase is her rock-star boyfriend of eighteen months. His music is great, but I've never been a fan of how he treats Steph. He makes her happy, though, so I keep my mouth shut.

After cleaning myself up a bit, I find some food in the kitchen that wasn't there yesterday. *Bless Cheryl's heart.* I grab a piece of toast and go outside to curl up in the hammock and stare at the waves rolling across the ocean—one of my other greatest fears.

I must have fallen asleep for a while, because the next sound I hear is a little girl laughing. I open my eyes and peer out of my hammock cocoon to see a family playing in the water.

They are far enough out that all I really see are their silhouettes against the morning glare on the water. It looks like a mom and dad and a young girl whose age is impossible to tell from this distance. They splash and laugh like they're so happy. So relaxed. I want that. I want my shoulders to release some of the tension I've been holding onto for too long. The little girl heads toward the shore, and I watch as she comes running out of the ocean and onto the sand. Her parents stay far out in the water, and I watch as the husband puts his arm loosely over his wife's shoulders.

I don't even realize I'm staring until a little voice tells me I am. It's not the little voice inside my head—it's an actual voice from a little person. "Why are you staring at my mommy and Dee-Dee?"

My head jerks toward the little girl, who is now on the back porch with me. "I'm not! I mean, I am. Or I was." I try to take a deep breath. "You're right. I was staring at them. They looked happy." I smile at this delightful girl, which feels so good because the smile feels genuine, even to me.

"Yeah, they are happy. My name is Eloise Maxine Huntsman, but everyone calls me Lou. I'm five."

Five? Wow. The way she introduced herself—and the confidence she exudes—makes her seem much older. "Does that mean you go to kindergarten?"

"Yeah, but I'm homeschooled." She looks out to her parents, who are still out in the water together. "We moved here last week. Or maybe last year. I can't remember, but it's one of those." That sounds more like a five-year-old. "I really like it. How old are you? Do you go to school?"

By this point, I think I'm in love. I want to take this little girl with me everywhere I go. "I am thirty-one, and I do not go to school anymore, but I did for a long time."

"My name is Lou," she says again, but this time a little slower and with raised eyebrows. It's like she is expecting something.

"That's right. You said that a moment ago." Now I'm a little confused. She's starting to sound like Dory from *Finding Nemo*. Does she not realize we already covered that?

She sighs a little, as if she's exasperated with me, but she still has a smile on her face. It's a look I'll bet she learned from her mom. "My mom says that if someone introduces themselves to you, you should introduce yourself back. That is called being polite. Do you not have a mom to teach you to be polite? If not, my mom can teach you. She's the best, and I'm sure she wouldn't mind being your mom too." Her face is complete innocence, and I know she is serious.

"You're right, Lou. That was not very polite of me." I give her a look to convey my appreciation that she's keeping me on the path of politeness. "My name is Samantha."

"You don't look like a Samantha. You look like a Penelope." She grins like she's just solved Fermat's Last Theorem.

I smile back. "Penelope is a great name." Penelope is not a great name. What is it about me that made her say that? At that moment, her mom comes out of the water and calls to Lou. I hadn't noticed her wading back to the shore.

"Lou, baby, it's time to go inside. We're going to work with Dee-Dee this morning." After wrapping a towel around Lou, she gives me a full and welcoming smile. "Hi, I'm Amber and this little scallywag is Lou." She roughs up Lou's blonde hair and gives her a little tickle, making Lou scream with delight.

"Hi. I'm Samantha." I reach over and shake Amber's hand. "Do you guys live in the condo next door?"

"Yep. Just the three of us. Is it just you in the condo?" When I nod, Amber signals to their side of the condo. "Well, we would love to have you over tonight for dinner. I don't really cook, but I make a mean frozen pizza." One of her shoulders goes up in the universal sign for *it's not much, but you're welcome to it.*

I start laughing. "Cheryl, from the management company, made me feel like I'd be living next to grannies who were going to bake me cookies everyday." I crouch down to Lou's level and give her belly a few tiny pokes, which elicits outrageous giggling, "But this is way better." I look up to address Amber and realize that, even though my hangover is mostly gone, I feel a little unstable looking up while also crouching down, so I stand up and wiggle my legs and arms to get some circulation going. Lou seems to think I'm trying to entertain her, and she throws her head back and goes full belly laugh! Did I already mention I'm in love with this girl? I wiggle my arms and legs again to see if I get the same result. I do, but this time Lou tries to wiggle her limbs in the same way, and both Amber and I start laughing along with her. Lou's laugh is contagious. When Amber starts wiggling too, Lou practically collapses on the deck with laughter. Other than Steph, who was the last happy person I was around—when was the last time I heard real laughter? It's been a long time. Too long.

"Thanks so much for the invitation. As much as a frozen pizza sounds delicious, I'm going to have to take a raincheck. I just got in yesterday and haven't even finished unpacking."

"No problem." Amber's smile is generous. So genuine! I can tell there is nothing fake about this woman. She looks the opposite of how I have been living my life for so long—and exactly how I wish I could be living my life now. I never really had a role model growing up, but is it strange to say that I already want Amber to be one? "We don't really stand on ceremony, so feel free to drop by for dinner anytime."

"Thank you. It was really nice to meet both of you, and you have a beautiful family."

"Thanks." At this, Amber beams. "Sometime I'll have to introduce you to Deacon—if I can ever pull him out of the water." Her head leans toward the ocean, where her husband is still just a distant silhouette.

Lou's eyes light up. "Dee-Dee is the best!"

Amber smiles as she looks out at him. "Yep, he is." She turns her attention back to me. "I guess we'll be seeing a lot of you if we are neighbors. Let me know if you need anything." She starts walking inside, but Lou runs and wraps her arms around my legs in a knee-crushing hug. At least as knee crushing as possible for a five-year-old.

"Mommy, I love my new best friend. Can I sleep at her house sometime?"

Amber rolls her eyes at Lou's question, and I get the feeling that Lou blurts out a lot of things like this. But I gently put my hand up to stop Amber's protests while I address Lou. "I'm so glad we're new best friends. I would love it to the moon and back if I could spend some time with you and your mom sometime. But instead of a sleepover, maybe your mom could join us while we do nails, facials, and all the fun girl things." I make a large sweeping motion with my arms, making eye contact with Amber to let her know I won't be doing anything without her permission.

Lou's eyes go huge as she turns to address Amber. "Mommy! She loves to the moon and back too!" She gives me one more hug and runs inside. After Amber follows, I can't seem to pull my eyes from their closed door. A new sensation stirs inside me; it's a little bit calm and a little bit happy. I'm not sure what to do with it, so I force my gaze to the ocean and take a deep breath. A subtle scent that I can almost recognize fills my nostrils, but I can't quite put my finger on what it is.

I see Amber's husband far out in the water, and suddenly realize that he is looking this direction. And I think he's touching his chest. Maybe scratching a spot? I want so badly to change from my regular, stiff office persona to something less . . . stiff, so I decide to give him a big and friendly wave. He cocks his head to the side then tentatively waves back, like he's not sure what to make of me. Too big of a wave? I wonder if there's a possibility he thinks I'm insane. Or worse, flirting with him. It's so sad how awkward I am at simply waving to a stranger. But at least I can finally name the floral scent I couldn't place a moment ago. *Oleander.*

I then decide that it's okay to be awkward about a few things. I'm here to make some changes, and my ability to wave to strangers will have to, apparently, be one of them.

Look at me! I'm still calm after a random married man in the water either thinks I'm insane or flirting with him. This island is already working its magic! Unfortunately, my head wishes that I wouldn't have tried to find that magic inside a colorful drink last night.

CHAPTER 5

Deacon

I'M GLAD AMBER AND I had a minute to talk away from Lou's little ears. I swear she can hear through walls sometimes. Trying to figure out life with the three of us isn't always smooth sailing, so it's helpful when Amber and I can have some good, grown-up conversations. Some days it seems the three of us take one step forward only to take two steps back. I'd do anything for them—they're my whole life—but some days I feel the weight of it more than others.

I watch Amber as she wades back to shore toward Lou and notice that Lou is talking to Samantha . . . Sam . . . ? I need to iron that out. I can't see any details from this far away, but I can tell, even from here, that sober Sam is as beautiful as drunk Sam . . . er, Samantha (whatever). Luckily, I was able to take in all the details last night when I took her home.

She's a complete enigma to me, because even passed out in my front seat, drooling, and making little whimper sounds as she adjusted from time to time, she still managed to look so . . . I don't know what the perfect word is, but it lands somewhere near adorable, sweet, cute, beautiful, alluring, and compelling. Yeah, it's obvious words aren't my thing right now. Anyway, when I got back to the condo, she was still too drunk to walk, so I carried her in. When I picked her up, she settled into my body like I was a memory-foam mattress, and now that I'm looking at her again, my body starts craving that feeling again. All I know about this woman is her drunk version, so why do I feel this way?

Drunk Sam was definitely a combination of entertainment and disaster. I couldn't look away—I was way too curious about what was going to happen next. But now I can't look away because of the way she's interacting with my family.

I look over at Lou and see her bright eyes—or really just sense them from her body language—as she talks. She lets out a giggle I can hear from here, and my heart melts. And the way Samantha (or Sam) is engaging with Lou does something else to my heart. I can't explain exactly why, but it's important to me that people recognize how special Lou is, and I think my new neighbor is a quick study. I can feel the ridiculously big smile on my face.

I look from Lou back to . . . I'm going to go with Sam. I look at Sam, and she bends down to talk to Lou on her level and gives Lou's belly a few little pokes, which make Lou giggle even more. Is she for real? Somehow I can't reconcile the drunk woman from last night with the woman I am watching interact with Lou. Geez, I wish I was close enough to see any details about her face, but I'm too far out in the water.

When Sam stands back up and does some silly thing with her long legs and arms, Lou belts out a huge laugh. Then Lou starts wiggling. Now all three of them are doing it, and Lou is laughing so hard it looks like she might fall over. What is going on up there? I'm both dying to go up and see for myself and afraid of moving and breaking the spell.

I don't know why, but a spot on my chest starts to tingle. I bring my hand up, thinking there must be a bug to shoo away, but pause as I remember the little bug that was there last night. Well, not a bug, but a lobster. And this spot is where she gave that lobster a long, lingering kiss before she passed out.

I suddenly feel a need to get to know my new neighbor. She intrigues me in a way I can't name yet. Not in an *I want to grab her and kiss her* way—though, remembering her full smile last night, I have a feeling that kissing her would be incredible. I've never been a guy who is just about physical looks. Don't get me wrong, I want a physical connection as much as anyone and I'll kiss a beautiful woman if she wants me to—and I'll do it well—but when I date a woman, I want there to be a connection that goes deeper than that, and . . .

Wait. Amber and Lou are gone, and Sam's looking out at me now. Does she remember last night enough to know that I'm the man whose chest she poked, repeatedly? How can she tell? She was pretty far gone when I showed up, and I'm pretty far out right now.

Her wave is big, friendly, and warm, matching the smile I can sense on her face. So she must remember me. And, based on the enthusiasm of her wave, she is really happy to see me, even though she has every reason to be embarrassed about last night's poking, singing, and lobster kissing.

My head cocks to the side as I try to figure it all out. All I can do is lift my hand, which had still been touching the place she kissed, and wave back. I know it's a weak wave, but it's the best I can do. I'm already preoccupied with the idea of asking her to dinner . . . and of calling her Sam all night. I don't think she'll like it. And for some reason, I think it would be fun to ruffle her feathers a little bit, just to see what happens.

CHAPTER 6

Samantha

AFTER I GET CLEANED up and my head clears a little, I leave the condo to explore the island for the next hour. It's not a large island, so it doesn't take much time and I end up at my final destination fifteen minutes early. But now that I'm here, I can't seem to make myself get out of the car.

There were many reasons for my self-imposed exile from work. One of them being my state of constant fear. Fear of not being taken seriously. Fear of losing relationships because I am not enough. Fear of being ridiculed for things out of my control. Fear of being abandoned. There are a lot of fears that I allow to control many of my actions, and I don't want to keep giving them power over my life. I want to work through them until they are just a speck in my metaphorical rearview mirror.

So that brings me here, to Breathing Under Water. It's a snorkel and scuba school here on the island. I'm terrified of water, and I thought conquering this fear would be a small (HUGE) but good first step.

Nine months ago, when I first googled "getting over fear of water," a lot of things popped up. As I scrolled through the options, I came across this scuba school and its name spoke to me: *Breathing Under Water*. It didn't feel like I was breathing above water, let alone under it, so I was intrigued. After reading so many reviews from people who credited this place with helping them get over their fear of water, it seemed almost like fate—if that was something I believed in. It was right then that I decided I was going to take a leave of absence from work and come live on this tiny island and sort my life out. And now I'm here. It took months of scheduling and planning to get my workload down to where I could either finish up cases or pass them off to other attorneys without disappointing clients.

Now I'm ready to conquer my fear of water.

I'm absolutely ready.

Yep.

I'm ready as I sit here in my car . . . gripping my steering wheel so tightly that my knuckles are white.

Nope.

Not ready.

Not sure I can do this.

I'm so worked up right now that I am either going to pass out or cry. And since I haven't cried since I was ten years old, I guess I am going to pass out.

I'm about to start my car, go back to my condo, pack up, and leave the island when a literal ray of sunshine comes beaming out of the building and shines straight on my car. And when I say a literal ray of sunshine, I mean a metaphorical ray of sunshine named Lou.

Lou is running straight at my car, yelling at the top of her adorable lungs. "Penelope!!"

I seem to forget that I was about fifteen minutes away from booking a flight back to Boston, because I get out of the car, squat down to the ground, and open my arms wide to catch my new best friend, Lou, as she launches herself into my arms. I spin her around as she hugs me like I am the key to free Disneyland tickets for life. I've never acted like this around children, but there is something special about Lou.

She starts talking at rapid-fire speed without even breathing. "I was telling Dee-Dee that I wanted to have a playdate with you, but Dee-Dee said we had to stay here for the morning classes of teaching people about water, and then Mommy said when we got home I had to take a nap after Dee-Dee makes me mac-n-cheese shaped like dinosaurs, because they are my favorite, especially when Dee-Dee makes the dinosaur noises—they really are my favorite after you."

I don't understand most of what she said, but I did catch the part about mac-n-cheese. "Mac-n-cheese shaped like dinosaurs? That sounds amazing! I've never had it, but I bet it would be my favorite too."

"Nooooo!" She drags the word out and rolls her eyes, all while giggling. "The dinosaurs are my favorite after *you*. You are my new favorite!"

At this point, if this girl asked me to swim to Florida, get her an alligator, and swim back with it, I'm pretty sure I would. Except for the fact that I'm afraid of water. Which brings me back to why I'm here. And . . . why is Lou here all by herself?

"Lou, where are your mom and dad?"

"Mom is inside and Dee-Dee is getting the waters ready. Don't tell Dee-Dee you are my new favorite. He was my favorite and might not want to share being my favorite with you."

I reach up a finger and boop her nose. "I would not dream of it. Dee-Dee will never know."

"What won't I know?" The voice comes from the office door, and when I turn to see who is walking out, my insides feel like they want to be on the outside, and my outsides definitely want to be anywhere but here—somewhere on the dark side of the moon comes to mind. Because all of a sudden, I remember jukeboxes, singing, bleeds, lobsters, poking and . . . oh no. I look at the man's shirt and see he is wearing a rash guard with a lobster and the words *Breathing Under Water*. He stops about ten feet away from me and seems to be waiting for me to speak.

No, no, no, no, and NO! This man can *not* work here. I flew over 1,500 miles and uprooted my life to live on this tiny island because I felt like

Breathing Under Water was speaking to me through the Google search engine. It was going to help me find a new outlook on so many things and be the start of not running from the humiliations of the past—yet here stands an employee that happens to be the man I had the second-biggest humiliation of my life with less than twenty-four hours ago!

"No!" Wait . . . did I shout that out loud?

He cocks his head to the side. "No, what?"

Okay. I guess I did. "This can't be happening. I came here for you!" I gesture vaguely his way.

His head cocks the other direction, and a slow smile spreads across his sun-kissed face. "Wow. I'm the reason you moved here?"

Kill. Me. Now. I hadn't realized I said that out loud either.

"I'm incredibly flattered, but I think we should at least have a proper introduction that doesn't involve you groping my chest and proclaiming that it's firmer than Trevor's."

Crap. I *did* do that! Could this get much worse? And I wasn't even talking to him when I said, *"I came here for you."* I was talking to the name on the building and how it called me here and . . . it doesn't matter what I was talking about. What *does* matter is that I take control back of the situation. Which is quickly spiraling out of my control.

Control. That's all I need. I take a deep breath, stand up a little taller—which is hard while balancing a five-year-old on your hip—and instinctively put on my best business voice. "I need to speak with the owner." I need to get my money back and go to another snorkel school.

He smiles back at me. "No problem." He doesn't move a muscle, like he has no intention of going to get the owner.

"I'm sorry if this is an *inconvenience*," I say, the last word dripping with sarcasm, "but I really do want to talk to the owner." Sarcasm has never been a weapon I've used at work. I have always been unflappable under any amount of pressure, but for some reason, this situation, and this man, seem to be undoing my self-control piece by piece. And I'm grasping at anything to try and find any amount of it back.

He straightens up and moves toward me, closing the remaining ten feet between us. I can't describe what he's doing as walking, because it's more like a strut. Or a saunter. Or something with confidence, but not quite cockiness. He . . . *meanders* over like he doesn't have a care in the world. I'm even more flustered than I was a moment ago.

I am the most sought-after lawyer for mergers and acquisitions in the state of Massachusetts. I can take any opponent and make them practically cave with the lift of one carefully sculpted eyebrow. Why is the sight of a smiling man in swim trunks, a rash guard, and flip-flops meandering toward me making me feel defenseless and the need to go on the attack?

"Hi." He extends his large hand and looks me square in the eyes. "My name is Deacon, but some people call me Deke. I own this fine establishment. I heard through the grapevine that you wanted to talk to me." His crooked smile never slides off his face, and his crystal-clear, blue eyes never look away.

"Deke? That sounds completely juvenile. What kind of a nick-name is that?" I give a small "humph" as I look down at his extended hand—without shaking it—and then back up to his face. I know everything I'm doing is rude, but I'm in new territory here, and I'm reacting in ways that are completely foreign, even to me!

"It's the kind that suits me well." He shrugs his shoulders and lets his hand fall back to his side. "Did you want to ask me any other personal information? Like when I'll be showing up at Sam's tonight so you can serenade me again?" His eyes brim with entertainment at my expense, and I can feel my cheeks turning to lava. "Or were you interested in poking my other . . ."

"NO!" I blurt out before he can finish his sentence. "I think you know that my behavior last night was not an accurate representation of my normal demeanor."

"That's too bad. Because I liked you better last night. You weren't as rude." He still has a smile on his face. I don't know what that means, and I'm not sure what to do. He just stands there, somehow challenging me. I lift an eyebrow to show that I accept his challenge—whatever it may be.

I set Lou down but keep hold of her hand. Then I squat so we are eye to eye. As I start to speak, Lou squats down like me, and I can't help but smile at her, as this eases a little bit of my tension. "Lou, why don't you run inside and see Dee-Dee while I have a nice talk with this man."

"But . . ."

"Just for a minute, okay Lou?" Lou stands up and looks at me as she shrugs her shoulders. I look back at Deke with a smug look. He knows that once little ears are out of the way, I will be sharing my full, unedited version of what I think of him. Although, the truth is, he has been nothing but kind to me, while I have been huffing and puffing and completely flustered. Using my highly refined attorney skills, I'm sure I can come up with some very articulate things to say while Lou is inside with her Dee-Dee.

Lou lets go of my hand and takes a few steps, until she stands right by Deacon. Then she reaches up and takes his hand. She looks up at me and shrugs with a smile.

Deacon looks down at her and says, "Good girl, Lou." Then he lifts his chin in challenge, and his blue eyes sparkle with something that says *your move.*

This is the man I not only groped at the bar but also enthusiastically waved at earlier this morning? This is Amber's husband and Lou's father? My jaw drops open in shock. I find my voice but can only utter, "You're Dee-Dee?"

He smiles as he answers me. "Yep."

CHAPTER 7

Deacon

I NEED TO KNOW what her next words will be. She's staring at me with her jaw hanging open, her hair distractingly gorgeous in the sunlight. She's so flustered at this point that I almost feel bad for her. Almost. I don't want the woman to have another embarrassing moment when I'm around, but I don't know what to do. I came outside when I heard someone mention my name, and I don't think I've done anything other than answer what she has asked. But for some reason, I get the sensation she is furious at me, and it's fascinating.

I hope I'm wrong, because—for reasons I can't explain—I really was going to ask her out to dinner the next time I saw her, and if she's furious at me, it would put a damper on things. I try to put an end to whatever awkwardness she is feeling. "Look, Sam . . ."

"Don't call me that!"

I let go of Lou's hand so that I can put both of my hands up in the *I'm innocent* pose, and then I look down at Lou. "Hey, Lou, why don't you run inside and see your mom. Okay?" Luckily she agrees and runs inside to find Amber. "Look . . . ," I have no idea how to finish that sentence. I just sigh. "Let's start over. Hello," I extend my hand in a friendly gesture, "my name is Deke." She opens her mouth like she's going to make another rude comment, so I cut her off. "Yes, it might seem like a juvenile name, but it's a nickname that's stuck over time, so

I've kept it. Except with Lou. She calls me Dee-Dee because she couldn't say my name when she was little. I own this place. It seems you have some business with me, but may I ask if it can wait? I have a bunch of five-to ten-year-olds waiting for me to start teaching a class." Then I go for broke. No sense putting off until tomorrow what you can do today. "If you wouldn't mind, maybe we could have dinner together so that you can 'ask the owner,'" I say that using air quotes, "whatever it is you want."

Like some switch has been flipped, her angst toggles to complete confusion. "You said the class was for five- to ten-year-olds?"

Now I'm confused. Why would that affect her so much? "Yes. It's a beginning snorkel class. It's for kids." My brow is definitely furrowed at this point. I cannot connect all I have seen about this woman into one person.

"But I'm signed up for that class, and I'm not any of those ages." She lets out a large puff of air, and her shoulders drop in complete defeat.

"Sam . . ."

She looks up with pleading eyes. "Please don't call me that."

"Why? It's your name?"

"My name is Samantha. I prefer to be called Samantha."

I can't help it, but I start to smile. For some reason I am captivated by her. She has more facets than a well-cut diamond, and every one of them is as vibrant as the last. "I will admit that we have spent very little time together and that I don't know you very well. But I can tell you this with absolute certainty," I step closer, close enough to touch her arm if I wanted to. "You are no Samantha. It sounds too stuffy. Someone who sings Andy Gibb so badly but plays air guitar so well is anything but stuffy."

She stands there staring at me, and I get the distinct impression that she is battling between slugging me and hugging me, but I have no idea which side will win out.

When she finally speaks, it's so soft I can barely hear it. "You don't think I'm stuffy?"

My brows furrow as I try to digest what she said. Of all the things I thought she might say or do, this surprises me. I slowly shake my head. "No. No, I do not."

As I stand there looking at this woman who I've barely had any interaction with—and none of it including what I would call normal conversation—something happens to my brain. It's like it short-circuits and then rewires itself the very next second, and then, all of a sudden, I need to know. I wish I didn't, but I do. I close my eyes and breathe deeply. When my sister finds out I asked Sam this question, I will have a *lot* of explaining to do. "Look, I was serious about the class. I really do have to teach it, and it really is for kids between five and ten years old. But first, Coke or Pepsi?"

"I'm sorry. What?"

"It's a simple question. Coke," I extend one hand to my left, "or Pepsi?" I extend the other to my right.

Please say Pepsi.

"Neither." She shrugs.

"Wait. What? You have to pick one!" I feel the need to press for an answer. It needs to be one or the other!

"I'm a Dr. Pepper girl." Her brows are furrowed, and she looks so confused by my line of questioning.

I'll admit, I'm throwing myself off a little bit by how much I wanted to know this detail about her; but her answer causes a large smile to gradually slide across my face. This is very satisfying to me in ways I really don't want to examine.

"Perfect," I say slowly. There is a part of me that really hopes she will hate what I'm about to say. "Then I'll call you Pepper-Girl."

Her feathers look as ruffled as I hoped they would, and she opens her mouth to protest, but I stop her by putting a finger to her lips. "I can see how excited you are about this, but I have one more question." Her eyes narrow at me. I think she knows that no matter what she says, I'm going to call her Pepper-Girl, or maybe just Pepper, from now on, so she sighs and lets me continue.

I slowly lower my finger.

"Why did you sign up for a kids' snorkel class? No judgments. No criticism. I just want to know."

She looks down and closes her eyes, almost like she's gathering energy for a fight. When she looks up, her chin is slightly raised and I can see steel in her eyes, as if this is costing her some pride to say out loud. "I didn't know it was for little kids, but I am very afraid of the water. I am here to conquer that fear." She takes another deep breath and lifts her chin a little more. I can tell our temporary truce is over, as the fight in her eyes is back. "I feel that due to our . . . interactions last night, I would not be comfortable being taught by you. So, even if you don't give me back my deposit, I would like the name and directions to the nearest snorkel school. This is, for very personal reasons, important to me." When she finishes, I can tell that she is done talking and that I will not get one syllable more from her.

"If you want your deposit back, I will give it to you, but I want you to know that last night doesn't bother me. I would feel completely comfortable working with you. If you don't feel the same, the next closest is probably Scuba Max." She sighs and her shoulders relax, but she doesn't know what's coming next. "You can get there by getting back on the puddle jumper that brought you here and traveling about three hours east to the next island." The shock on her face is about what I expected. "Yep. I'm the only scuba shop in town. So, *Pepper*," I'd be lying if I said I didn't like seeing the little flinch in her body as I put some extra weight on that last word, "I'm going to go inside and teach my class. Why don't you think it over, and if you want to take a class here, come back tomorrow at the same time and join us."

She still says nothing, so I give her a little head nod, turn around, and head to teach the kids—but I can't help but notice that my finger is still zinging from where I touched her lips.

CHAPTER 8

Samantha

I FEEL LIKE I am a completely different person since I landed on this island, but not in a good way. I feel like I don't have control of anything. Not even my emotions. I've almost cried three times since just this morning!

I don't know how to explain it, but when Deacon said he didn't think I was stuffy, I could barely reign in my emotions. I feel like everyone else in the world thinks I'm stuffy, with the exception of Steph. I can't blame them, because I do act that way, but I've grown tired of it.

No one actually uses the word *stuffy*, but they say things like, "Samantha probably doesn't have to starch her shirts—they stand at attention for her naturally." Or one I used to love, "Samantha takes out the opposition as if she doesn't have a heart." How did I ever think it was okay to not only be perceived like that but to actually act like that? One I heard recently was, "Samantha is so cool under pressure, it's like she's an iceberg." It wasn't meant as an insult—all of these things were said in admiration, as if I was something to aspire to. I used to feel that way too—until I didn't.

Now I hate it. I hate it all. But I don't know how to change. I can't seem to release the pressure I feel to act that way, because people expect it from me.

My relationship with Trevor was the perfect example of how out of touch with the human experience I was, and it was my wake-up call.

So when Deacon said I wasn't stuffy, I wanted to hug him for being the first person to notice I might not have a heart made of ice. But since I knew that would make me look insane, I thought about slugging him instead. But again—insane. Hence the standing there trying not to cry. And not to look like I was trying not to cry. The emotional dam I've built over the years to keep back my tears and feelings and create an image of someone who is unflappable and . . . well, stuffy . . . is eroding. There are cracks all over the place, and I'm afraid that one big push is all it needs to come crashing down in a wave of emotional disaster. That's why I need to figure this out. Quite frankly, I'm tired of the energy it takes to constantly stay in control of what I've locked up tight in the deep recesses of my mind.

And now, my plans to conquer my fear of water went down the drain—no pun intended—unless I suck up my pride and go back to the snorkel class in the morning.

I'm sitting on the back porch, looking out into the ocean as the sun goes down. It looks like diamonds have been sprinkled across the surface of the water. It looks so inviting and peaceful, but I know it's not. I love looking at the water. I love listening to the water. I love the smell of the water. I just can't go in it.

Instinctively I grab my phone and dial.

The next voice I hear is thickly accented and gruffly masculine. "Good day to ya, Cap'n. Hoist the sails, cuz there be a storm comin' quick." And all of a sudden, the voice changes to a completely contemplative feminine voice. "Hey, Babe, if a storm is coming, do you *hoist* the sails? Or do whatever the opposite of *hoisting* is?" Each use of the word *hoist* is emphasized and still slightly accented.

No one can put a smile on my face like Steph. "Well, if I knew any proper pirates, I would do some research on that, but since I don't . . ." I let my sentence die off as I hear Steph sigh with disappointment.

Her voice immediately peps right back up. "I wasn't expecting to hear from you twice on your first day there, but when I saw it was you, I knew I needed to do something properly seafaring for you. Ya know, since you are with the sea," her laugh tells me that she thinks she's hilarious. "And a pirate accent was the first thing that came to mind." She slips back into the accent. "I hope I wasn't a disappointment to ya, m' lass."

"You're the best, Steph. You can put a smile on my face when the world wants to knock it off." I sigh a little.

"Spill it, Sister! This morning you were hungover, and now you're a squeaky grocery cart. What's going on?"

I actually managed to laugh at the accuracy of her assessment. "It's pretty bad. You know I have some tough challenges to work through, which is why I'm here, but ever since I arrived, it's like my brain has forgotten that I am an incredibly educated, successful, capable, and put-together person. I've either been crazy, lashing out and rude, or a mushy baby who wants to cry. I don't even recognize myself today!"

"What was the crisis today?" Steph asks in her *I am all business* tone of voice, like she's an FBI agent taking a statement from someone.

"I . . ." I knew I would tell her eventually, but I wasn't planning on it this soon. "I . . . went to a beginner's snorkeling class." The silence on the other end of the line lets me know she understands what that means.

"Samantha," Steph only calls me that when she drops all her silliness and is just her. No flourishes, no crazy. Just her. And it happens when she senses that I really need her. "Wow, I'm a little speechless here. I knew you were going to tackle some issues, but on day one?!" Her voice fills with all the tenderness I need from my best friend in the whole world. "How did it go?"

"Not well. I didn't even make it into the front office. I sat in my car and psyched myself out until my five-year-old next-door neighbor came running out and gave me the biggest hug. Then this man came outside and . . . ," I close my eyes and my shoulders drop as I let out a big sigh. "It was the same guy from the bar last night. What are the chances?!" I throw a hand in the air as if she can see me. "I couldn't do it! He'd already seen me during the second most humiliating night of my life, and I couldn't bring myself to have him teach me snorkeling. OH! The class was for kids by the way. Ages five to ten!" I hear her give a little chuckle, but I'm okay with it because I know she's not laughing *at* me. She's laughing at the ridiculousness of the situation. "I can't even explain what happened, but he got me all flustered, and I forgot I was an adult who could act with a level head. One moment I wanted to lash out at him, and the next I wanted to hug him because he said something nice to me. But in the end, I think I was just defensive and rude because I felt all the humiliation from the night before."

"I promise you, you didn't lash out at him for any reason other than the fact that you are there to make some big changes. That makes you feel vulnerable, and that means you don't have control, and you hate not having control. That's what this is all about, so cut yourself some slack." She elevates and punctuates each of her next words to make sure I understand her next phrase clearly. "You don't want to be the Ice Queen, remember? What you are experiencing is something others call *emotions*." She draws out that last word. "Say it with me: E-MO-TION."

"Steph! Stop it." My voice is raised, but it's not because I'm mad. It's because I'm nervous—almost terrified. She's not wrong though. Keeping control of my life and my emotions has practically been my number-one goal for many years, and she's probably the only one who knows it. Vulnerability is the feeling, or e-mo-tion, I have avoided more than any other. The second I sense it, I stomp it down and move on to something I know I have complete control over. "You know this is hard for me . . ."

"Samantha Joy Turner, this will be the hardest thing you have ever done, but you can do it because you know how to do hard!" She calms her voice and starts her *ticking off a list* tone of voice. "One, you graduated from law school at the top of your class. Two, you were hired at the most prestigious law firm in Boston. Three, you are now the most sought-after lawyer on the East Coast in your area of expertise. Do I need to go on? You are all those things because you are fierce and brave and strong. You are a woman warrior and can do anything!"

At this point, I am on the verge of tears. Again. "Steph, this is different."

"How?"

"Because."

"Because how?" Her voice is challenging. She's trying to push me to the edge of something that I don't like.

"Don't push like this, Steph." I hate that my voice breaks.

She keeps her matter-of-fact tone of voice. "Why did you call me?"

This was not the question I was expecting. "I don't understand."

"It's a simple enough question. You called me. Why?" When I don't answer, she goes on. "You called because somewhere deep down you want a kick in the butt to get going, and you know I am the only one brave enough to do it! You are a goddess of strength, you beautiful creature! You have a heart of gold, and I feel like I am the only one lucky enough to see it. It's been under lock and key practically your whole life, and it's time to let it out of the cage."

"I don't feel very brave right now."

"But you are brave. You've been avoiding and deflecting every day for a couple decades to protect yourself, and now you will work every day to take down the wall you built."

She's right about everything, but I try one last time to justify forfeiting what I've been planning all these past months. "It would be so embarrassing to go back to the snorkel school in the morning and see that man again! Last night I was a mess, and this morning I was rude."

"You were only rude because you were humiliated to see him again after last night and you got defensive. Apologize and all will be well. Speaking of last night . . . ," her voice changes, like she's about to discover something scandalous. "Did he bring it up?"

I roll my eyes. "Yes. He said something about how he liked me better last night because I wasn't as rude." Steph's laughter on the other end of the line is so annoying, but I'm smiling at it anyway.

"You ran into the same man twice within twenty-four hours? And he gets your feathers ruffled? I gotta meet him! NO ONE gets your feathers ruffled! Tell me about him!! Is he tan? Does he have abs of steel? When are you going to kiss him? Is he beautiful? When you have his babies, will they be gorgeous? And will you name one of the babies after me?" Each question is emphasized by a different-sounding tone of voice, which has me both laughing and shaking my head at her.

"Stephanie! You have no idea how inappropriate almost every question you asked me is!" I'm still laughing at where her mind goes. "First, he is tan. Second, I've never seen his abs. Third, I am positive I will never kiss him or have his babies because he is unavailable, so I am sorry that I can not name one of our babies after you. I will admit that he is objectively gorgeous to look at—but in the same way Chris Hemsworth is. Yes, a gift to everyone's eyes, but, again, unavailable."

"WHAT?!?" I can hear equal measures of outrage and disappointment in her voice. "How unavailable are we talking? Does he have a girlfriend?"

Only Steph can take me from gut-wrenching to smiling in the same phone call. "He's married with a five-year-old daughter, and they all live next door in the attached condo. We share a washer, a dryer, and a common wall, and it's all very domesticated."

When I hear the disappointed sigh on the other end of the line, I can tell I've crushed her dreams. "Fine. We will find you another man to have babies with so that you can name a child after me!" She says it like it's a call to battle.

"I think I have higher priorities when looking for a husband than having a child to name after you."

"Then your priorities are out of whack! For now, swallow your pride, go apologize, and then do the snorkeling class! *Don't think, just do.*" Her Yoda impression is actually fantastic. "You are only there for a few months. Who cares what anyone on the island thinks?"

"Steph, thanks. I miss you and I love you."

"Love you back, Wallaby Woman." I will never tire of her nicknames.

I go to sleep that night with her words traveling around in my mind: *You are brave*, and *Don't think, just do.*

And that's how I find myself outside my car the next morning in front of Breathing Under Water.

CHAPTER 9

Deacon

SHE'S STANDING IN THE parking lot.

She got here forty-five minutes early. She spent the first thirty sitting in her car, but now she's been standing next to her car for fifteen minutes. I guess it's time to go out and talk to her. I'd be lying if I said I didn't spend more time last night than I should have wondering if she would show up this morning. And I stayed away from Sam's—just in case she showed up. I wanted to give her some space, and after my *Coke or Pepsi* moment, I think I needed some space, too.

I walk outside and head for her car. When she sees me, she looks . . . I actually can't tell what's going through her mind, but at least she looks me straight in the eyes. Why not see how far I can push? "Good morning, Pepper." I smile like I don't know she hates my nickname for her.

"That's right. I forgot to tell Steph about Pepper."

I get the feeling she did not mean to say that out loud—something I suspect happened a couple of times yesterday. "Steph? Is that a boyfriend?" *Please say no.* "Or are you personal friends with Steph Curry?"

"What? Are you insane?" She looks slightly disgusted and completely confused by my question. She also seems to have no problem being rude again. I don't know her, but I can tell this is not who she really is. There is a lack of practice in her rudeness, as if it doesn't really fit her. Jet lag?

Or maybe heightened emotions? She did tell me she's afraid of the water, and she's here for a snorkeling class, so maybe nerves?

"Last I checked, I was not insane." I shrug my shoulders and let my head fall a little to the side, like I'm contemplating what she said. "But sometimes the crazy ones are the last to know," I stage whisper, smiling to let her know that I'm teasing.

For the first time, she looks as transparent as a jellyfish, and I feel I'm about to see her unfiltered version. She takes a deep breath, as if she is walking to the gallows.

"Steph stands for Stephanie. She's my best friend. I told her all about you when we talked." She told her best friend about me? Suddenly I've never been so interested in anything a woman has said to me. "I called her yesterday morning, and she instantly knew I was very . . . hungover." Sam seems to teeter on the edge of something, but I don't know what that is. I stay silent, not knowing if I'm supposed to respond or not.

After a pause, she continues, "She asked about that, since I've only had one other hangover in my life, and I told her how I made a colossal fool of myself in front of a man. Then, when I called her yesterday afternoon, I told her how I went to a beginner's snorkeling class to get over my fear of water, but it turned out to be for children, and the man who owns the company was also the man I humiliated myself in front of the night before. And after he had seen me during my second most humiliating night ever, I was so embarrassed that I became flustered and was rude to the man. Who is you. Then Steph and I acknowledged that I should apologize . . . which I would like to do. I also informed her that I would never kiss you or have your children or name said-children after her. I'm also incredibly nervous right now, which is a feeling I am completely unaccustomed to, but I am trying very hard to allow my emotions to be both felt and acknowledged. And for reasons beyond my control, it unfortunately falls upon you to witness this moment, which is—as I said—unfortunate. Due to that fact and that I am feeling very vulnerable—another feeling I have been avoiding for many years—I would very much appreciate you not responding to me with any words. If you would just . . . ," she breaks eye contact with me for the first time and closes her eyes, "teach me how to get over my fear of water. I would like to be done here and move on from the uncomfortable encounters I seem to have with you."

She doesn't acknowledge, or even know, that tears have been coursing down both of her cheeks, and her nose has become slightly rosy because of it. She simply starts walking past me toward the front office.

I begin to process some of the things she said, when she turns back around to me.

"And I would also like to apologize to you, your wife, and your child for anything I may have said or done while inebriated that was inappropriate or crossed the line. I can assure you I meant nothing by . . . whatever it is I may have done." Then she turns around and walks into the office.

I stand in complete silence as she disappears through the door. I had been trying to process the, what felt like, one-hundred different things she said—including that she told her best friend that we will never kiss or name any of our children after her—but then she threw out that last comment and it's all I can think about. *Since when did I get married and have a child?*

CHAPTER 10

Deacon

As the class starts, I have no idea what to say to Sam. It's obvious we need to have a discussion—she has come to some very wrong conclusions about my life and I very much want to set her straight. I'm trying to figure out how to do it in the middle of a snorkel class full of children, but I'm working with the kids and she's on the opposite side of the pool. It took some coaxing just to get her in the water, but after promising that she wouldn't have to go past her knees, she stepped in.

I have already finished my demonstration on the different parts of the mask and snorkel and how to fit them to their faces and given them some activities to get used to breathing under water. Now my teenage employees are helping all the little kids, so I am able to move over to where Sam has been standing.

"It's time to fit a mask to your face. The ones that will fit you are inside, but you can use mine." I push my mask toward her, but when she reaches for it, I don't let go. "Before I give you my mask, I have a few questions."

She replies with a business-like tone of voice, though it's mixed with something I would call *the tremors.* She's definitely nervous and trying to hide it. But is she nervous about my questions or the mask? "Are you going to test me? Because I was listening to all your instructions, and I don't feel like being tested like a child."

"Don't worry," I say with a calm voice—I don't want to get her defenses up again, but at the same time I'm not entirely sure how to have this conversation. "My question is not class related. It's on a more personal level." Her eyes shoot straight to mine and narrow in suspicion. "I was wondering why you think I have a wife and child, because I can assure you I don't have either." Her mouth drops open like she might speak, but no sound comes out. "I wanted you to know that, so you don't worry about what happened at the bar the other night." When she doesn't speak again, I try to clarify. "I mean, I don't have a wife to be upset about the way you were . . . touching me." I sigh because that came out *so* wrong, but I don't know how else to phrase it.

"But . . . she . . . and she . . ." I have never seen anyone deflate so fast in my life. This poor woman cannot catch a break. It's like the universe is trying to find every form of embarrassment known to mankind and cram them into a thirty-six-hour period, and all in front of the same person: *me.*

I keep my questions simple. "Is this because of Lou?" The nod of her head is almost imperceptible. "And because she calls me Dee-Dee?" Her nod is slightly bigger this time. "And also because she and Amber live with me?" She nods again. "Amber is my sister, and Lou is my niece. When Lou was learning to speak, she called me Dee-Dee because she couldn't say Deacon, and it has stuck ever since. It does not mean Daddy, Dada, or any other form of Father. They moved in with me about eighteen months ago. I am not married. I am not dating anyone. I am very much single."

"You are not married?" Her voice is a cocktail of thoughts that I can tell she's trying to sort out.

"Very much no. And it is important to me that you know that."

Her brow furrows and she tilts her head slightly. "Why?"

Once again, I might as well go for broke. "Because I am planning on asking you to dinner, but if you thought I was married . . ." I let my voice trail off, not sure what to say next. "I just think it wouldn't go over very well if I asked you to dinner again and you thought I was married."

"Again?" Her voice is laced with confusion.

"I asked you yesterday. I admit, my timing was bad, but I told you maybe we could have dinner together so that you could *ask the owner,*" I point to myself, "whatever you wanted to ask me."

"But I thought you were asking for a business meeting. I never thought it was a . . ." She lets her words trail off and then looks even more confused, if that was possible. "Why would you want to ask me out to dinner?"

"That is a compelling question to which I have no direct answer other than this: you intrigue me. You are interesting and I find myself wanting to figure out what makes you tick." At this, her jaw drops open in shock—again. I could tell her other things that would be more flattering. I could tell her she's the most beautiful woman I've seen on this island, or maybe ever. That the combination of her dark-red hair and green eyes are affecting me more than anything has in a long time. I could mention that it's more than her hair and eyes. That I didn't mind one bit that she poked me, kissed the lobster on my shirt, passed out on me, and "let me" carry her home. I could tell her a lot of things, but I get the feeling that right now is not the time for flourish and flattery. So I'm going to stick with what I've already said, because that's also the truth.

"Makes me tick?" Her forehead is creased and her eyes look lost.

My head falls slightly to the side, and I take a beat before speaking again, but I keep looking directly in her eyes. "I think there is a lot more to you than what I've seen so far. I wouldn't mind a chance to spend some time with you and figure out what that is." She's still looking at me in stunned silence. "So, Samantha Sam Pepper," I say this like it's her full legal name, "you intrigue me, and at some point, I want to have dinner with you."

She stares at me like I've grown a second head. I get it, though. A man she thought was married five minutes ago now wants to have dinner with her sometime. It would take a moment to digest. And I know, I should have waited to bring up going to dinner. Oh well, I've never been patient when I'm this curious. I clap my hands once in a way that means *let's table that discussion for now*. "In the meantime, how about we get this mask on your face?" I hold my mask out and, this time, let her take it.

She takes the mask from me, but I can tell she's still processing. Without me saying a word, she does everything she needs to do and fits the mask perfectly to her face. I guess she really was listening during class.

I point to where the kids are still floating and using the equipment. "The rest of class today is what they are doing. It's getting used to putting your face in the water and doing things like blowing bubbles while wearing the mask, taking a few breaths with the snorkel—things like that."

"No." Her answer is short but absolute.

"No?"

She doesn't even look at me as she takes the mask off. "No. I won't do that."

"For clarification, what are you saying no to? Putting your face in the water? Or going to dinner with me sometime?"

"Both."

Ouch. She looks quite resolved in her answers, but I need more explanation. "May I ask why you won't put your face in the water?"

"Because it terrifies me."

"I can accept that answer, and from what I remember you saying yesterday, that is what you are trying to overcome by coming here. Now, may I ask why you will not go to dinner with me sometime?"

"Because."

I nod my head like I understand, but I honestly have no clue. "So the water gets more of an explanation than I do? Interesting. May I ask why that is?"

"You might not like the answer about you, so I chose not to give it."

I shoot her an amused smile. "When Heather West rejected my request to go steady in the seventh grade, it only took me a couple weeks to get over it, so I feel I can cope pretty well with whatever it is you have to say."

"Fine." She takes a breath, resigning herself to say something unpleasant. "I could never go to dinner with a man that I keep finding new ways to embarrass myself around. I don't blame you for any of this—I seem to do all the work myself—but I can't help but think it would happen again, and that doesn't appeal to me."

"Give me one dinner sometime." I hold up a single finger and flash her my most flirtatious smile. "One. And if you sense anything embarrassing is about to happen, please notify me and I will gladly jump onto the table and recite a Shakespearean sonnet, taking all the embarrassment on myself."

She gives me the smallest amount of hope, as one side of her mouth tips up in an almost-smile. "Cross your heart and hope to die?"

I falter a little on her turn of phrase, but I nod and cross my heart with my finger. She looks down at my chest to watch, but her eyes continue a bit farther down my body and freeze, her face going a little pale. "Umm . . . is something wrong?" I don't think she even realizes I said anything. I snap my fingers to get her attention.

Her eyes pop back up to mine—they are big as saucers. "Yes. No. I'm fine. I'm sorry. I . . ." Her cheeks are as red as a sunburnt tomato, and her words are suddenly choppy. "So just bubbles? Okay." And then she quickly puts the mask back on and bends at the knees until her face and mask are in the water. She blows one big bubble, stands up, takes the mask off, and hands it to me. "Thank you for the use of your abs today. MASK! Thank you for the use of your *mask* today. I appreciated the class." With that, she gets out of the pool and starts to leave.

Then the pieces click into place. I'm not one to flaunt my body, but I don't hate the reaction I just got from her—in fact, it put a huge smile on my face.

I look back toward her, and she has stopped walking and turned back to look at the pool. I can't tell if she is crying again or if the water is just dripping from her curly red hair.

After she stays motionless for several moments, I get out of the pool and walk over to her. "Are you okay?"

Her gaze jerks to mine, as if she'd forgotten I was there. "I just stuck my face in the water."

I furrow my brow, trying to decipher what I'm missing. "Yes you did. I was there and saw it. Was that . . . a problem? I thought you did great."

Her eyes cloud over. "I haven't been able to do that in a very long time." When she is done revisiting whatever she was thinking about, her eyes come back to mine. "Thank you." She turns to leave but then stops to look at me again. "And you can pick me up at seven."

CHAPTER 11

Samantha

THE SELF-LOATHING I FEEL right now is at a never-before-seen level. Since I've been on this island, I've changed my entire persona—from polished and professional to . . . something I can't even name. But whatever it is, I hate it. At the same time, I can also see that I'm such a disaster it's practically comical.

I don't have the emotional bandwidth to even call Steph and fill her in on what happened today, because I wouldn't even know where to begin. Nothing about this is believable. It's like I'm the leading lady in a slapstick comedy that I didn't know I was starring in.

I can't believe I made a fool out of myself. Again.

Could this get any worse? Unfortunately, the answer is probably yes, and it will happen sometime tonight on the date I didn't want to go on. I had already told him no! But then, out of nowhere, I told him what time to pick me up!

I was half way home when I realized what I had done, and I nearly careened off the road. I had been so embarrassed at getting caught gawking at Deacon's abs that, without thinking, I stuck my face in the water and blew one big bubble, hoping to hightail it out of there. *I put my face in the water.* I guess I'd been hit with an unexplainable surge of gratitude for his distracting abs, and I blurted out that he could take me to dinner.

I've always been very proud of the fact that I am not a woman who ogles and gets flustered seeing a man's physique. I go to the gym five times a week and see very fit men all the time. It's even commonplace to see many of those men shirtless, but I've never had the desire to look and take inventory of every perfectly chiseled dent and curve. When he crossed his heart, though, I noticed for the first time that he didn't have a shirt on. Steph's voice jumped into my head, telling me to take a good look so I could go into full detail later, and—in my emotionally weakened condition—my eyes complied. I started looking. I mean, *really* looking. I'd never allowed my eyes to rake over a man's torso like this before. It's like I was walking out of the desert and his abs were a nice, tall glass of refreshing ice water that I wanted to dive into. And to make it worse—he'd caught me doing it.

I've seen Trevor without a shirt on, but I'd never been tempted to devour him with my eyes like that. Honestly, I don't even know how Deacon and Trevor are the same species.

It was so humiliating!

I'm so enraged at myself and, once again, so embarrassed—it's almost entertaining. Almost. I have stayed inside my condo with the drapes closed since I got home, because I didn't want to see Deacon if he walked by one of my windows on his way home.

So, here I am, loathing myself for the situation I am now in and hoping he doesn't show up. But, on the off chance he does, I have dressed for a dinner date. I have a peach-colored sweater, which is a color I look good in but not great. And I've paired it with long, linen pants with a slight flair at the bottom, which is a style I look fine in but that doesn't really accentuate my figure as well as other styles. My hair is in a simple ponytail, which is fine but not great, because it never takes long for some of my curls to find their way out of their scrunchie confinement and look a little unruly. It's all very calculated. I have on a nice outfit, but not too nice. Casual, but not too casual. I need to send the right signal—which is no signal at all.

I've never been so hopeful that a date wouldn't show, but unfortunately, at seven o'clock sharp, there is a knock at my front door. My shoulders drop because, despite my hopes, Deacon is here.

Deacon, the not-married, not-a-father man whose chest I have poked, groped, and now ogled at—to the extent of being rendered temporarily insane and agreeing to a dinner date—is here.

I take a deep breath, compose myself, and open the door.

I'm not prepared for what I see. Deacon looks very casual—but not the good kind. At least not for a date. He's dressed in old, mid-thigh shorts; an overly worn Journey T-shirt; and flip-flops. For a date!

And his hair! I will admit that he normally has fantastic hair. It's blonde with golden sun-streaked highlights—not surprising due to his job—and has gentle waves that turn a little curly at the ends. It's long enough to almost touch a collared shirt but short enough to still look professional. It's actually amazing hair that I would normally find incredibly attractive. But right now, those waves look like he just rolled out of bed, and some of them are falling over his forehead.

There are romance books that talk about how a woman wants to reach up and "move an errant curl" off a man's forehead or "run her fingers through his hair." I've never understood that feeling until now—but in the books it's meant for sexual tension and chemistry. I want to move the errant curl that has fallen in front of his eyes so that he can see the glare I am giving him right now. And I want to run my fingers through his hair because it looks like it hasn't even been combed! It's annoying because he looks like he put no effort into his appearance.

I didn't want the date, but at least I put effort in. Granted, that effort was simply to make sure I made no impression at all. But at least it was something.

He must sense my thoughts, because he reaches up and moves the errant curl off his forehead and runs his fingers through his hair. In a very unfair result, his hair all of a sudden looks fantastic, and now I can see just how blue his eyes are. I won't be telling Steph that they are the exact color of Chris Pine's eyes. She wouldn't let that one go.

He must see how speechless I am, because he is the first to speak.

"Good evening, Deke. Don't you look nice and comfortable." He says this in a voice that is obviously supposed to be his best impression of me, or what he thinks I sound like. When I still don't speak, he continues, but in his own voice. "Thanks, Pepper. I have been told many times that I'm nice, and I am, in fact, very comfortable."

I hate that he's using that nickname for me, but I feel like he's doing it just to get a reaction from me, so I can't show it. I simply respond with a perfectly executed arched eyebrow and fold my arms across my chest in a slightly challenging way. I want to convey that I'm not impressed, but he deciphers my actions to mean I want him to continue this two-sided conversation all by himself.

"Why, Deke," again in his interpretation of my voice, *"I'm really looking forward to tonight. I don't know many people on the island, and so I'm thrilled you accepted when I asked you out on a date."* His voice changes again and he continues.

"Pepper, it was my pleasure. Thanks for asking." Then he leans against the doorjamb, folds his arms across his chest in the most relaxed way, and gives me the kind of grin that could charm a space heater from a freezing man. It's so gorgeous it's almost disarming.

Then I realize what he said. "Wait. What? I didn't ask you out for dinner. *You asked me.*"

"No I didn't. I told you I was planning on asking you to dinner, but I never actually asked, because you said you were going to say no. Somewhere during our compelling conversation, you obviously decided that dinner with me was too tempting and commanded that I pick you up at seven. It was a little demanding and unconventional—but hey! I'm all for an empowered woman." The smile creeping across his face is like that of a sly jungle cat. "I guess I won you over with my great wit and charm, and you were too excited to spend the night with me."

His smile tells me that he knows the double meaning of his last sentence. He's trying to bait me, and I won't fall for it. For once I will hold myself together around this man. I have stared down the most defiant of judges, mediators, lawyers, and high-priced executives, and for the first time since arriving on the island, I feel like I can successfully tap into that strength, which makes me feel suddenly giddy.

"One point to Deacon." I lick a finger and make an imaginary tick mark in the air with a completely straight face. "Now, if you're done being funny, I'm hungry. Where are we going for dinner?"

"You think I was kidding? Pepper, I can honestly say that I didn't plan a thing." He looks so smug. So pleased with himself. His crooked smile sits so comfortably on his tanned face, like it was created just to torment me.

He's starting to affect me, and it makes me want to smile back at the ridiculous situation we are now in, but I don't. "Deacon, you now know for a fact that I did not intend to ask you out, so you also know that I made no plans." If I was frustrated with myself earlier, I'm even more so now because, as much as I try, the corner of my mouth lifts just a little.

He smiles back for a moment before speaking again. "Okay, we can think of something." Then he shifts his gaze, looking off into the abyss with squinty eyes. It's the look someone gets when they're trying to come up with an idea. Then he abruptly stands up straight and starts rubbing his hands together. "I've got it. Put your swimsuit on and meet me on the back deck. You've got five minutes." His smile is open and sincere. He's not trying to tease, poke, prod, or bait me. He turns to leave.

"Wait! Swimsuits on the deck? This is supposed to be dinner! And full disclosure—I'm hungry. I didn't have lunch."

"Pepper," his tone of voice is so teasing and playful and dripping with sarcasm that I know—whatever he says—he's full of it. "It's adorable you were so nervous to go on a date with me that you couldn't even eat lunch."

"You couldn't be more wrong. I was so nervous because I was hoping you wouldn't show up." I don't even try to hide how smug I feel proving him wrong, and the raised corner of my mouth shifts into the smallest of smiles.

"You've wounded me." I can tell he's not even a little bit wounded. "Why wouldn't you want to have dinner and get to know me better? Check my Yelp reviews. I get at least a 3.5 rating on all my first dates."

At this I actually laugh out loud. "You know why. I already told you. I can't stand to embarrass myself around you one more time, and it seems that is all I can do. Tonight proves my point!" My head is shaking in an *are you for real?* kind of way, but I can't wipe the smile off my face.

He's had an air of fun teasing in his voice, but at my words, he tilts his head a little, and his smile turns from teasing to curious. "Are you embarrassed about this?"

"Yes!" I can't hide the shock on my face that he would think otherwise. "How can you not see what a fool I have—once again—made of myself in front of you?" The words might seem like a defensive stance, but my face shows that I clearly find some part of this amusing. "I made an assumption that you had asked me out to dinner, which you hadn't. And when you show up, it turns out you think I asked you out!" A small, exasperated kind of laugh escapes my lips. "Let the record state, your honor, that yes, I should be found guilty of being embarrassed by that."

"Let the record state?" He starts earnestly laughing. "I'm not sure this situation demands the legal system to sort out."

"I'm sorry." I can feel a blush rising up my neck. "I am, in fact, a lawyer. Courtroom talk is second nature to me."

"Lawyer, huh?" He gets very serious and takes a step closer. "I need to know, have you ever pounded your fist on a table and yelled, '*You can't handle the truth!*' like they did in that movie?"

I can't help the full belly laugh that escapes now. "Are you serious? First of all, I do mergers and acquisitions, not courtroom law. Second, it was Jack Nicholson's character who said that line, and he wasn't the lawyer. He was the witness." There is some kind of strange banter going on between us right now, and, though it's not second nature to me, I'm actually enjoying the challenge and rising to the occasion.

"Pepperrrrrr," he draws the name out and has such a look of anticipation on his face, like he's about to drop a truth bomb on me, that I feel little butterflies swooping around in my belly, anticipating what he's going to say.

His voice is quiet, but his eyes still sparkle with a kind of playful mischief as he takes one more step toward me. "You lied to me." I have no idea what he is talking about. He adopts a tone that sounds like some trial lawyer on a cheesy TV series. "*I move to strike your testimony. Let the record state that you,*" he points at me, "*Pepper Smith . . .*"

"WHAT? My last name is not . . ."

Deacon turns the full force of his energy toward me, and I step back in shock. "*Silence, or I will hold you in contempt of court!*" His attempt at sounding authoritative falls completely flat, since his smile is large and his blue eyes are bright and sparkling. He starts slowly circling me as he talks. I can't help but rotate my head and body as he circles, so I can keep my eyes on him. "As I said, I move to strike your testimony. Earlier you said, 'Courtroom talk is second nature to me.'" He returns to his fake, TV-lawyer voice and adds, "*But then you admitted you are not a courtroom lawyer. Therefore, Pepper Smith, you have been found guilty of falsely representing yourself.*" He stops moving and takes a step closer to me.

"You're ridiculous." I hate that my voice has a smile in it and gives away that I find him more entertaining than ridiculous or annoying. "I did not insinuate I spent my time in a courtroom. I simply meant that legalese, or legal jargon, or whatever you want to call it, is second nature to me."

He ignores me completely. "I hereby hand down your punishment, to be served immediately. You now have only three minutes to put on your swimsuit and meet me on the back deck." He looks directly into my eyes, like he's laid down a challenge and is checking to see if I take it up. Up close I can see flecks of gold in the blue of his eyes. He casually looks at his watch and back up at me. Then he winks and turns to leave.

"Wait! No. I don't understand." I was never good at being spontaneous like this. I need a plan. I need to know what to expect, so I can mentally prepare and get a grasp on the situation. And "*meet me outside in your swimsuit in three minutes*" is definitely something I don't have a grasp of yet.

He turns around and speaks in a very matter-of-fact way. "You gave me less than one minute to come up with a dinner plan for the date you asked me on. I was serious when I told you that I was going to ask you out because I wanted to get to know you. That would mean we need to talk to each other—so Sam's is out because it's too loud. Therefore, I'm calling an audible and bumping tomorrow's dinner plans to tonight, which requires you to be in a swimsuit because I'm hoping dinner is in the lobster trap I set out this morning. So, Pepper," I can tell he loves calling me that—only because he knows how much I hate it. "You now have," he looks at his watch, "two minutes."

And then he turns and leaves.

CHAPTER 12

Deacon

DID I REALLY THINK Sam had asked me out to dinner? No. But I wasn't about to pass up a chance to tease her when she told me to pick her up at seven o'clock.

Every interaction I've had with Sam has shown me a different side of her. I've seen a drunk version of her who is not only full of spunk but also worries when she thinks others are hurt. A version who is fantastic with kids. One who gets defensive and rude and tries to pick verbal fights when she's thrown out of her comfort zone—only to come back the next day and apologize with tears flowing down her cheeks. I'm honestly not sure she knew she was crying while she was giving me her speech, because she never reached up to wipe a single tear away. And that brings up another version I've seen: the one that nervous-talks. After apologizing, a lot of things came spilling out of Sam's mouth that I am pretty sure she didn't mean to tell me.

Then the version who was in the pool this morning was the most different. She was quiet, nervous, scared, and kept to herself in the corner, like a baby deer standing before a hunter. But she still stayed and put her face under the water. That's actually a big deal for someone who has a fear of water, and it made me respect her bravery. Conquering any fear is a big deal. I should know. I'm working on that right now myself, though I don't always feel as brave as I saw her be this morning.

When I showed up at Sam's house tonight, it took her a moment to relax, but after she did, I saw the version of her I like the best so far. It's what my mind is already referring to as her *authentic side*. I saw her spunky version at the bar, but tonight she was also willing to banter and spar with me in a way that felt like we had both won by the end. And while her smile was intoxicating that first night, her sober smile and laughter produce a light that could power the space station, which is probably what Lou saw in her when they first met. Lou has always been a great judge of character.

I know I've just met her, but I can tell she is incredible. She's the type of person I want to spend time with. A lot of time. More time than I want to admit to myself. And that's ridiculous, because—again—I've just met her.

I feel my phone buzz in my pocket and take it out to read a text.

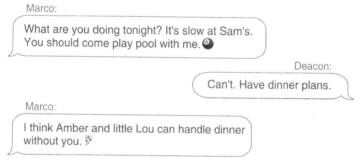

Marco:
What are you doing tonight? It's slow at Sam's. You should come play pool with me. 🎱

Deacon:
Can't. Have dinner plans.

Marco:
I think Amber and little Lou can handle dinner without you. 🌭

How much do I want Marco to know? If I tell him the truth, I might regret it. If I don't, he might make me regret it when he finds out. I decide to try and stay as vague as possible.

Deacon:
My plans aren't with them.

Marco:
ARE YOU SERIOUS? You're dating Samantha?!?!?!?!?!?!?!!?!? 😱

My heart leaps out of my chest, and I frantically look around as if someone could actually hear the words and see the emoji on my screen. I can't have this conversation via text, so I call him. It only rings once.

"Can I please plan the bachelor party?" I can hear not only the jukebox in the background but also the smirk on his face.

"You used the bride emoji? You're an idiot." His laughter rings through the phone much louder than the jukebox does. "Yes. I'm having dinner with Samantha. No, we are not dating. This isn't even a real date, and I'm expecting her outside with me any second, so I don't have time to explain that to you. Also, excessive punctuation on that text. You need to seek help."

"Put her on the phone. I'll make you sound better than you actually are, and then she'll be begging you for a ring!"

"Again—you're an idiot. She's not even out here yet, which is why I should get off the phone."

"Wait! What are you having for dinner? Should my feelings be hurt that you didn't bring her here?"

"It's a twisted story, but it boils down to my lobster traps and a lobster dinner. And how did you know my plans were with her anyway?

"Deke, I'm the only person you've had dinner with since you've been on the island, outside of Lou and Amber. It wasn't that big of a stretch—Samantha and Cheryl are the only ones on the island who are better looking than me." His laughter booms through the phone again. I love that Marco doesn't take life seriously. He keeps people grounded in what's important, even if he is a pain in the butt right now.

"Marco, I really should get off the phone."

"Wait! I just need to know—is she a good kisser?"

"You're an idiot."

"A little harsh don't you think?" a feminine voice asks. I spin around so fast that my phone almost slides out of my hand. Sam is standing behind me.

How much of that did she hear? I need to get off the phone. "Marco, don't worry, you're just as pretty as all the other girls at the ball." I hang up on him. "Sorry, that was Marco. Been standing there long?"

"Nope, just got here. So where's my dinner?" Her look is a little challenging and a little playful. I'm glad she didn't lose the fire I saw from her when we were inside, because that was something I could definitely get used to. Then my eyes take her in. She's wearing very tailored and starched linen capris. Some kind of floral shirt is tied in a knot at her waist, and all of the buttons are undone, showing off what seems to be a light-pink one-piece swimsuit with a classic scooped neck. It suits her more formal side and not what I now think of as her authentic side.

"I told you to be out here in two minutes. You took ten. If you want dinner now, it's going to cost you." I'm smiling, so she knows I'm not upset, but I make sure my voice has enough of an edge that she knows I'm pretending to be serious.

Her eyes narrow the slightest as she tries to figure out my meaning. "Cost me? How?"

"If you want dinner, you give me a secret." I shrug my shoulders like this is the easiest thing in the world, but if I'm right, it will ruffle her feathers a little bit. Which, I will admit, is my goal.

She stands still for a moment. Very still. Then she adopts some kind of carefree attitude and nonchalantly says, "I'm an open book. Ask me anything."

She's full of it. By her reaction, I can tell she has secrets that run deep. Not that she's killed someone and is the only one who knows where the body is, but she's definitely holding onto things she doesn't want to talk about. I don't want to make her uncomfortable—I want her to trust me—so I give her my most-serious stare down as I ask for my secret. "Football or basketball?"

I can tell I've taken her by surprise, and I see her shoulders release some tension as she rolls her eyes at me. "My sports preferences aren't a secret."

"I don't know them, so they're a secret to me. Let me try again, *Pepper-Girl.*" I can see the corner of her mouth fight hard not to turn up at my use of the nickname, and it makes me feel like I've won a little prize. I take one step closer. "Football or basketball?" I keep my stare fixed on hers.

"If you must know," she folds her arms and adopts the most adorably smug look on her face, "neither."

"I object!"

"Overruled." She rolls her eyes at me as she lets out a small laugh. "And besides, you're badgering the witness." She's pretending to be outraged.

"Your honor, I ask permission to treat the witness as hostile." As my voice echoes very serious undertones, I take another step toward her. I'm only an arm's length away, which is an arm's length closer than I should be but—frustratingly— also an arm's length farther away than I want to be.

She shakes her head and, once again, rolls her eyes at me. "You are ridiculous! I can't be both the judge and the witness. You'd make a terrible lawyer." She starts laughing. "I'm going to regret telling you I'm a lawyer, aren't I?"

"Probably." I drop the fake lawyer voice and smile at her. Then I take one step back, to the safety zone. "Okay, how about this—why don't you tell me why you're afraid of water?" I hope the sound of my voice lets her know that I'm also okay if she doesn't tell me.

We stand facing each other, and I hold her gaze. It's not a staring match. It's not uncomfortable. I can tell she is mulling the question over in her mind, deciding whether or not she wants to tell me.

After a moment, she seems to resign to something and opens her mouth to speak. "I need a certain amount of control in my life. Having it makes me feel safe and comfortable." She's silent for a moment, but I don't say anything, hoping she'll go on.

"I don't feel like I have control in the water. It's stronger than I am, and that terrifies me." I can tell there's more to that story, but I know it's all I'm going to get tonight.

"Okay." I nod my head, letting her know that I'm satisfied and won't pry anymore. "That earned you dinner. But if you want dessert, I'll need another secret." I throw her a snarky smile and start to move away, but she reaches out and puts a hand on my arm to stop me. She just initiated physical touch. I'm okay with that.

"Not so fast." When I turn back around, her emerald eyes bore into mine with a challenging look. There is a slight lift to her brows and a sly grin shimmering on her lips. My heart reacts in a way I wish it wouldn't. "If I had to spill a secret to get dinner, then you do too."

She wants to know something about me. This is . . . unexpected. "Sorry. My dinner. My rules." My words are harsh. My tone of voice is not. I can tell she doesn't believe a word of what I just said.

"Then I will say goodnight and hope you enjoy dinner by yourself." With that, she smiles and turns toward her door, moving to go in. The little tease. I like this side of her.

I wait until her hand reaches for the latch before I cave in. "Okay, okay. Can I tell you any secret I want? Or is there one in particular you want to ask me?"

Her body language shifts just a little. If I wasn't so good at reading people, I would have missed it, but it was definitely there. Whatever she wants to ask also makes her uncomfortable. "I want an honest answer about why you really wanted to take me out to dinner."

I can feel the shock register on my face. After I recover, I slowly start to answer. "Okay, here is the truth." I take a breath and hold it for a moment, not knowing how much I want to tell her. "At first, when I saw you at Sam's, I thought it would be fun to tease you a little bit." I see her bristles coming out and a protest forming on her lips. "Don't worry! I never would've been mean. It was like . . . wanting to hang out with someone who just had their wisdom teeth taken out, hoping they'll say something funny. Then, even in your drunken stupor, you wanted to help me when you thought I was bleeding, which was really nice of you. But you were also outrageously singing along to the jukebox with more passion—and less skill—than anyone I've ever heard." I can't help a small laugh escaping as the memory passes through my mind. "Then you got all worked up about your name and why you hated Sam and wanted to be Samantha . . ."

She interrupts me and awkwardly tries to stop whatever it is I'm saying. "It's fine. You don't have to finish answering. It was a dumb secret to ask for."

I watch her physically and emotionally stiffen, her relaxed version from earlier disappearing. My brows crease in concern, and I raise my hands in a show of innocence. "I feel like I've said something wrong, but I don't know what it is. I'm sorry if something I said upset you." I look to her for any clarification, but she remains silent.

My mind starts scrambling for better words than the ones I'd been using. "Look, Sam, or . . . sorry, Samantha. We all need people in our lives who can make us laugh and put a smile on our face. Every time I've met you, you make me want to laugh and smile. It's really that simple. I want to get to know the woman who puts a smile on my face."

We both stand in complete silence for a few moments. I hear the waves lapping up on the beach behind me and nothing else. I can't tell what she's thinking, but her gaze hasn't left mine.

Then she reaches up and wipes away a tear that I hadn't noticed before. "So," she quietly and slowly starts talking, "after seeing me in my drunken stupor, I made you smile?" Her brows are furrowed like she doesn't understand. "So you were laughing at me?"

"No!! Sam, no! *I wasn't laughing at you.* You made me laugh, and there's a big difference between the two! It felt more like laughing *with* you." I don't stop myself from walking over to her, putting my hands on her upper arms, and holding her in place while looking earnestly into her eyes. "Please believe me that I have never—not even once—laughed *at* you. I'm just someone who wants to get to know you better."

When she doesn't move or say anything, I try one more time to help her understand. "When you are drunk or bossy or rude or tender or nervous or brave, you still have a way of making me feel happy and relaxed. Or you did . . . until right now. Because I'm not relaxed, and I'm definitely not happy. But I think that's all my fault. Maybe?"

Her eyes are soft pools of green liquid when she starts to speak. "Even though I said and did things that were embarrassing? Even then, you wanted to be around me because that made you happy?"

"Yes."

"And when I acted strange and was so rude to you the first day at the snorkeling school?"

"Yes."

"Even when . . ."

"Yes, Sam," I interrupt her. "Yes to whatever you are going to say, because there is nothing I've seen you do that has made me not want to be your friend and get to know you better."

More tears slide down her cheeks when I say this. I have no idea what, but I feel something profound is going on behind her emerald eyes.

Quietly, and without any pomp and circumstance, she rises up and places her lips on the corner of my mouth in what feels like a very intimate gesture. She simply holds her lips there, locked in a tender kiss, for a long moment.

This kiss isn't about seduction. It's not even about romance of any kind. She is only holding a kiss to the side of my mouth in what feels like an acceptance of what I've said to her.

When she finally pulls away, she takes a soft step back and looks me in the eyes. "Deacon, I don't want you to think I'm upset at you or mad at you, because I'm not. But I'm not going to have dinner with you tonight. I'm going to go back inside my condo now. I've actually had a really nice time getting to know you better, and I think I'm glad we're neighbors." And she once again turns to leave.

"Sam . . ."

"Not tonight, Deacon." Her voice is gentle. "I can't tell you what's going on, because I think it's too big for even me to grasp right now." She must see on my face that I'm willing to let her go but still desperate for answers. "What I can say is that I've spent the last ten years building and maintaining a wall around myself. But it's been starting to crack and crumble and," she pauses for a moment and looks down at the ground as she thinks. Then her eyes come back up to mine. "I think a chunk just fell off."

"I'm . . . sorry? Is that my fault?" I'm not even sure what I'm asking.

"Yes." Then she gives me a small smile. "It is very much your fault. All these years, I thought it would be devastating if any part of my wall came down, but I actually feel . . . *hope*." Another tear slips down her cheek. "Thank you, Deacon. That's what the kiss was for. It was a thank you."

I stand still as she walks inside her condo. I have no reply, no response, no reaction. I feel like something just happened, but I have no idea what. I stare out to the ocean for . . . I actually have no idea how long.

"Deacon?" I turn around to see that Sam has opened her door back up and is standing in the opening. "I want you to know that you can ask me about this later. It's not that I don't want to talk to you about it. It's that I don't know *how* to talk about it right now. Does that make sense? I need a little time and maybe a little space too." I nod to her. She smiles and retreats back inside her condo.

CHAPTER 13

Samantha

NOTHING ABOUT LAST NIGHT seems real.

When I came in from the "date" with Deacon, I went straight to bed and laid down. At first I thought I might toss and turn all night, but I fell asleep immediately and slept until morning.

After having some breakfast, I comb through my hair with my fingers, put it in a simple ponytail at the base of my neck, and go to my closet to get dressed. I let my hands run across the clothes hanging there, and when I see a yellow-colored sundress, I stop. It used to be one of my favorites because I thought it looked good with my complexion and red hair, but I haven't worn it in years. Back in Boston I found it at the very back of my closet, along with other dresses like this, when I was packing. So far, I've still been wearing some variation of work-casual, but this morning, I can actually see a time when I might wear something like this again.

Now I'm sitting on the bottom stair off the back deck with my toes in the sand, trying to make sense of so many things.

Back at my office, when I couldn't make sense of something, it motivated me to action. It was like a battle call that I eagerly took up and devoured. I always lead the charge with my colleagues, and we combed through documents, spreadsheets, contracts, or anything we needed. I would spend multiple late nights, and sometimes all night, at the office until everything was in its place and we'd crossed all the t's and dotted all the i's—both literally and metaphorically. It was an adrenaline rush of the best kind, and I loved it.

This is distinctly different on every level. I feel no need to go and conquer, but also no desire to retreat and hide behind my emotional fortress—which is completely foreign to me.

I feel resigned, like it might be okay if my walls come tumbling all the way down and I have to sort through and deal with the hurts and humiliations of the past. It's time to face my fears and see if I recognize myself when I'm done. I don't really know how to move forward because I've never allowed myself to be here. I can't run away though—it's why I came here.

"Samantha!" I turn and see Amber, dressed in a mint-green and white striped swimsuit and holding a couple of towels, coming out of her back door. "How are you? I didn't see you at all yesterday."

I don't know how much Deacon has told her, so I'm not sure what to say. "I'm good. Soaking up the morning sun. Where's Lou?"

"Inside. I told her she had to clean her room before we played on the beach."

"Then come and sit down with me." I scoot over and pat the space next to me.

She sits, and a comfortable silence sets in until Amber speaks up. "I thought I heard voices as I was falling asleep last night, but I wasn't sure. Were you and Deacon out here?"

Falling asleep at seven and still sleeping in? She wasn't kidding when she said she'd been tired! "Yeah. When our dinner date didn't turn out the way . . ."

"You and Deacon had a *date*?" Amber interrupted. The look on her face is one of total confusion.

"Yeees." I draw the word out and say it more like a question. I thought she would have known, and now I'm not sure what to say. I think Amber can tell I'm taken back by her reaction, because she quickly shakes off her surprise and reaches over to put her hand on mine.

"I'm sorry. That was probably an overreaction on my part. I didn't know he asked you out. He's not gone on a date since we've been on the island, and I was just taken by surprise."

"Oh. Well . . . he didn't really ask me out." I involuntarily roll my eyes, remembering the conversation that ensued when he showed up last night. "I guess I sort of asked him out, but I didn't mean to. It was a big mix-up that was basically my fault, but in the end, it was actually a nice evening."

A nice smile sits on Amber's face as she looks back at me. "I'm so glad! He needs to take more time to himself and to get out and have fun. He's too focused on taking care of Lou and me and forgets to have a life sometimes."

"If I'm being honest, I didn't want to go out with him. I thought it was going to be a disaster."

The look on Amber's face makes me think there are battling thoughts going on inside her head. "Now I have so many questions and don't even know where to start!"

I laugh out loud—I was feeling the same way before she came out: where do I even start? "Well, let's pretend I'm an open book. Ask me whatever you want."

"Why wouldn't you want to go out with him? I mean, I know he's my brother, but I can impartially say that he's not only a really good guy but also incredibly good looking!" Her eyes tell me that she thinks I'm crazy.

"I'm not going to argue either point. He actually does seem like a good guy and is, in fact, very easy on the eyes, but . . ." I search my mind for what to say next. "What has Deacon told you about our interactions so far?"

"Well," she tilts her head a little as she thinks for a moment, "he said he helped you out the first night you were on the island. . . . Then he said you were going to take a class from him, but something came up and so you didn't. . . . But then you came back and took the class the next day. He said you did really well at the class." She pauses for a moment and then concludes with a shoulder shrug, "Nothing else comes to mind."

He could have told Amber so much about me—and most of it could have been very unflattering—but he has remained almost entirely silent about my embarrassments. And he "*helped me out*" my first night on the island? That's not how I would have phrased it if I'd been retelling the story. A feeling from last night comes back to me—how I felt when I was with Deacon. He felt . . . *trustworthy*? Is that the right word? Like he was safe. I guess he really is a good guy?

"Well, let's just say that no one on the island would ever think I'm a professional woman whose life was consistent, organized, put together, and lacked any and all drama. I feel like drama has been my constant companion since I've been here, and your brother seems to be around for every embarrassing episode."

Amber laughs a little at my confession. "I wouldn't worry if I were you. Lou and I provide so much drama that you probably seem like a breath of fresh air to him." Her smile is big as our eyes meet, but she must see the storm inside me, because her smile softens and she reaches to give my hand another squeeze. "Samantha, can I be completely intrusive right now and pretend we've known each other for years instead of a day or two?"

My heart picks up pace, and I don't even know why. Even though I have no idea what she's going to say, the tenderness in her face is so unlike what I'm accustomed to that I feel a terrible prickling behind my eyes. Not again. My tear ducts are standing at attention, ready to hang on Amber's every word, and I feel completely helpless to them. I squeak out a small, "Sure."

"You looked pretty deep in thought when I came outside. I kind of get the sense that maybe you're here to work through some stuff?" She says it like both a question and a statement. I give a small nod. "I don't know what your stuff is, but I've had plenty of my own. And whatever it is—if you're willing to embrace it, everything can be okay." Her voice is coated in tenderness and feelings on my behalf. I'm not sure anyone has ever looked as concerned for me as she does right now.

"You don't even know me."

"I know. At least, not yet. But I can tell we are going to be the best of friends."

My heart can't take it! "Cheryl wants to have lunch with me. Lou thinks I'm her favorite. Deacon wants to get to know me better. And now you? I can't piece it together." My tear ducts are loading every cannon right now, getting ready to fire all they've got, while my mind is wandering in a fog of disbelief.

Amber starts nodding like she has now figured it all out. What does she have figured out? Can she tell me? Because I just feel more confused! "Well, that tells me a lot about the people you've spent time with." She gives my hand another squeeze. "And don't try to piece everything together right now. Just lean in and trust yourself."

"I don't even know what that means."

Before she has time to answer, Lou comes tearing out of the house in a little pink swimsuit with ruffles on the sleeves. She starts talking a mile a minute, her sentences running into each other and each containing the energy of two exclamation points. "I made my bed so now we can swim!! Penelope!! I love my new best friend!!" She throws her arms around my neck before returning her attention to Amber. "I didn't find my other jelly shoe, so I got my polka-dot sandal instead,"—I look down and see that she is, indeed, wearing one polka-dot sandal and one purple jelly shoe—"but it will be good because the sand isn't hot yet, so I don't need either one!! And I thought Eli could come with us!!" She holds up a tattered teddy bear with a blue-knit scarf around its neck, a missing eye, and stuffing coming out of an armpit.

Thank goodness Lou showed up when she did, because it gave my tear ducts time to unload the cannons and put the tears away.

Amber sighs. "Lou, we've gone through this before. Eli needs to stay inside. He's not a beach toy."

"What about these?" Lou produces a backpack filled to the brim with different toys, none of which look beach appropriate.

Amber and I share loaded looks as we begin to stand. Her's says, *Sorry, I guess I need to parent right now, but I wish we could keep talking.* Mine says something like, *Amber, you're amazing. Thank you. How can you see into my soul like that? Do you have x-ray vision?*

Just as I head back inside, my phone starts ringing and I answer it. "Hi, hold on a second." I put my hand over the phone and look over at Amber, who's still rummaging through Lou's backpack. "Amber," she turns her head around to look at me, "for what it's worth, I'm glad you're my neighbor."

Amber smiles back. "I am too."

I walk into my condo and put my phone back to my ear. "This is Samantha. What's up?" I cringe at how casual my greeting is, but it flew out of my mouth before I could think of something else.

"My Sweet Little Samantha!" Cheryl's voice is like sunshine on steroids. "I'm so glad I got ahold of you. First off, how are those dead bolts? Did they get installed on all the doors?"

"Good morning, Cheryl. I was going to call you today and thank you for getting that done so quickly. I don't know how you do it, but you're one of the most efficient people I know."

"Oh stop it!" It's like I can hear her blushing on the other end of the phone. "The other reason I was calling was to see how you're doing. Are you all unpacked and settled?"

"Yes, and I also meant to thank you for the food you brought over my first night here. It was just what I needed the next morning to get me back up on my feet."

"What food?"

"The food you brought over . . . to my house . . . that was here after my . . ." A chilling sensation runs over me as I realize that there was only one other person who knew where I lived and who might've known I didn't have any food in my house. It was the man who brought me home that night. Deacon. "Cheryl, are you sure you didn't buy food for me and bring it over sometime on my first night here?"

"Sweet Pea, I think I would have remembered that." She has a chuckle to her voice.

I suddenly have a situation that is equal parts a puzzle that needs piecing together and just plain confusing. Usually Steph helps me out in situations like this. She sits and listens, and I talk until all the pieces magically fall together. Steph is a great listener that way. I don't know how good Cheryl is, but I need someone right now, and she's the best I've got. "Cheryl," I take a deep breath, because I normally avoid reaching out to others for help, "are you still interested in going to lunch with me?"

"Oh my word! I would love to go to lunch with you! Name the time and place!"

CHAPTER 14

Samantha

As I PULL UP to have lunch with Cheryl, I'm curious and anxious at what I will find. Curious because, for the life of me, I still have no idea how old she is or what she looks like. Anxious because, for me, reaching out to another person voluntarily to spend time with them socially is something I don't do anymore. Even with Trevor, I knew him for over two years before I went on a date with him, and I still kept things casual for another three.

When I asked Cheryl for a lunch recommendation, she suggested Sam's—again. So here I am, returning to the scene of the crime.

I walk in and start scanning the place, wondering if I'll know Cheryl when I see her. There is a man sitting at the bar eating peanuts who has a scruffy beard and skin that looks like 150-year-old aged leather. So, not Cheryl.

A man and a woman are sitting with half-empty drinks and an empty basket that once held food. Also not Cheryl.

In the corner by the jukebox is a woman who looks to be in her mid- to late-twenties. She has blonde, shoulder-length hair with highlights that look like they come from the sun, not from a bottle. Her lips are full and covered in bright-red lipstick. Her fitted dress is as red as her lips, and the black belt cinching her waist accentuates a gorgeously curvy figure. She is barefoot, so her shoes must be tucked under the table where I can't see them. To top it off, she has large black earrings and flaming red nail polish. This woman looks larger than life—even though she's only sitting in a chair. Her face says young, but her outfit says vintage 1950s with a touch of . . . something.

So, this is Cheryl.

I can't help but smile because, now that I see her, I can't imagine her looking any other way.

When I get a little closer to her table, I clear my throat. "Cheryl?" It comes out more as a statement than a question.

She jumps up and throws her arms around me with no hesitation at all. The top of her head hits the bottom of my chin, so I'm guessing she's around five feet even.

"My Sweet Little Samantha, let me look at you." Knowing that she's obviously younger than me and using words that should come from my grandma makes me love the pet name even more. Cheryl reaches up and grabs the sides of my face with her hands to inspect me. She moves my head gently from side to side then has me turn all the way around.

"You. Are. Perfection." She smiles at me. Is someone going to give me a trophy now? I feel like I won a contest for something.

I smile back. "It's so nice to meet you in person. You have no idea how much I've loved our phone calls. My work calls can be a little intense, and so talking to you is a breath of fresh air." I stand there and drink in this woman, who I all of a sudden want as my confidant and the newest member of my very small, but growing, list of friends on the island.

Cheryl motions for us to sit, and we do, facing each other with the table between us so we can talk. Luckily the jukebox isn't on, so we can hear each other.

"Now, I hope you don't mind, but I already ordered. I got a little bit of everything—so you can see what you like." I nod in agreement. "I didn't know your drink preference, so I got my regular drink," her eyes dance a little at this, "and you a special Dr. Pepper."

I smile that Cheryl guessed correctly on my drink preference, then my brows crease at the word *special*. "What makes it special?"

"I had Marco add coconut cream, a dash of vanilla syrup, and a squirt of lime. It's delicious. You'll love it." It's a statement. Her eyes instantly shift to something more serious, and it makes their bright-blue color seem darker. "Now, we are here to talk. So . . . spill it, Sister." I don't answer because I'm genuinely confused. Then her eyes shift, and they are no longer serious and bossy, but something I can't name. It feels like a truth-serum-Jedi-mind-trick that I didn't know humans could possess.

Without thinking about the repercussions, words start flying out of my mouth.

I tell her every detail of my interactions with Deacon the first night on the island. I move on to how rude I was the next morning and how I thought he was married. By the time I get around to how I ogled his chest and told him he could take me out to dinner, I've been talking uninterrupted for a solid ten minutes.

Cheryl remains silent and looks incredibly invested in what I'm saying, so I continue talking to this woman who, for all intents and purposes, should feel like a stranger to me but doesn't. "He showed up at seven," I go on, suddenly shifting from every detail to a quick recap, "and we went out on the back deck, and . . . he was . . . nice." The finality to my tone tells her I'm done.

She is quiet for a moment. "Explain '*and he was nice.*'" She puts her last words in air quotes.

I think through how I want to explain it, while she sits quietly. It's the first time since I've sat down that I've done my thinking before speaking. "I've had experiences in the past where people I thought were friends . . . abandoned me, in all the ways a person can be abandoned, when I did something embarrassing. It was as if I was no longer worth their time or attention—or maybe they thought they would somehow be tainted by their associations with me. This has caused me to act in ways that," I pause, looking for the right words, "assure me I won't do anything embarrassing or humiliating again." I choose my words carefully and am happy with how I'm explaining but not overexplaining.

Cheryl surprises me by chiming in. "Yes. You built bigger walls around yourself because of what happened ten years ago. But right now, explain '*and he was nice*.'" Again, the air quotes.

Without my permission, my jaw drops completely open. How did Cheryl know that the *something* was ten years ago? After a moment, I almost hear Mary Poppins in my head saying, *Close your mouth, Samantha. We are not a codfish.* I close my mouth. Cheryl is right, but I don't know how she's right.

"It's just that . . . ever since I met this man, I have done nothing but embarrass myself in front of him or be rude to him. But he hasn't judged me or wanted to laugh at me and move on, even though my actions would have made that easy for him to do. Instead, he said he wanted to take me out to dinner sometime and get to know me." The tone of my voice betrays that I'm still having a hard time understanding it all. And also, how is this woman still pulling everything out of me? And why is my mind so willing to comply? "I was so taken aback because . . . well, he was nice. I've not been around *nice* in a really long time. So I leaned in and gave him a kiss on the cheek . . . or the mouth. It was a little of both. I just wanted to thank him for seeing something in me no one has seen for a very long time—maybe ever. Not even myself. And the funny thing is that I'm not embarrassed about the kiss." For the first time, I'm unsure if I've said too much. I wish I could go back and edit my words.

Cheryl smiles at me. "That's because it was a moment of genuine, unfiltered emotion. You don't feel a lot of those." Cheryl's voice is strong and confident with a gentility that wraps me in a blanket of warmth and affection. "Is this the first time you've cried today?"

Her question takes a moment to register, then I reach up and am shocked to feel wet cheeks. "I don't know! I didn't even realize I was crying."

"That's normal." She shrugs like it's not a big deal that she can see into my soul. "Unpacking old emotions can be a wet business." She smiles and hands me a napkin to wipe my cheeks with.

At this moment, a familiar-looking man and teenage-looking boy arrive, each carrying multiple trays covered with all kinds of food. Cheryl wasn't lying when she said she ordered a little of everything. There are chips with salsa and fresh guacamole, several different kinds of fish, shrimp, sandwiches, carne asada tacos, appetizers, some kind of curry that smells amazing, and a few things I don't recognize at all. The familiar-looking man excuses the younger boy, then he places my drink in front of me. The lime resting on the edge of my glass has been cut and twisted in a way that makes me think it's a piece of art and not a simple lime. It's what you'd see in a place that also has intricately carved, four-foot ice statues. "This is amazing!" I can't hide the admiration in my voice.

"Thank you." The man delivering the food sets the last dish on the table and smiles up at me. He's probably six foot three and easily over 200 pounds, but it's all muscle and broad shoulders and toned thighs. His hair is dark brown with loose curls that almost hang into his eyes, which are just as dark brown as his hair. He looks like he should play football—not carefully cut and create the type of lime decor that's sitting on the edge of my glass.

He raises a large hand toward me. "I'm Marco. We didn't get introduced the other night when you . . . ," his voice trails off as he starts to look a little sheepish. "Well, I just want to say welcome to the island, and I'm really sorry about the other night."

That's why he looks so familiar. He's the bartender. I reach up and shake his hand, not sure what to say.

He releases my hand and looks over to Cheryl, and I see something I can't name flicker in his eyes. "I hope everything is to your liking, *Cherie*."

Cheryl's entire body tenses, and from the look on Marco's face, I can tell it's the response he was looking for. There is something going on right now, but I have no idea what it is. "Don't call me that." Her gaze is icy and cold and could be weaponized by hostile governments looking for world domination. I'm a little scared for Marco right now. Without breaking eye contact, she reaches down, grabs a nacho chip, and takes a bite. After chewing for a moment, she swallows. "Chips are a little salty today, Marco. You're off your game."

Marco appears to be completely unfazed by her comment and holds her gaze for a few more seconds before turning to me. "This is my place, so let me know if you want to try anything else."

"You own this place?" He nods. "But it's called Sam's."

"You're right." Then he nods and walks back behind the bar.

Cheryl picks up her fork and takes a bite of the curry dish like this wasn't a very strange encounter. Her voice is flat when she finally speaks. "Don't waste any time wondering about Marco. He's nothing like what you might expect." Then she dips a chip in the guac and takes a bite.

"Well, he's not who I would have expected to make shapes with limes, so I'll take you at your word."

Cheryl lets out a little chuckle. "Yes. Marco is full of a looooot of surprises." Her eyes sparkle, and a mischievous grin slides across her face. I don't even want to know. Cheryl takes this moment to lift her glass for a drink.

"NO!" I startle Cheryl enough that her glass stops halfway to her lips. "Don't drink that! It's some kind of toxic waste! I don't know what's in it, but it's the drink I had the first night I was here." I recognize all the colors in it. My voice drops in volume and pitch. "I think it's poison."

Cheryl's head flies back as she lets out a loud, long, genuine laugh. I can tell this woman doesn't hold back anything in her life. Not her fashion choices, her interrogation tactics, or her laughter. "My Sweet Little Samantha, Marco doesn't have anything strong enough for me, so I helped him *invent* this baby right here." Then she takes a long drink from her glass as if it's simple ice water.

How can this tiny woman drink that without even a wince? Will she ever stop surprising me?

Cheryl puts down her glass, places her elbows on the table, touches her fingertips together, and leans toward me. "Let's recap. Ten years ago, you had an incredibly humiliating experience that you feel caused the people around you to abandon you. Since then, you've reined in whatever fun side you had and replaced her with a boring—but successful—woman." She takes an easy breath and continues. "So, you've been keeping your emotions sterile, your life sterile, and your relationships sterile."

She sits back into her chair, squinting in a way that lets me know she's still thinking. "Something happened in the last year to make you realize you needed to make some changes in your life, but you needed a fresh place to start and ended up here, where you started having embarrassing experiences—the very thing you've been avoiding all these years. All of that—coupled with the fact that you'd already started cracking open your Pandora's box of issues, which has spanned *twenty*," she looks me pointedly in the eyes, "years—made you feel vulnerable in a way you never have before. It's why your behavior has been different, which is also embarrassing to you."

Her bullseye streak comes to an abrupt stop. I correct her, but in a voice that is smaller than I would have liked. "Ten years. It's just been the last ten years."

"That's sweet." When I open my mouth to protest, she holds up a hand to stop me. "I promise, it's twenty years of issues. You said you haven't cried since you were ten. That means something. But that's also for another day." She lowers her hand to the table and rests it against the glass of toxic waste.

She's a witch. It's the only explanation.

I sit completely stunned. "We've had less than half a dozen phone calls and met in person for the first time today. How did you figure out all of those things? I hadn't even figured them out!"

Cheryl throws a coconut shrimp into her mouth. "It's my superpower." She smiles as she chews. "And my parents are both psychiatrists. They've had me in therapy since I was a kid, and I've picked up observation skills."

"Do your parents live here? Will I meet them?"

"My parents? Heavens no! They divorced when I was sixteen, but probably should have when I was six. My father turned into a drunk, and my mother is so terrified to fly that she's never set foot on an airplane, and never will. So the day she sets foot on this island is the day I play center for the Los Angeles Lakers. I visit her every eighteen months to keep her off my back about moving home and giving her grandbabies."

She takes a long drink of toxic waste and sets her glass down. "You kissed Deacon because he made you feel safe for the first time in . . . who knows how long!" She grabs a bite of her carne asada taco and another sip of radiation and sits back for more observations. "Put that all together—and the fact that he really is a nice guy—and you wanted to kiss him. Maybe not because of the romance, but you wondered how it would feel to kiss someone who makes you feel safe."

As I continue trying to process her words, she goes on.

"You couldn't kiss him on the lips because you didn't want to give him the wrong idea, so you went for what I call *the safety zone*." My eyebrows draw down in confusion. "It's that zone where you leave it up to him to decide if you were going for the cheek but missed, or if you were going for the lips but missed." She dips a chip in the salsa and takes a bite.

I sit stunned—at not only everything Cheryl has deciphered from the few conversations we've had but also at the amount of food she is consuming. She's so small that I don't know where it's all going.

Did I really want to kiss Deacon on the lips? Have I ever been kissed by someone who made me feel safe? What would that feel like? There are so many questions swirling around in my brain now.

I waited years to give Trevor a small slice of my trust, so what is it about Deacon that made me feel so safe in just a matter of days? Especially considering everything that happened during those few days! After everything Cheryl said, why are these the first things I'm questioning right now?

I turn my questions to Cheryl. "Earlier, you told me to spill it. How did you know I had something to spill?"

Cheryl takes another bite of something. "It's my gift. You're a woman who has needed a dump for years. I could tell the first time we talked. I could also tell that we would be best friends, and I was right about that too." She takes another long swig of her drink without even flinching, and then she picks up her phone and starts typing. "Done!" She sets her phone down and looks up at me with complete satisfaction. "I added you to my calendar. I now have a lunch date with my new best friend every Friday at eleven." She smiles at me and takes a bite of something else.

A small laugh escapes my lips as I realize she's right. "We really are going to be good friends, aren't we?" She nods.

I have Steph. Then I met Amber. Now I have Cheryl? How did this happen?

She just peeled back more of my layers—completely exposing them—than anyone has in years, so why do I feel okay? Why am I not packing a bag and running for cover?

And why am I still wondering about what it would be like to really kiss Deacon?

CHAPTER 15

Deacon

"Amber," I shake her a little till she wakes up, "we need to talk." She looks up at me with sleepy eyes.

"What time is it?" Her voice has that rough, unused, morning sound.

"It's 8:30."

Amber sits up abruptly. "Oh my word! It's almost time to go! Why did you let me sleep so late?"

"Because I'm a nice guy." I hand her a glass of orange juice. "We do have a slight issue. Lou is running a low temperature and says her throat is a little sore. It's going to be a long day, and if she's coming down with something, I'm not sure we should take her."

Amber nods her head in agreement. "You're right. Can you go ask Samantha if she can watch Lou today? She's offered several times to watch her if I ever needed it."

Sam . . .

It's been almost a week since our not-date. She made it obvious that she needs time and space before we dive into whatever happened that night, but I don't know how much—or for how long. So even though I've wanted to pound on her door and make her tell me so I can make it right, I haven't.

I still get to see her everyday, though. She's started spending time with Amber and Lou every morning, and I pass them on the deck when I come in from my morning dives. A few times, they've been deep in a conversation, so I've just walked by with a "good morning" and gone inside. Other mornings, they've been laughing like school girls, and I've joined them, chatting for sometimes up to an hour before I've had to go to work.

The rude Sam is gone entirely, and in the last week, I've seen more of that authentic Sam I always knew was in there. It's hard to explain exactly how I knew it, or how I've noticed the changes in her, but I have. A lot. It's in the way she speaks less formally. The way she is starting to knock on the back door of our condo and then just let herself in. The way her shoulders look less tense. Even her makeup and hair styles seem more relaxed. Her smile makes more appearances, and her laugh . . . oh man. Her laugh is something else entirely.

If I could bottle up her laugh and sell it on Amazon, I would make more money than Jeff Bezos himself. It's intoxicating. It's mesmerizing. And it has me plotting different ways to make her laugh again. I've started categorizing them, too.

She has one that's more of a light chuckle and involves a slight eye roll. I first noticed it when I was doing something juvenile to entertain Lou. She has a short and abrupt one for when she's taken by surprise. The first time I heard it was at a market we'd all gone to. A vendor quoted Amber a ridiculously low price for a purse. The short laugh said, *So, the vendor has a thing for Amber.* (She was right. He does.) She has another laugh just for Lou. It drips with kindness and includes big smiles and bright eyes. And I've even seen her starting to laugh a little at herself, too, which I can tell is the hardest one for her because it still sounds a little reserved and stiff. But her biggest, and most genuine, laugh comes when she's talking with Amber.

The first time I heard it, I was walking up the beach from my dive. The two had tears streaming down their faces, and Sam was in the middle of a deep belly laugh. It made me jealous of the friendship she has with Amber. I want to be the one making her light up like that.

A couple nights this week, I've found an excuse to walk down on the beach when I've noticed her sitting on the deck. It's so juvenile, but I hoped she would invite me to sit and join her, like she does with Amber. After a couple nights with no invitation, I realized she probably still needs some space, so I've stayed inside, even though I didn't want to.

My plan was to be patient and let her approach me on her timeline, but I guess that plan just went out the window, because now I need to knock on her door and see if she can watch Lou today.

I knock, and when she opens it, I stare. The morning light is shining on her hair. It's braided and coming up and over one of her shoulders in an explosion of dark reds, but with dark browns that I've never noticed before, and they're all woven together like a gorgeous tapestry. It's not the first time her hair has captured my attention, and my fingers twitch because they want to reach up and touch it and see how soft it is. I fist them and resist the urge. I never thought I was a hair guy, but she has me rethinking that.

Her makeup is minimal and her skin is glowing from the way the sun has kissed it since she's been on the island. I smile because she is still wearing a white button-up shirt, like she might wear to the office. But today the sleeves are rolled up, it's untucked, and it's a little wrinkled—not starched to perfection. This is the most casual I've seen her.

She's wearing denim shorts that show off toned legs. Not skinny sticks that some girls try for, but legs that have an actual shape. They have curves. *She* has curves. And they are all over her in all the right places. Aaaand she's barefoot. What is it about a woman who's barefoot?

"Uhmm . . . is something wrong?" She snaps her fingers to get my attention, and my eyes snap up to hers. She has a slightly amused look on her face.

Crap. Did she just catch me ogling her legs? She just said and did the same thing to me that I said to her when she was ogling me in the pool. Yep. She knew exactly what I was doing.

"Hi." My voice sounds like I'm a sixth-grader talking to a cute girl I didn't think I was worthy to speak with.

"Hi back." Her head tilts a little to the side. "Did you need something?"

"Yes! Sorry." I don't mean to, but I physically shake my head to clear out the images of her legs I'd been focusing on. Real smooth buddy, real smooth. "I don't know what your plans are for the day, but Amber and I have got this thing we've been planning to do for awhile, and we were going to take Lou, but she's a little under the weather. We were wondering . . ."

"Watch Lou? I'd love to do that."

She catches me off guard with the way she reads the moment. "Well, I should give you all the details first." My tone of voice lets her know that there's more to my request. "We are going off island for the day, so we won't be back till dinner."

"I'll still do it," the grin on her face grows, "but now there's a price." Her look has all the bite of a toothless baby.

I'm glad she's feeling comfortable enough with me to joke a little bit. I back up and lean my hips against the deck table, cross one ankle over the other, and fold my arms across my chest. "A price? Can I afford it?"

She adopts a similar pose by crossing her arms and ankles while leaning against the doorjamb. "We'll see." Her grin is wide and playful. "I need another secret from you."

I take a moment to mock-think about it, reaching up to scratch my chin as if pondering the offer. "What kind of secret?"

"Your choice, but if it's not good enough, I won't watch her." She tries her best to look serious, but I know she's bluffing.

I try to fake-ponder, but then I'm pondering for real. What do I want to tell her? I don't want to go deep, but I still want to surprise her. "Okay, my secret is that I've never seen *Star Wars*."

I thought it was an okay secret at best, but her reaction tells me otherwise. "What?!" She stands up straight with total shock in her eyes. "Are you serious?"

"Serious as a heart attack. Never seen one of them." I shrug my shoulders.

"Wow. We need to remedy that sometime." She pauses for a few seconds, still whirling over the fact that there's a human on earth that has never seen *Star Wars*. "That was a worthy secret. I'll watch Lou." She holds out her hand for me to shake. "Deal."

I stand and move to shake her hand, but I soon realize that this is the closest I've been to her in the daylight. Her eyes are still a brilliant emerald color, but up close and in the sunlight, I can see flecks of gold in them. I realize I'm looking longer than normal when she cocks an eyebrow as if waiting for my response.

"Deal." I reach out and shake her hand.

As I walk away, she calls back to me. "I'm willing to share a secret if you want one." This is not the same woman I practically had to wring the tension out of last week. Whatever has happened this last week, I'm a fan. I wait for whatever she's about to say with an anticipation I shouldn't feel but revel in anyway. "My secret is that I would have watched her for free. I didn't actually need a secret from you, but I'm glad I got one anyway." She gives me a little wave and walks inside.

I stand staring at the door she retreated into. I can feel the smile on my face.

As I turn to go back inside, I notice Amber standing there. Looking at me. I don't know how long she's been there, but I don't like it. Amber has always been too observant for her own good, and I'm still trying to figure out how to navigate what's going on, so I don't need her getting any ideas.

"You know it's okay, right? You can have a life."

I try to play dumb, even though I know I'm not fooling anyone. "It's just your imagination, Little Sister." As I walk inside and pass by a smiling Amber, I stop to give her a hug and kiss the top of her head. "Just your imagination. Now let's go get ready. It's going to be a long day."

CHAPTER 16

Samantha

I STEP OUT OF the shower the next morning feeling refreshed. Deacon called around three yesterday afternoon saying the puddle jumper that they were coming back on had experienced mechanical problems, and they didn't know when they'd be able to get back. I told him not to worry about it and that I could stay with Lou overnight.

After putting her down, I stayed up to wait for them but ended up falling asleep on their couch. I woke up at seven the next morning and didn't know if Amber and Deacon had made it home. Their bedroom doors had been closed when I went to sleep, and they were still closed when I woke up—but they could have come home in the middle of the night, and I might have slept through it.

Lou was still asleep when I woke up, so I left both back doors open and came over to my place for a quick shower. Right now, I've got a towel wrapped around my head and one around my body, and I'm stepping into the kitchen to grab some breakfast.

As I'm buttering my toast, I see movement on the counter that catches my eye. I turn and see a giant lizard on my kitchen counter. He's at least four-feet long. I freeze, not knowing what to do.

Suddenly, its tongue pokes out at me and I scream, jumping back several feet. This creature slides off my counter and slithers toward me with its stubby legs, scaly skin, and beady eyes, and I start screaming again. I don't know where this thing came from, and I don't care. All I know is that it's crawling toward me like it thinks I'm some kind of snack, so I keep screaming and jump up on the couch.

Suddenly Deacon runs in through the back door looking disheveled, his blonde waves going several different directions. "Sam! Sam! What? What is it? Are you okay?" He looks frantic but still half asleep.

I'm crawling and jumping around on my couch cushions, frantically trying to keep away from the devil creature. It's currently crawling up the side of my couch, stalking me like it's a heat seeking missile and I'm the sun. "DEACON! He's trying to eat me!!" I frantically scream.

Deacon calmly walks toward the couch, and I jump on his back to save myself. He starts trying to get the beast out, but he can't while my arms and legs are wrapped around him—or while I'm screaming in his ears.

"Pepper, let go." He's too calm. He has no idea of the gravity of the situation!

"NO!! He's trying to bite me! He keeps following me around—no matter where I go! Get him out! Get him out! GET HIM OUT!" My screams become more and more frantic, and the giant lizard creature is still coming after me, its long tongue flicking out as if it's hoping to get a little taste of my skin. I tighten my grip around Deacon's neck and start a scream that sounds like the tsunami alarms I've heard in the movies.

"No . . . he . . . isn't." Deacon stops walking toward Godzilla and tries to loosen my grip around his neck. "Pepper . . . you are choking me. Let go!"

"NOOOO!!" I am terrified and will never let go of this man's neck until the beast is gone and vanquished.

"Pepper . . . ," he tries to pry my arms from around his neck. "Give him your toast! Give. Him. Your. Toast!" he yells in between my screams and his breaths.

I realize I am still holding my toast, so I hurl it at the creature and quickly bury my face into the back of Deacon's neck, like the toast was a hand grenade and I was now shielding myself from the inevitable explosion.

Godzilla immediately stops his advancing attack, gathers up my toast into his mouth, and slowly meanders out the back door without even glancing back at the wreckage he's leaving behind. And to be clear, that wreckage is my nerves, because I feel like I will never be able to get my heart rate under 200 again!

My grip on Deacon's neck is still a vice.

His voice is barely a whisper. "Will you please let me breathe? He's gone!"

I comply and Deacon's breathing starts to normalize.

"Want to get off my back now?" His calm demeanor is unsettling. It's like he doesn't realize how close I was to being bitten—or eaten—by a lizard creature that came into my home and stalked me like his prey.

I slowly let go and slide down his body until both my feet are on the ground, but my legs are uneven and shaky. Deacon turns around to face me, and we see each other for the first time this morning. I mean, *really* see each other. The towel that had been around my hair is long gone, having fallen during the struggle with Godzilla. The other towel is still around my body, but, after jumping on Deacon, it's open in the back, so I have to use both of my hands to keep it up in the front.

Deacon obviously jumped out of bed and ran straight over when he heard me screaming, because he's only in his boxer briefs. Jet-black boxer briefs.

A towel and boxer briefs. These are the only forms of clothing in the room, and for a moment, I forget that I was almost a reptile's breakfast.

We stare at each other, afraid to look anywhere but each other's eyes once we realize how the other one is dressed. Or, I guess, *not* dressed.

Even though my towel and his briefs cover more skin than a swimsuit would, there is something that feels too exposed right now. My body feels exposed. My nerves feel exposed.

Deacon is the first to break the silence. His voice is calm but has a slight tremor to it, as if he's trying to hold back an emotion of some kind. "That was Alex. He's a Savannah monitor lizard. He's a harmless, non-poisonous lizard that lives on the island. If you are cooking with the door open and he is near, he will come inside for a snack. A food snack, not a human one." The corner of his lip twitches as if it's fighting to curl up. "Next time, give him food and he will go away." Then Deacon ducks his head in an effort to hide his face from me.

Suddenly Cheryl's words from our first conversation about installing dead bolts make more sense: *We don't get many unwanted house guests, and even then, most are pretty harmless.*

Alex must be what she was referring to.

"Deacon!" I spit out at him with, apparently, more venom than Alex the Savannah monitor lizard ever had. I try to catch Deacon's eye, but he's still looking at the ground. His shoulders start to shake a little, and he puts his hands on his hips as if that will conceal what he's doing. My eyes track the movement of his hands, but now I'm looking at his hips. His *only clad in boxer briefs* hips. I can't help it if my eyes linger for a fraction of a second. But then they snap back to his face. "Are you . . . laughing at me?!" My voice is loud and full of accusation.

"Oh come on, Pepper!" Deacon throws his arms open while still laughing, as if the reason should be so obvious as to why he's laughing. "That was funny!"

"Deke, so help me—if you do not stop laughing this very second, I will . . ." I am desperate to come up with something so threatening that it will shut him up for the rest of his life, but all I see are his laughter-filled eyes and big, easy smile trying hard to get control of his laughter.

"Pepper-Girl!" His voice is giddy with joy. "That's the first time you've called me Deke! That's either pretty juvenile of you or we're becoming friends."

I'm still trying to come up with something threatening to say and don't appreciate his attempt at lightheartedness. I end up glaring at him instead.

"What are you gonna do? Throw things at me?" His bright-blue eyes are still smiling. He's not even the slightest bit worried. "Come on." I hate his voice. It has a tone that's inviting me to see the humor in the situation, which is literally the last thing I want to do. But my body doesn't get that memo, because one corner of my mouth starts to turn up and my shoulders droop a little as they let go of the tension from the Godzilla attack.

"That's better," he says as he instinctively moves in for a hug. It's meant to be one of those hugs you give a buddy. You know, a *here's a hug with a pat on the back to culminate this hilariously good laugh I just had at your expense, and don't worry, buddy, you'll be able to laugh at it someday too* kind of hugs. But the second his hands make contact with my back, that all changes.

His arms are around me now, but it's obvious he didn't remember all the fine minutia of our situation. Namely that my towel had come undone in the back and was only being held up by my fisted hands in the front. The fisted hands that were flattened out of their grip when Deacon abruptly pressed his body against mine for a hug.

I no longer have a hold of my towel.

If he moves—it falls.

The only silver lining is that the two ends of my towel decide to flap backward instead of forward, giving me the slightest bit more privacy.

His hands are on my very bare back, and my hands are pressed up against his very bare chest. He is looking up at the ceiling. I am looking at the wall, because my hands aren't the only thing being pressed flat against his chest—my face is too. I'm literally cheek-to-pec with him, and if I turned my face toward him, I would be looking at the exact spot I kissed on my first night here. We both stand frozen for a moment, not knowing what to do.

After an awkward few seconds, I speak up. "So . . ."

"Yep."

"You're aware . . ."

"Yep."

"That if you move . . ."

"Yep." At that, he looks down at me and smiles.

I shift my face and tilt my chin up to look back at him, so now I'm chin-to-pec. Is this supposed to be any better? Because it doesn't feel like it. My hands are still flat against his bare chest—and they're confirming what my eyes suspected the other day. This man is fit. I don't let my mind linger there longer than . . . well, I'm only human, so it might have been for more than one second. But I really need to extract myself from this man before my hands start trying to take a tour.

"So," his head nods slightly, like he's figured something out, "this is what it's like." I have no idea what he's talking about, and my look must convey that because he goes on. "When you do embarrassing things in front of me. This must be what it feels like."

"What?" My answer comes out with a laugh. "Why are you embarrassed? I was the one jumping on your back because I thought Godzilla was trying to eat me!"

"Pepper-Girl, have you seen the precarious situation we're in? This is alllll me. I swear, I was only coming in for a quick, buddy-hug kind of thing, and I wasn't even thinking. I should have gone for a high five."

"And which hand would you have suggested I use for a high five?" I cock my eyebrow in a challenge.

When he realizes what I'm implying, his body starts shaking again with laughter. "DON'T!" he yells. "Don't make me laugh anymore. We can't afford it."

And while we are standing there in a hug that includes only an open-in-the-back towel and boxer briefs, laughing until tears fill both of our eyes, Amber and Lou make an appearance at the back door.

CHAPTER 17

Samantha

AMBER IS SILENT. HER jaw has dropped to the floor, and she's staring.

Lou, on the other hand, keeps walking in, like this is the most normal thing she has ever seen. "Hi Dee-Dee. Hi Penelope. I woke up by hearing screams." When she sees what we are doing, her reaction is typical for a five-year-old—but not helpful in this situation. "Group hug!" She runs over and wraps her arms around us, so we are now in a very awkward kind of group hug. Her little arms reach around each of us, and her face looks up at us in total satisfaction. I'm so grateful she's not taller, because my bare butt is hanging out back there. Her arm only comes halfway up my thigh, so all is well.

At this point, Amber finds her voice, though her eyes still say she's looking at a three-headed giraffe who's smoking a daisy while wearing a leather jacket. Her voice comes out slow and curious. "Are you guys . . . ?"

"NO!!" Deke and I yell in unison before starting to give our explanations.

"I got out of the shower and there was toast . . ."

"There was a scream from somewhere . . ."

". . . a giant scaly monster was stalking toward me . . ."

". . . she was jumping around on the couch, and I tried to calm her down . . ."

". . . he showed up, and I jumped on his back . . ."

"STOP!" Amber puts her hand up to silence us both.

We both look at her in desperation, like we're waiting to be sentenced for a crime that we didn't actually commit.

Amber looks at Deke. "Is this about Alex?"

"YES!" we both yell.

"So you came over to help?"

"YES!" Again, we both answer.

"Aannnddd . . ." Amber starts speaking slower, trying to piece the puzzle together. Deke and I both shoot her encouraging looks, like it should be easy for her to understand what got us in this position. "So naturally, you two ended up like this becauuuuuse . . ."

We wait for her to finish, but the look on her face tells me she has no idea how a lizard home invasion would end with Deke in his boxer briefs pressed up against me—and with only a towel, that neither of us have a hold of, separating us.

She finally shrugs her shoulders. "Yeah, I got nothin'." She motions to Lou, who has left the "group hug" and made herself at home working on the puzzle we started last night. "Lou, Honey, let's go."

As she turns to leave, both Deke and I start speak-shouting at the same time. Again.

"I thought I was going to get eaten . . ."

"She was choking me, and I didn't realize what she was wearing . . ."

". . . so I threw the toast and the towel almost slipped off . . ."

". . . or what she *wasn't* wearing . . ."

". . . and I can't wrap it back up, because my hands . . ."

". . . then I gave Pepper-Girl a friendly hug . . ."

Amber raises her hand in the universal *stop talking right now because you both sound like idiots* way. She looks at Deke with raised eyebrows. "You gave *Pepper-Girl* a friendly hug?" For some reason, he looks like a kid who got caught with his hand in the cookie jar. Then Amber turns to me. "Does your favorite drink happen to be . . . Dr. Pepper?"

"Um, yes?" Why is this the question she's asking me? Then she looks back at Deke with very raised eyebrows. I have no context for this silent sibling conversation, and Amber gives no reaction to any explanation we've given.

"Samantha, would you like some help with your towel?" she asks politely.

"YES!" Both Deke and I yell. I'm sure the desperation in his eyes mirrors my own.

Amber walks over to me, picks up the two flapping towel ends, and wraps them around my back, tucking one edge into the top of the towel to secure it in place. Then she walks over to the towel on the ground, the one that my hair had been wrapped in, and throws it at Deke. "You might want to wrap that around yourself. Your little undies are kinda tight." And with that, she starts to walk out the back door with Lou, who is waving at us like this was all another day in paradise. Before her exit, Amber turns around and looks at me with admiration in her eyes. "Your tattoo," she nods toward my backside. "I like it. It's sexy."

"Thanks." It sounds more like a question. My face is on fire.

Then she smiles at me and turns to Deke with steel in her eyes. It's a semi-evil glint I've not seen on her before. "Just my imagination, Big Brother? I think not." Then she winks at Deke and leaves.

CHAPTER 18

Deacon

I FINISH SECURING THE towel around my waist just as Amber mentions a tattoo and nods to Sam's butt. I freeze in place, trying as hard as I can to not imagine what it is—or exactly where it is.

When I inadvertently trapped Sam's body up against mine and realized the situation we were then in, I tried to not react, but it took every bit of my will power. She felt so comfortable in my arms. It was all I could do to not pull her even closer, rest my head on top of hers, and see if I could discover the scent of her shampoo. I didn't want to let go of her, even in that ridiculous situation.

I find myself smiling again, thinking about how absurd, embarrassing, and funny the whole morning has been.

I don't know why Sam has such an effect on me, but I'm embracing it. Unfortunately, due to my slip of the tongue, Amber knows just how much of an effect that is. I can tell she's going to have a lot of questions for me when I get back to the condo. She knows the story of the day my parents met as well as I do.

They were in college and neither was looking where they were going. They bumped into each other, and my dad's Coke spilled all over my mom's white shirt. Mom always said the thing that made her the most mad was that my dad's drink was a Coke—she was a Pepsi girl through and through. She always said it with a glint in her eyes, so we knew that she was never really mad at all.

Dad told us that after he spilt his drink on her, he walked her straight to the campus store and bought her a new shirt. My mom wouldn't tell my dad her name at the time, so he called her Pepsi-Girl until she finally caved and told him that her name was Janet. They grabbed lunch together at the cafeteria, laughed the entire time, and never looked back. It didn't matter that he'd found out her name was Janet. He called her *Pepsi* from that day on.

I've never seen a couple as in love as my parents were. They were what everyone referred to as "couple goals." I once asked my mom when she first realized that she was falling in love with my dad. She said it all happened without her even realizing it. One day he spilled his drink on her. Then he was her best friend. Then he was the love of her life.

My dad always said he knew right away, and that's why he called her . . . well, it doesn't really matter. All that matters is that they had this connection that was immediate. And they've never been apart since. Not even in death.

My dad died of lung cancer three years ago, and a month later my mom went in a freak car accident during a particularly harsh winter storm. We all think Dad sent the storm because he couldn't be without his Pepsi for even a month.

When my parents talked about their love story, I always thought they were romantics who were prone to exaggeration for the sake of their story. I didn't think people really had immediate, first-encounter connections that turned into love, marriage, babies, and everything else.

I'm not so sure anymore.

I'm not saying I'm in love with Pepper! I'm not insane! I've known her for a total of a week and a half, so love isn't on the table. But I am saying this: I can tell something is there. It's a connection and pull I can't describe, but that connection is trying to be something.

There is no other explanation as to why I've been drawn to Pepper since the moment I saw her.

Man, she's even Pepper in my mind now.

Yes, she's one of the most beautiful women I've ever seen, but I've seen a lot of beautiful women in my life. I usually appreciate how beautiful they are in the same way I appreciate a painting at a museum—I can look at it and notice its quality, but that doesn't mean I want to buy it and bring it home. But Pepper? She makes me want to not only buy it and bring it home but also keep it with me wherever I go so I can talk to it, laugh with it, look at it, and smile at it. Just knowing it exists makes me happy. Okay, this painting metaphor might be getting out of control, but I don't know how else to describe the pull I feel to spend as much time with her as possible. Without seeming like a stalker, of course.

But then there's my life with Amber and Lou. We've got a plan, and despite the pull I feel toward Pepper, nothing is more important than that. It's part of what brought us to the island. Can I blend Pepper into that plan? It's not as easy as it would have been a couple years ago, but I don't have control over that anymore.

I close my eyes and sigh, because for some reason, that's all I can muster up right now. This situation—my life—keeps having that effect on me.

"I'd say penny for your thoughts," Pepper's voice startles me back to the present, "but I'm more interested in wearing something other than this towel. So I'm going to scoot back in there," she points with her thumb toward her bedroom, "and get dressed. Thanks for your help today, and sorry . . ." She looks off like she's trying to decide what to say, then she looks back and continues, "I actually don't know what I'm sorry about, but I feel like it should be something. Anyway, thanks for the advice: next time, give Godzilla the toast."

She's going for humor. Shaking off a situation like this is a big deal for her. It makes me happy that she feels like she can do that with me.

She looks at me like she expects me to say something, but I'm so caught up in my thoughts that I don't move or speak, and she starts walking back to her bedroom.

When she's almost to her room, I call out to her. "Pepper!" She turns and looks at me with raised eyebrows. "Get dressed and then come over. I'm going to start making breakfast for Lou and Amber, and I can easily make enough for you as well."

She takes a moment before answering. "Okay," the smile on her lips gets a little bigger, "can you give me twenty minutes?"

I nod my head and walk out the back door, a towel around my waist and a lot to think about.

CHAPTER 19

Samantha

I TAKE ANOTHER SHOWER, because after Godzilla it seemed like the right thing to do. As I get dressed, I decide to make another subtle change for myself. I grab that yellow-colored sundress. I'm ready to see how it feels to put the cotton and starch away. As I put my hair up in a high, messy bun, I think back over everything that has happened with Deke. *Deke* . . . I guess that's what my brain is calling him now. I'm thinking about not only this morning's disaster but all of the other disasters I've had around him in the last week and a half.

These kinds of situations would have made me run for the hills even a few weeks ago, but now I find a small smile slipping onto my lips as they play back in my mind. It's not that I no longer look at them as embarrassing, because—there's no way around it—they were! But Deke has a way of making them all seem . . . okay? Is that the right word? I know it's not, but I'm still trying to piece my feelings together.

Something about Deke makes me feel like it's okay to show my cracks and flaws. I don't understand how it's different from what I feel around Steph, Cheryl, or Amber, but it is. Maybe it's because I feel like he . . . cares? About . . . being nice?

For a lawyer whose job it is to craft and write intricately woven contracts, I sure can't think of any words right now. Maybe because it's not about the words but the feelings. It's like I've been unexpectedly thrown off the roof of a ten-story building and the sensations in my body are terrified and don't know what to do. They're running around colliding with each other due to the shock and panic of it all. My head tells me I'm going to crash violently down to earth, but Deke is one of those giant air pads waiting for me at the bottom, and he's telling all of my nerve endings that I'll be okay. Everything feels foreign and scary, but he's telling my feelings that it's okay. He makes it okay. He makes it safe to land.

Land?

I realize I have the sensation of safely landing.

A boat can drift or maneuver on the ocean from one place to another, but it is always fighting. Fighting against the current, the wind, the storms. But once it lands in a port, it gets tied onto the dock and can rest from the fight.

I've been fighting and fighting against elements for most of my life. Elements like my parents, false friends with hidden agendas, the need to prove my worth, the push for perfection in both school and work, the desperation to avoid the feeling of being alone or abandoned. Even Trevor! He was my wake-up call to finally make some changes.

But then Deke comes along and makes me feel like I've landed. Like I can finally rest. Like I can stop fighting and . . . breathe.

I remember being in Clarice's office before I left and wondering why I couldn't breathe—or why my soul couldn't breathe. Now I understand why.

I close my eyes and take a deep, cleansing breath.

For the first time, I can sense what is around me. The smell of the ocean, the citrus from the trees, the coconut from my shampoo, the clean air. If calm had a smell, I think this might be it, in combination with the sound of the waves brushing up against the sand in a steady cadence.

All of a sudden I . . . feel.

It's not like I've never had feelings, but this is different. This is new. I'm not sure I've ever felt *this* feeling before. I search back to my earliest memories, and I still can't find it.

It's a feeling of . . . peace.

It's a feeling of . . . safety.

It's a feeling of . . . belonging.

My mind starts to rake over the changes I've experienced since being on the island. What do I have now that I didn't have before?

I remember the pull I felt toward Cheryl from the very first conversation I had with her. How much Lou loved me from the moment she met me. The warm invitations from Amber. And Deke.

He's stripped away so many of the fears I've carried with me for so long. Since long before my desperation to be the absolute best in my career. Before my drive to be top of my class at law school. Before the humiliation of my first drunken night with friends that were idiots. Even before my parents' ugly divorce.

Deke seems to see me—and life—in a way I never have. He laughs with me, not at me. He actually notices me instead of ignoring me. It's like I have someone in my corner, but it's still different because for the first time my corner feels a little crowded, but in a way that feels really good. There's Steph, Cheryl, and Amber there too. But everything about Deke feels . . . well, it feels.

You have *got* to be kidding me! I'm crying. Again.

They aren't sad tears or happy tears. They're the kind of tears that find their way out when you finally relax after a really, really long fight with all the elements of life.

I've tried to avoid any more alone time with Deke since our talk on the back deck at the end of our sort-of date, because there is an energy between us that I don't know what to do with. Maybe I need to stop fighting and embrace it.

Crap.

Now I want to kiss Deke again—but this time, I know where I'd aim.

CHAPTER 20

Deacon

". . . AND then Penelope made me cheesy dinosaurs for dinner before we made a mermaid puzzle and started a soda-pop-can puzzle, then we played Candyland again, but then I had to go to sleep, then she screamed and woke me up, and we had a group hug." I'm at the stove cooking bacon with my back to her, but I can tell Lou's smile is brighter than a million-watt bulb. She's been giving me an incredibly detailed version of everything she and Pepper did from when Amber and I left yesterday to when Lou walked in on our group hug. "I think Penelope is the best. I think you do too. You smile at her different than you smile at other people."

Curse how observant this child is. "Yeah, but let's keep that between us two for a while. Okay?"

"Okay." She hops down and runs back to her room.

"Back door was open, so I figured knocking wasn't needed." Pepper says the last part like it's a question.

My mind starts spinning, wondering if she heard what Lou said. Would it be a problem if she did? "No worries. I'm finishing up some bacon, and then we're ready for breakfast."

"Bacon? Wow. I haven't had a home-cooked breakfast in years! It's usually toast or a coffee on the way to the office."

"Don't get too excited. It's bacon and Lucky Charms." I turn around with a smile and see the most beautiful version of her I've ever seen. I can't help it—I stare.

Her hair is freshly showered and up in a high bun that is both a complete mess and total perfection. She has no makeup on, and her face is glowing. She is wearing a yellow dress that compliments the olive in her skin, and the slight ocean breeze coming through the door is giving it the slightest amount of movement. Luckily she is no longer barefoot—because I don't think I could have handled it—but the cream-colored flip-flops on her feet aren't doing my heart rate any favors. It's mesmerizing. *She's* mesmerizing.

I'm in so much trouble.

I don't know how long I've been staring at her, but I'm suddenly aware that she is staring back. The look on her face is both serene and contemplative. I would give anything to know what she's thinking right now. At the same time, I've never been so glad that my own thoughts are hidden. They are hidden, right? I don't know what the look on my face says, but she's starting to smile at me like she's puzzling something together. Am I okay if she puzzles me together? All of me? All the aspects of my life that very few people know about? Neither of us say anything, but the moment still feels completely comfortable.

"Mom says you need a room," Lou says—shocking us both out of our comfortable staring contest—as she walks back into the room with half a dozen stuffed animals. "Penelope, why don't you have a room? You can share with me if you want. I have a tent in the corner." She shrugs and starts to set up her animals at the kitchen table.

"LOU!" Amber yells from the back of the condo, "Lou, you do *not* need to repeat everything I say!"

I look over at Pepper to gauge her reaction at what my family just flung at us. She simply has a little blush on her cheeks, like she doesn't know what to say or do.

Amber slowly emerges from the hallway with the audacity to look not even a little bit embarrassed by what Lou said. She looks over at us both and shrugs her shoulders.

Amber looks tired this morning. The circles under her eyes are a little more pronounced, and there is a sag to her shoulders that I rarely see.

Lou's voice catches my attention. "Dee-Dee, you are burning the bacon." I turn back around to see that the bacon is smoking and burnt to a crisp. Pepper comes to my side and looks down into the pan.

"Lucky Charms it is." Then she looks up at me with a smile that is more than a smile. It's saying something, but I'm not sure what. An invitation maybe? But an invitation to . . . what? I close my eyes and take a deep breath to calm my heart.

"It's okay. You don't need to be embarrassed." When my eyes snap open and down to her gaze, she gives me a little smile and joins Lou at the table, where Lou starts animatedly introducing Pepper to all her stuffed animals.

Pepper must have mistaken my deep breath for embarrassment and not what it was: a need to get control over my growing feelings for her so I can give her the space she asked for.

Once again, I have to physically shake my head to clear it before I can join the ladies at the table.

CHAPTER 21

Samantha

So FAR, MY MEALS with Deke have consisted of our not-date dinner—that ended with no food at all—and a breakfast of Lucky Charms and burnt bacon. I don't mind either one.

Honestly, it's one of the best breakfasts I've had in years, but that's because of the company. Lou is the perfect five-year-old combination of breath of fresh air plus category-five hurricane. Her enthusiasm and joy for life can't be stopped, and I can't imagine anyone ever wanting it to.

Amber dotes on Lou. It's heartwarming to watch her interact with her daughter. She balances discipline and fun in a way my own mother never did. Or at least, what I imagine my mother would have been like had she ever paid attention to me.

And Deke . . . he's so good with both of them. I don't know what happened to Lou's dad, but Deke loves Lou as much as any dad ever could. It's obvious he would do anything for either one of them.

We've been lingering around the table, chatting and laughing, for some time now. The bowls of cereal have long since been consumed, glasses of orange juice are empty, and even the burnt bacon is mostly consumed. Now Lou is giving us all a puppet show with her stuffed animals.

Everyone is laughing and enjoying themselves. Amber and Deke are acting like mornings like this happen every day. That this is normal for them.

This is not normal for me. I've never been part of a family where happiness and laughter ever existed. I have no siblings, and my parents divorced when I was young. I've never seen this dynamic, and I want it. I want it badly. I want laughter and smiles and what feels like the emotional embodiment of sunshine. I want this happiness and goodness and light and peace and love.

And more than that—I want it with these people. I want all three of them!

Lou had my heart from the moment I first saw her smile. And when I met Amber, it was like I had a sister all of a sudden. She's taken me under her wing in a way I can't describe. Our morning and afternoon talks have meant the world to me. She's not one whit behind Cheryl in soul-seeing ability; even though I've remained vague and nonspecific during our talks, she's helped me so much. She's also reminded me that I can laugh!

Steph laughs most of the time. She doesn't always have an easy life either and I know sometimes she does it to cover up the pain, but she still laughs. I watch her, and I smile with her, but I'd forgotten how good it feels to join in the laughter, not just watch it.

And Deke. The way he doesn't judge or condemn.

I want to live next to this amazing family for the rest of my life. Can I adopt them? Would they adopt me? Is that the relationship I want with Deke? A prickling on the back of my neck shouts at me that adoption is the last thing I want with Deke. I tell that prickling to mind its own business, then I stomp on it and tell it to go away. It doesn't listen.

I don't want the partnership at the law firm or to deal with Clarice or to make rich men richer while they step on the lives of other hardworking people. I don't want the day-to-day grind that suffocates souls as it slowly pollutes them with an inability to breathe.

I want whatever is here.

On this island.

In this room.

With these people.

All of these realizations hit me one after the other, after the other, with a force that should feel dangerous for how powerful it is—but I'm not scared. If anything, I'm more than willing—anxious and excited, even—to start learning what it feels like to live this way.

What's more, this family seems to be more than willing to embrace me into whatever it is they have. And that's what I need.

Lou finishes her puppet show, and we all clap and hoot and holler as she takes her bows, then dissolves into giggles.

Eventually Deke—how is it that in one morning I've gone from "Deke is a juvenile name" to "Deke is perfect for him"? Anyway, eventually Deke interrupts the fun of the morning. "I hate to be the wet blanket on this party, but I need to go to work, and someone," he starts giving Lou little pokes in all her ticklish places, "needs to get dressed for the day."

"Can I pick my own clothes today, Dee-Dee?" The anticipation that he might say yes is written all over Lou's face.

He bends down until he is on her level. "Nope. Not until you pay me." Then Lou wraps her arms around his neck and squeezes as tight as her little arms will let her.

"An-a-con-da squeeze!!" Lou screams as she holds tight to Deke's neck.

Deke fakes that her hug is the strongest thing in the world, and my heart reacts to see him be so cute with her. When Lou breaks the hug, she steps back, waiting for the word from him. "That was the best anaconda squeeze, and now that you've paid me—yes. You can pick out your own clothes today." They high-five each other, and Lou runs screaming down the hall like she just found the golden ticket to Willy Wonka's factory.

Deke starts clearing the table and taking dishes to the sink to wash, so I join him. I have so many thoughts swirling around in my brain—it might short-circuit.

Deke breaks through my brain fog. "Can you please stop thinking so loud? You're giving me a headache." I look over, and he's smiling at me.

I'm so confused. "Excuse me?"

"Pepper, you're thinking so loud that I think the people a mile away can hear your brain working."

"Wait, what? Did I say something out loud?" I'm aware that I've done that several times since I've been on the island.

He gives a small chuckle. "No worries. You didn't say anything. Your secrets are safe, but your face has the look of someone very deep in thought. What's up?" His look is so sincere that I decide to listen to Steph and be brave.

"I was thinking that I've never seen a family like yours before."

"What, totally insane? Crazy? Loud?"

"No. That likes spending time together—that likes each other." Just saying that out loud makes me feel vulnerable. Brave—but still vulnerable. And my tone of voice betrays that, because I sound as uncertain as I feel about sharing personal family insights.

"We don't like each other all the time. I mean, we are siblings, after all." His smile is a little cheeky and playful. "I'm sure you fought with your siblings, but I'm sure there were other times you got along fine."

"I'm an only child." I shrug my shoulders. "So no siblings to fight with." He stops doing the dishes and turns to face me completely.

"Pepper, when you say you've never seen a family like ours, what do you mean?"

I shoot him a glare. Fine, it's not a very threatening glare, since I also have a small smile on my face. "You know I hate that nickname, right?"

"I know you *claim* to hate it, but I don't think you really do. I think you secretly love it. And whenever I say it and you wince a little, pretending it gets under your skin, I secretly love that. So for me, the nickname is a win-win." He wags his sun-bleached eyebrows at me while a cheeky grin spreads over his handsome, yet smug, face. "So, are you going to tell me why you're asking about my family?"

I think over my answer and realize it's not a quick one. "When do you have to leave for work?"

He checks his watch. "I lost track of time! I gotta leave in about two minutes, and I'm not ready. Sorry, can we rain check this discussion?"

"Sure. You go get ready, and I'll finish up the dishes."

"Thanks." As he starts down the hall, he yells out, "Lou, if you want to go to work with me today, you've got about two minutes!"

The next minute Lou comes walking into the kitchen wearing a green camo T-shirt, pink shorts with unicorns on them, rain boots, and a tiara on her head. "Hi, Penelope. I'm going to work with Dee-Dee." Her smile is gorgeous, and she looks delighted.

Deke comes in wearing swim trunks and water shoes and is pulling a T-shirt over his head. My retinas burn with the image they're seeing.

While I'm sure it runs in real time, my eyes take it in slow motion. Deke's arms raise up to pull his T-shirt over his head. His torso is stretched, and his muscles are moving and rippling and showing off every gorgeously sculpted angle of his physique. His pecs pop and his lats step up and gloat their perfectly defined shape. His biceps are also on display as he pushes his arms through the arm holes in his shirt. Once he gets the shirt on, he realizes it's inside out, so he has to rip it off, turn it right side out, and repeat the process.

I'm not mad about it.

Deke yells down the hall. "Amber, I've got Lou!" And then he turns to me. "Thanks again for an adventurous morning, but remember, next time, surrender the toast." Then he nods and goes out the door holding Lou's hand.

Once I'm done with the dishes and am getting ready to leave, Amber comes walking in the kitchen with a towel wrapped around her wet hair. She's wearing a jumper so yellow that it makes her look like a smiley-face emoji. And the color does nothing for her complexion.

She must be able to read my mind. "I know, I look like a banana." Amber rolls her eyes. "Lou wanted me to buy it, and I'm a sucker when she begs."

"I was thinking more happy-face emoji, but banana works too." We smile at each other. "Amber, do you have any plans for the next little bit? With Deke and Lou gone, I wondered if we could talk?" When she nods, we go to the back deck and relax on the deck furniture.

I sit trying to collect my thoughts—and there are many—as Amber waits patiently for me to speak. When I finally do, I only partially know what I'm going to say, and I have no idea where my thoughts will take me, but I begin anyway.

"I want to ask for some advice, but I think I need to give you some history, so you can understand where I am coming from." Amber's nod gives me the courage to start. "I've always been a very independent person and have worked very hard to get where I am. I graduated from high school at sixteen. In college I took over twenty credit hours each semester and had my bachelor's degree by nineteen. I graduated from law school at twenty-two and started working right away. Now, at thirty-one, I've done well enough that on the day I started my leave of absence to come here, I was given an offer to be a partner at my firm. The kind where my name ends up on the stationery." At this, Amber makes a whistle to show she's impressed. "Yep. If I accept, the law firm would be Parker, Jenkins,

Snow, and Turner. It's pretty unprecedented at an established firm, but I'm very good at what I do, and I make them a lot of money. They don't want to lose me." My tone of voice lacks any enthusiasm for what I've said.

"Why do you sound like you're not proud of your accomplishments? You should be! I'm over here bursting with pride for you!" She's beaming with sincerity.

"But that's just it." My voice betrays my sadness. "Yes, I've built a career. And if I'm being honest, I've actually built what would be considered an amazingly successful career. But Amber, I have no life. Other than this time with you, I don't know how to slow down and relax. I watch you and Deke, and I get the feeling that this is normal for you, not one random week out of your life. I sat around your table this morning and realized that I've never had a morning—in my life—where my family gathered for a puppet show or laughed about burnt bacon and Lucky Charms." I take a moment to compose myself before speaking again. "I'm asking . . . for help." The words burn in my throat and mouth. Have I ever said them before? I don't think so, but Steph's voice keeps me going: *be brave.* I don't feel brave, but at least I'm trying. "Does that sound stupid?"

Amber lightly laughs, but I know she's not judging me. "It makes perfect sense. Sounds like you've been pushing yourself for so many years that you forgot how to slow down, enjoy life, and build relationships."

"I'm not even sure it's that I've forgotten—I don't think I've ever known how."

"Have our talks this week helped?"

"More than I think you could ever know. When I'm with you, or Cheryl, I can actually see a light at the end of the tunnel."

"And what about Deacon? What do you see when you're with him?"

My mind goes completely blank. I have no idea how to answer that. There is a possibility that sweat is gathering in my armpits right now, forming a gigantic waterfall that will start falling in the next sixty seconds. What do I see when I'm with him? Does she mean in life as a general statement? Or in more literal terms, like what his hair color is? "I have no idea what you mean." I'm serious, and I also don't want to answer any more of her questions. So I grab my glass of orange juice and start gulping it down. There, now my mouth doesn't have to speak.

Her eyes dart over to me. "I see a shirtless man in some black briefs. That's what I see."

The orange juice comes spurting out my mouth and up my nose. "AMBER!!" There is orange juice all over my face, my clothes, and the chair. Amber roars with laughter while I sit in stunned silence. What am I supposed to say to that?

I go inside to clean myself up the best I can. If Amber was going for shock value, then bullseye! I'm sure my reaction told her more than any words could have, and I'm wondering if that's what she was going for. When I come back outside, Amber is still laughing, and my nose still burns from its orange-juice invasion.

"Amber, I'm starting to think you might be a little devious." I look at her with assessing eyes.

"Devious? I call it observative. And after this morning, my list of observations is overflowing, because there were a whole lot of things going on that had nothing to do with Alex." She slides her sunglasses onto her face in a move so smooth it belongs in a James Bond movie. Then she looks over at me and starts giggling, which only makes me laugh, which makes her laugh harder. We both end up laughing till we're crying and forgetting about what started it all.

When her laugh has mostly subsided, she stands up and pulls me into the biggest bear hug I've ever had. "You are such an amazing person," she whispers into my ear. When she pulls back, there are so many emotions on her face. "I thought you might need a hug. I hope that was okay. And yes, I will help you. I'll always be there for you."

I revel in her sincerity and the memory of the most incredible hug I've ever had before speaking again. "That was . . . a really nice hug. I can't remember the last time I had a hug like that."

"Thanks. I'm a mom. It's my superpower." Her shoulder raises just a little with the corner of her lips. "But from what I saw," her tone of voice drips with sassiness, "you got a *really* nice hug this morning from my brother." Her eyes are brewing with mischief.

And that's how the rest of the morning continues.

CHAPTER 22

Samantha

MONDAY MORNING, LOU COMES over bright and early, and we snuggle with a blanket on the couch, talking about how she wants to own a unicorn.

Then we all have breakfast together and Deke leaves for work. Amber and I move to the back deck, talking while Lou plays on the beach. We talk about how shoulder pads should never come back in style.

That night we have dinner together, and when Amber goes to put Lou to bed afterward, Deke and I talk on the back deck. It's the first time we've talked alone since the non-date—or the rain-checked family discussion—and I thought he would bring up those past conversations.

I'm pleasantly surprised when he keeps the convo light and silly.

He makes me laugh while telling me stories of funny things kids have said and done while learning to snorkel, and they all make me feel better about my first (and only) attempt. I can't explain why I haven't gone back, and I appreciate that he's never asked.

When it's finally late enough that we need to go in, he walks me to my back door, opens it, and looks me in the eyes. "Goodnight, Pepper."

I love his eyes. They are like the bright sky on a cloudless day.

CHAPTER 23

Deacon

TUESDAY MORNING, PEPPER JOINS us again for breakfast—after she and Lou have cuddle time for the second day in a row. I couldn't be happier for Lou and am not jealous at all. At least that's the lie I've been telling myself.

Lucky for me, I don't have to teach today, so I get to stay home and be there for what the girls have started to call "deck talk."

A heated discussion commences about the best Marvel superhero. Amber says Black Widow. Pepper says Thor. Lou says Elsa because . . . well, she's Lou. They are all wrong—it's Captain America, and I go on a long speech about why I'm right. I don't convince anyone, but I make Pepper smile. It reaches her eyes and goes down to her toes, so I'd say I won the argument.

That night, Lou runs over and begs Pepper to join us for dinner, which she does. I may have sent Lou over.

After dinner, Pepper and I talk on the back deck until it's time to go to sleep. I walk her to her back door, open it for her, and look her in the eyes. "Tomorrow's breakfast is something special. I got Cap'n Crunch. You wanna join us?"

"I wouldn't miss it for the world." She smiles and walks inside her condo.

I could stare at her smile all day.

CHAPTER 24

Samantha

WEDNESDAY MORNING BEFORE BREAKFAST, Lou joins me for snuggles again. We wrap up in a blanket on the couch, and she tells me she wants to be the first person to walk to the sun. If anyone can do that, it's Lou.

When we go over for breakfast, I notice Deacon's hair is still wet from his shower. I wonder what kind of shampoo he uses and what it smells like.

After a Cap'n Crunch breakfast, Deke and I do the dishes together and get in a water fight.

Best. Breakfast. Ever.

And I don't even like Cap'n Crunch.

CHAPTER 25

Deacon

THURSDAY MORNING, PEPPER COMES over for breakfast and brings Eggo waffles. Man, that woman can work a toaster.

Afterwards Amber goes back to bed, and Pepper and I sit on the deck talking while Lou plays in the sand.

Later, Pepper surprises us by showing up with dinner. She'd picked up shrimp nachos from Sam's.

After Lou and Amber go to bed, Pepper and I stay up late lying on the beach, looking at stars, and comparing favorite things.

Her favorite museum is the Museum of Contemporary Art Chicago, while mine is the beach (I don't like museums).

My favorite thing to listen to in my car is 70s classic rock, while hers is a legal podcast.

Her favorite ice cream is butter pecan, while mine is double chocolate brownie.

My favorite car is a '69 Mustang, while hers is anything black with tinted windows.

But we both have the same favorite weather—sunny and warm.

Pepper is a new addiction. I have started and ended every day with her this week.

She is my new favorite thing.

CHAPTER 26

Samantha

FRIDAY MORNING, LOU WAKES me up, pulls me out of bed, and drags me to the couch for another cuddle session. These have become my second-favorite part of my mornings.

My favorite is about to happen. Lou and I are done talking and we are about to head over to Deke's condo for breakfast. The first thing I always do when I walk into his condo is search him out. I want to be looking at him when he first notices me, because he always stops whatever he's doing and smiles. The smile is indescribable, and something about his energy always seems to shift when he sees me. Even if he's already standing still when I enter, something about him changes. There's an intensity about it that always makes my heart shutter.

For someone who has spent most of her life trying to avoid spending time with people, that's all I want to do with Deke. I want more time. More talking. More laughter. More arguments about superheroes. More breakfasts. More dinners. More accidental touches.

Every time we do the dishes together, our hands brush as we pass dishes back and forth. It's like my body gets a shot of adrenaline every time. If I hand him a puzzle piece, his fingers brush against mine when he takes it. Door knobs, juice pitchers, remote controls (we've gotten through the first four episodes of *Star Wars*). Whenever anything is passing from his hand to mine—or vice versa—I can count on the fact that our skin will touch.

And everyday I'm reminded of a thought I had during my first lunch with Cheryl. *What would it be like to be kissed by a man I truly trust?* I want to know.

My heart rate picks up a little as Lou and I step out of my back door and in through Deke's.

I look around, but I don't see him right off.

"He's not here." Amber's voice comes from the kitchen.

"Who?" Considering there is only one *he* in our little group, that might be one of the dumber things I've said.

"If you don't realize that the first thing you do every morning when you walk in the door is look for Deacon, you aren't very self-aware." Amber is at the stove and has her back to me, but I can hear the smirk in her voice. "But never fear, he left you that." She points to a card on the table.

I don't even try to play it cool as I rush to the table and pick it up.

Pepper,

Sorry I couldn't be there to have breakfast with you. One of my employees called in sick this morning, so I had to cover an early morning scuba dive.

I didn't have time to pack a lunch, so would you be willing to grab something for me from Sam's?

Text me to let me know.

Deke

P.S. Marco will know what my order is.

I suck in my lips, trying to conceal the smile attempting to break across my face.

"I can hear your smile all the way over here. Did he leave you a sexy little note?"

"No! It's not a sexy little note. He was asking if I could pick up his lunch for him at Sam's."

"So that's what the kids are calling it these days." Amber turns around and leans back against the stove with a knowing look on her face.

I have no reply. What am I supposed to say?

Yes—his is the first face I look for every time I walk through her back door? Yes—even though he just asked me to pick up his lunch, I do, in fact, find that note pretty sexy? Yes—I think he's the most amazing man I've ever known? Or yes—I wish it was what the kids are calling it these days?

No, I don't think I'll be saying any of those things. So I roll my eyes. Obviously, my maturity game is on point this morning.

"Friday is usually my lunch date with Cheryl, but I'm going to see if she can meet up earlier. Then I could still grab lunch for Deke." I'm trying to sound casual. Do I sound casual? I don't know why my armpits are sweating right now.

Amber walks over and sits down at the table. "It's okay, you know. You can be super excited that my brother wrote you a sexy note asking for a lunchtime rendezvous, and I won't be grossed out."

"It is not a sexy note! Do you want to read it?" I try to shove it in her face, but she stands up and walks away.

As I head out the back door, I yell back at Amber, "You know I hate you, don't you?" I try to hide my smile so it sounds more threatening.

"Love you like a sister!" she yells back.

I send off a quick text to Deke.

Samantha:

I think I can pick up your lunch. I've got my lunch date with Cheryl today, but if she can meet earlier, I can.

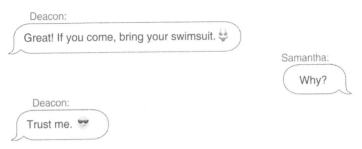

Luckily Cheryl is able to meet up earlier, so we don't miss our girl talk. I get there before her and head to the bar.

"Hey, Marco. Deke sent me in to pick up his lunch order, but Cheryl and I will be chatting for a while first, so maybe have it ready in an hour?"

Marco is in front of the counter wiping down barstools. His impressive size is on display, because his work T-shirt that says *Sam's Bar & Grill* looks incredibly new—and incredibly small. He turns to me, looking confused. "Deke never gets lunch here."

My mind goes blank as I try to think through Deke's note. Did I misunderstand something? "He said he needed me to pick up his lunch and bring it to him. I swear the note said to pick it up here." All of that comes out as a question.

Marco looks like a deer in the headlights until he starts shifting back and forth a little on his feet. "Oh. Yeah. I mean, of course. Deke gets his lunch here almost everyday. I just forgot about that for a moment." He looks like he's breaking out in a cold sweat, and I feel a little lost. "What did you say he wanted?"

I narrow my eyes at him, trying to piece together what's going on. "He said you would know."

"Of course I know! I do know. I just didn't know . . . if you knew."

I notice Cheryl walking in the front door, and she heads straight to Marco. "You left this at my house last night." Then she produces a very large, and very worn looking, T-shirt that says *Sam's Bar & Grill* and slams it down on the counter.

"That's where I left it!" And without more than a second's thought, he rips off the T-shirt he's wearing and throws it over the doors into the kitchen, yelling, "Hunter! Refold this and put it back with the others!"

Oh. My. Word. Marco's clothing covers up a lot. I mean, it was obvious that Marco is a fit guy, but I had no idea! This man is not just strong. He has the body of a Greek god. I realize I'm staring when Cheryl smacks me on my backside, snapping me out of my trance.

"You get used to it." Cheryl shrugs and walks away as Marco slips on the much better-fitting shirt that Cheryl brought with her. "And whatever he was telling you—he's lying. Marco is the world's worst liar. You can always tell because he starts fidgeting with his feet, and then he breaks out in a sweat and starts talking like an idiot."

When Cheryl and I sit down, I can't help but ask, "Why did Marco leave his shirt at your house? I mean, at what point was he even there, and why did his clothes come off? I didn't think you two even liked each other."

"We don't. At least, we don't anymore." A sly grin is all I get before she changes the topic and we discuss everything else.

CHaPTer 27

Deacon

WHY DO I FEEL nervous? I think Pepper is coming, but I'm not sure. She never followed up with a text to let me know if Cheryl could meet earlier.

Did I need someone to pick up my lunch? No.

Have I ever gotten lunch at Sam's? No.

Am I a liar? Yes.

But if you put together a jury of men, they would not only find me innocent—they would cheer me on with a "ya gotta do what ya gotta do to get the girl!" Or, in my case, find more time with the girl.

Finding as much alone time as I want with Pepper is not easy when I live with my sister and five-year-old niece, who seems to be as crazy about her as I am. We usually get the evenings, but I want more. So although I'm still trying to give her space, I may have gotten a little desperate and . . . yes, I concocted a lie about needing lunch brought to me. But I knew I wasn't going to see her at breakfast, and I didn't want to wait till I got home! I was hoping she would take pity on me.

All of a sudden, a conversation I had with Amber a few days ago starts playing back in my mind.

"Deke, I know where your mind is, but she doesn't have all the information she needs, and I can't tell her. You need to. And you need to before this goes any further."

"But . . . ," my protest died on my lips as I saw the look on Amber's face.

"I can't, Deacon. It has to be you."

I sigh, feeling the weight of the world on my shoulders. Amber was right. She usually is.

I guess today's lie is just one more thing I should tell Pepper about but won't. At least not today.

Crap! That reminds me—I need to text Marco and warn him that she might show up. I need him to cover for me! I grab my phone and send off a quick text.

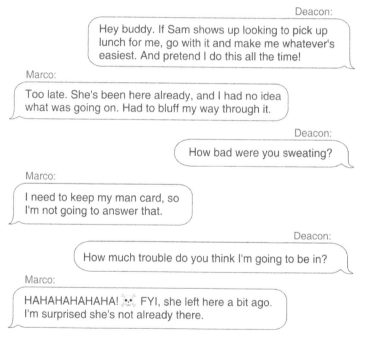

Deacon:
Hey buddy. If Sam shows up looking to pick up lunch for me, go with it and make me whatever's easiest. And pretend I do this all the time!

Marco:
Too late. She's been here already, and I had no idea what was going on. Had to bluff my way through it.

Deacon:
How bad were you sweating?

Marco:
I need to keep my man card, so I'm not going to answer that.

Deacon:
How much trouble do you think I'm going to be in?

Marco:
HAHAHAHAHAHA! 💀 FYI, she left here a bit ago. I'm surprised she's not already there.

I look outside, and sure enough, she's pulling up. Now I'm back to being nervous—if she figures out my little white lie, I don't know how she'll respond. This ploy to spend time with her is not necessarily a grand gesture, but at least it says I was thinking of you . . . right?

Pepper walks in with a to-go bag from Sam's and gives me a big smile. If my knees go weak at the sight of her, I hope she doesn't notice. I need to play it cool. "Hey." Wow, great conversation starter.

She puts the to-go bag on my desk. "Marco said this was your regular lunch order." She doesn't flinch or give herself away. Did Marco cover for me better than he thought he did? Or is she calling my bluff?

"Yep. I can say with complete accuracy that I have gotten this every single time I've ordered a to-go lunch from Marcos." I reach for the bag, but Pepper reaches out and puts her hand over mine, stopping me from opening the bag.

"So what is it?" She smiles at me.

"What is what?" I'm full of crap and know exactly what she's getting at.

"What's this lunch that is so good you get it every single time? I mean, Cheryl literally got me one of everything on the menu the first time I ate there, and everything is so good, I can't imagine sticking to one thing." She takes a few steps back and rests her hips against the desk behind her.

"Pepper, are you really going to do this to me?"

"Do what?" She knows! I know she knows. And by the satisfied look on her face, she knows that I know she knows.

"If I share my lunch with you, will you please not make me say it out loud?" I'm not pleading like a beggar, more like a used-car salesman trying to make a deal. And I can't say that's much better.

A mischievous smile spreads across her face. "I've already had lunch, but I'm willing to make a deal. You need to tell me a secret first."

The apprehension I feel at her question is real, because I feel like I might be walking out of the frying pan and into the fire. "Why do I feel like I've sold my soul to the devil?"

"Because maybe you did." I'm sure she doesn't mean to, but when she pushes off the back desk and walks back toward me, it's like she's slinking toward me, and it's one of the most alluring things I've ever seen. I die a little inside—but in the best possible way. Every nerve ending in my body stands at attention. I'm standing by my desk, and when she gets to me, she stops, reaches over to the bag of food, opens it, and starts taking my lunch out. "My first night on the island, I went to Sam's, as you know, because I didn't have any food in the condo. When I woke up the next morning, there was food in the kitchen. I thought it was Cheryl. When I thanked her for it, she didn't know what I was talking about." At this point, she's done getting the food out of the bag. She hands me some utensils and motions for me to sit down. "I can think of exactly one other person who could have figured out that I didn't have any food. Do you have any idea who that person is?"

"So you're saying if I admit to *that*, I can avoid admitting to *this*?" I point to my lunch sack.

"Yep."

"Fine. That was me. It was your first night, you were going to wake up with a hangover, and I knew you would need something solid when you woke up. I grabbed a bunch of stuff out of my condo and brought it over. I wasn't trying to keep it a secret. It's just a little awkward to say, '*Hey, I got you a bunch of food. Aren't I a nice guy?*'" I shrug my shoulders.

She smiles sweetly at me. "Yeah, but you are a nice guy. And now I can say thanks. Also, you owe me twenty-five dollars for lunch."

"He charged you for my food? He never charges me for dinner!"

"Does he ever charge you for lunch?"

"I've never had lunch there, so . . ." Busted. Her smile is all victory. "Oh. You're good." I point my fork at her then stab into my lunch. "You're good. Now go change into your swimsuit while I eat. You're finally going to get a proper snorkel lesson."

"What?"

I turn to look at her, and she's not the same woman who was standing there five seconds ago. She's suddenly uncertain and nervous. "No. Please not today." She's literally backing out of the room. I stand up and reach for her. I've got her by one hand, and I reach my other hand out in an invitation for her to take it. Reluctantly, she does. I can feel her hands shaking a little.

"Give me a chance. One chance. Everyone else is gone for the day. It will just be me and you, and we can take all the time you need." She looks utterly unconvinced. I muster up all the sincerity I can. "One chance, Pepper. Will you trust me?"

CHAPTER 28

Samantha

WILL I?

To me, being in water represents rejection, abandonment, and the sense that no one cares. It makes me feel alone and helpless.

When I don't respond, he asks again.

"Will you trust me?" His eyes are soft and kind. I can't speak, but I nod my head because I know that I *can* trust him. I already *do* trust him. So I guess I will at least *try* to try one more time.

He squeezes my hand. "Good. Now, put your swimsuit on and I'll finish up my lunch."

Twenty minutes later, I'm standing by the pool with Deke. I'm in a solid-black one-piece with a square neck and a deep, plunging back. I bought it because I look amazing in it and thought the low back would minimize tan lines. It was not to be used for swimming. Ever.

Deke is in nautical-colored swim trunks and a black, long-sleeve rash guard. I almost wish he had his shirt off again, because I could use the distraction.

Even though I stuck my face in the water my first day here, it doesn't help me at all right now. I'm physically shaking, can't move, and can feel a panic attack coming.

"Samantha." My gaze jolts up to Deke, and I can tell from his tone—and from the fact that he used my full name—that he must have been trying to get my attention for at least a little while. "Hi." He gives me a little wave. "I need you to know that this is a safe place and that you are safe while you're with me. Do you believe me?"

I look down at my feet. "I . . . I don't know. I mean, yes. Yes, I believe you."

"The first thing we will do is talk about how you feel around water. Then we will talk about you getting in the water."

My gaze snaps back up to him, my breath quickening and my chest tightening. "I can't get in. Please don't make me!"

He must sense that I'm unraveling, because he reaches out, pulls me into him, and wraps me in his arms. I close my eyes and revel in this cocoon of safety. "I promise you that we will only talk about you getting in the water and that you do not have to go in if you don't want to. You don't have to get a drop of water on you. I promise." He releases me and holds me away from his body, making sure I'm looking right at him when he speaks. "Nothing will happen here today that you are not one-hundred percent on board with. I need you to know that. Okay?"

I nod my head. It's all I can do right now, and he doesn't make me say anything.

He sighs a little before speaking again. "When I work with people who have a fear of water, I do everything I can to help that person feel as comfortable as possible. So . . . what do you want me to call you?"

My brain is running on fumes right now. "I don't understand."

"I have taken to calling you Pepper. I love it for several reasons, but one of them is that . . . ," he sighs in resignation. His eyes pierce into me as he seems to debate his next words. "I want you to know that you're making me give away one of my secrets right now!" His tone is one of exasperation, but the hint of a smile across his face takes all the bite out of his bark. "You seem to not like Pepper very much, and I will admit that I enjoy ruffling your feathers a little. That's maybe one of the reasons I do it." He then changes into snorkel-teacher mode. "But this place," he gestures to the entire pool area, "needs to feel safe to you, so I will use whatever name you feel the most comfortable with me using."

I'm not sure what to say. Knowing how much he dislikes calling me Samantha, I feel like it might take my mind off some of the anxiety if I knew I were ruffling *his* feathers for a little bit. "Call me Samantha, please."

CHAPTER 29

Deacon

I DEFLATE A LITTLE, but I make sure it doesn't show. I don't know what I'll do if she never gets used to Pepper. It's the only way I think of her now.

"Okay. Samantha. I am going to ask you some questions, and you can nod your head or answer a simple yes or no. I can see that your breathing becomes rapid and shallow around water. Have you ever been nauseated when thinking about getting in water?" She shakes her head. "Great. Have you ever had a panic attack when thinking about getting in water?" She nods her head. "That's fine. Do you have trouble sleeping when thinking about water?"

"Sometimes. A little. But not often." It's great that she's speaking. It shows she is starting to relax a little bit.

"I notice you can stand on the back deck and look at the water and be fine, but here, when we are next to the water, you're afraid. Do you know why?"

She takes a moment to construct her answer, but when she speaks, her voice is shaky, like she thinks she's going to get thrown to the sharks. "I can look at the ocean off the back deck because I know I don't need to get in it. When I'm here, I know I'm supposed to get in."

"That makes sense. Two more questions. First, when you think about water, would you describe it as dangerous or bad?"

"Bad!" Her answer comes lightning fast, and her voice comes out stronger than I thought it would. Whatever caused her fear has some pretty deep roots. Her breathing becomes more shallow again.

"Alright. Last question for a moment. I think I know the answer to this, but since thinking about conquering this fear, do you find yourself crying more than usual?"

Her eyes water instantly at the question.

I can't stop myself from reaching up and gently wiping her tears away with my thumb. I want to take her in my arms again, but I'm trying to be professional. And holding your student isn't really in the brochure, so I'm trying to avoid it a second time. "It's okay. You cry if you want to. There is no judgment here, and that's actually a normal symptom for people who struggle with aquaphobia."

"You . . . you are really good at this." Her voice is soft, but she looks up and meets my gaze, which shows me she's still doing okay. Not great—but okay.

"Thanks. Sometimes I think I breathe better under the water. So I've worked hard to help people with this fear, in case breathing under water helps them too." Her whole body starts to shake when I mention under water. "It's okay." I pull her into another embrace. *So much for professionalism.*

"Don't make me do that. Don't make me breathe under water with the mask."

"We aren't going to worry about that right now. We were talking about things that I like to do, not things you have to do. What I want you to focus on right now is BLRT."

"Blurt?"

"That's what it sounds like, but it's actually B, L, R, T, which stands for *breathe*, *look*, *relax*, and *touch*. The techniques are real, but I made up the acronym. I'm cool like that." I see a shadow of a smile on her face at my feigned cockiness, and I feel like I've won a gold medal. Getting her to smile—or at least think about smiling—at a time like this is a good sign. It's all about baby steps.

"First is B. *Breathe*. It's as simple as it sounds. Can you look at me and take a few deep breaths?" It takes several tries, but her breathing starts to even out. "Great. Do you think you can do the same thing while looking at the water?" Her breathing instantly hitches, but she at least turns to the water to try. Without thinking, I grab her hand and squeeze it. She squeezes back and doesn't loosen her grip until her breathing starts to even out.

"You're doing great." I reach up and wipe a few more tears from her face.

She looks up at me. "Okay. BLRT. I don't remember what the L stands for." Her voice isn't as shaky as it was a minute ago.

"It stands for *look*, and you already did it." I smile at her.

"I did?" Her voice sounds so hopeful. People who don't have this fear don't understand how debilitating it can be. I've never had it, but I've worked with so many that have. I can tell that her case is pretty severe, but I'm amazed that she's trying so hard—even when it's practically suffocating her.

"You did, because you looked at the water. That was all you needed to do. The next letter is R. It might be hard for you right now, but try to *relax*. Do whatever you need to do—close your eyes, take a breath, sit down, stretch. Just relax as much as you can."

She nods at me and starts to roll her head from side to side. Then she shakes out her arms and legs and takes a few more deep breaths. "Okay. That's as good as I can do right now."

"You did really well. You're still tense, but I can tell that you're more relaxed than you were. The last one is T for *touch*. This is when you would walk over and touch the water as much as you're comfortable with. But you don't have to unless you want to. And if you don't want to, then you're done for today." I try to sound very casual so that she won't feel bad if she decides to not go near the water.

She looks at me for a long time. Then she looks at the water for even longer. Her breathing is already so much better when looking at the water.

"Samantha, you seem more nervous today than you did last time you were here. Last time, you at least stood in the shallow end. Is today harder?" A small nod of her head is all I get. "Do you know why?"

When she doesn't answer, I decide to give her a little bit of room and start moving to the back of the decking.

Her head snaps around to me. "WHERE ARE YOU GOING?" Her voice explodes with panic!

"Nowhere! Samantha, I'm going nowhere!" I return to her side. "I was going to give you a little space to think. That's all." I don't know what happened, but she's in panic mode.

"You were going to *abandon* me next to the water?"

"No, I was taking a few steps back, that's all."

"But you were leaving, and you weren't even going to tell me! You were leaving!"

She's shaking so badly that I quickly step in and hold her before she collapses to the ground. "I'm not leaving you. I'm not going anywhere." Her entire body shakes in my arms, and she grabs onto my shirt. This woman is petrified that I was going to leave. "Pepper, I'm not ever going anywhere." My voice is soft, and I move my arms up and down her back to try and calm her. She is still clinging to my shirt when she takes one more shuddering breath, and the shaking subsides.

"Don't leave me by the water." It's a statement. It's also a plea.

"I won't. I won't ever leave you by the water—or anywhere else. I won't leave you." I'm still holding her. She's still clinging to my shirt.

After several moments, and when I feel very confident that she isn't scared anymore, I try to lift the mood.

"Would it help at all if I took my shirt off to distract you again?"

She steps back and gives me no reaction at all for a moment. But slowly, I see more tension in her shoulders release and a small (but pathetic) smile appear on her face.

"Too soon?"

"Maybe." Then she shrugs a little, and her smile grows the slightest bit more. "I don't know. Maybe not. That was kinda funny."

"*Kinda* funny?" I fake some outrage at her comment. "Come on, that was hilarious!"

Her chest moves with a small internal laugh, but her eyes dim a little as she does it. She looks down, rubbing her toe on the decking and holding her hands together while fidgeting with her fingers.

I try to make my voice sound quiet and non judgmental. "Do you want to be done today?"

Her eyebrows are raised and slightly pulled together when she looks back up at me, and her eyes are so hopeful.

I don't make her say it. "Why don't we call it a day and head back, okay?"

"Will you hold my hand for a minute?"

I step closer to her and reach down to entwine my fingers with hers. Then she looks at me and takes a deep breath. Slowly she turns, looks at the water, and takes a few more calming breaths. Then, with a vice-like grip on my hand, she starts walking toward the back of the pool where she was standing last time. When she gets to the edge of the water, she looks up at me like she's pleading for permission to move to the desert, where she'll never have to look at a body of water again.

"You don't have to do this if you don't want to." I give her hand a little squeeze.

She looks back to the water and slowly steps in, and I follow. I can see her concentrating on her breathing more than anything else—so frightened but so determined. Then she surprises me even more by taking a few more steps into the water.

When she looks up, we lock eyes. Her voice is soft, but stronger than the last time she spoke. "Okay. We can go home now."

I don't know if it's how stunned I am at her bravery or the way she's looking at me or that she used the word *home* like it's a place where we belong together, but my body inadvertently takes a step closer to her, angling itself to fully face her, our fingers still intertwined. If I pulled her into me and kissed her, it would feel like taking advantage of her emotionally compromised condition, and it would be the absolute wrong thing to do. But I've never wanted to do the wrong thing as much as I do right now.

My eyes roam over every inch of her face—from her eyes, to the few freckles I can only see when I'm this close, to how full and pink her lips are—and then back up to her eyes. Instinctively, I reach up and put my palm on her cheek, letting my thumb wipe away another tear.

I'm falling more and more, but this isn't the right time or place to do anything about it. I lower my hand, and we both walk out of the pool, dry off, and drive home.

When we both park and get out of our cars, she heads straight for her condo, and I follow her to the door. "You okay?"

"Yeah. I actually am. I just keep playing Steph's voice over and over in my head: *You are fierce and brave and strong. You are a woman warrior and can do anything.* It helps."

"I gotta meet this Steph. She knows what she's talking about." I smile and Pepper gives me a gentle eye roll.

"You two meeting would be a disaster." She chuckles a little at whatever is running through her mind, then she sobers up and looks at me. "Thanks. You really are good at what you do."

"It was my pleasure." I reach down and open her door for her. "And thanks for bringing me lunch, Pepper."

At the mention of her nickname, she does another eye roll, but this one has a little bit more sass. "I hate it when you call me that."

"And that's probably why I love doing it so much." I give her a little wink and then step back to watch her go inside.

Once her door is shut, I turn to my own door, wondering what I have to do to make her not hate that name. Then my phone lights up, and I smile when I see who's calling.

CHAPTER 30

Deacon

"Cooper! You have no idea how much I need you right now." Cooper Mallory was my freshman roommate, and we've been best friends ever since. We were even business partners until eighteen months ago when we sold our company and I moved to the island. He knows me better than anyone except Amber, and if there is anyone I need advice from right now, it's him. We have this way of reading each other that makes us constantly joke that we must be twins separated at birth. Sometimes he reads me so well that I'm almost not joking when I say it.

"It's always good to feel needed." I can hear Cooper's smile through the tone of his voice, which is like listening to the highest quality chocolate. If chocolate could speak. Women have been known to fawn all over him from a simple phone call. I've seen cashiers go slack-jawed at Chick-fil-A taking his lemonade order. Of course, those women also had the pleasure of seeing him in person.

I'm very confident in my looks, and it's a good thing, because a lesser man could lose all confidence standing next to Cooper Mallory. He's got dimples and a smile that ladies love. No matter how hard he tries to blend in, he just can't. He gets more attention from women than he wants, which has always been a bit of a problem.

"Cooper, I thought you weren't going to have phone service for a while."

"Plans change, and I'm happy about that because I'm going to get my first warm shower in three weeks."

"Where are you right now? Are you coming for a visit? Because your call is timely. I need some advice."

I hear chuckling on the other end of the line. "First of all, I have no idea where I am. I've gone through so many time zones in the last twenty-four hours that I can't even think straight. Second, I wish I could visit, but things didn't pan out the way I'd hoped, so I need to keep looking. Don't worry, I'm not giving up."

He's been working on a surprise for Amber, and the amount of time and resources he has put into it have almost been more than my heart can take. "Coop, you know you don't have to do this, right?"

"Deke, what good is it being a gazillionaire if I can't help the people I love? And you know how much I love Amber."

Neither of us says anything for a moment. Finally I choke down the lump in my throat. "And she loves you back, but you don't deserve her!" I try to sound like an intimidating big brother, but unfortunately nothing intimidates Cooper.

"Please, who does? She's an amazing woman. I just want to be able to give her everything she wants. But let's not talk about that anymore. Let's talk about your woman troubles." There's that twin intuition. I didn't even need to say anything, and he knew. "How deep is it?"

I only need two words and he'll know everything. "Mariana Trench."

Cooper and I have been diving together since freshman year, and somewhere along the way, we started using ocean depths to compare how much we were interested in a woman. *Snorkel day trip* meant the date was fun but we didn't see a second date happening. I dated a girl once for six months, and she was considered a *60-meter dive*—the depth divers call a "deep dive." That was usually when Coop and I started thinking of the relationship as committed. Anything above 60 meters meant we were still testing the waters, no pun intended. *Great Blue Hole* is the deepest I've gone at 124 meters. Her name was Holly, and I thought she might be the one, until we got some news and she bolted. She was almost four years ago, and the last diving I've done. Till Pepper.

Cooper is silent for a long time. I don't need to say anything because I know he's processing. "Deacon, we talked on the phone three weeks ago. Three weeks. Holly stayed at twenty meters for a couple of months, so to say I'm taken back is an understatement."

I love that Cooper doesn't tell me I'm crazy and try to talk me out of anything. He just accepts and tries to process the shock. I can't blame him—I'm still in shock about it all.

"What's her favorite . . ."

"Dr. Pepper. I used it the second time I saw her."

"So much better than Fanta!"

"I know! But she hates the name."

Cooper knows the story of my parents meeting. When I felt things getting serious with Holly, I wanted to make the nickname work as an homage to my dad, but her favorite drink was Fanta. Fanta is a stupid nickname and it never worked.

"That's rough. Maybe she'll get used to it? Have you . . ."

"Nope."

"Is she . . ."

"I don't know, but when I make her laugh, I feel like I've won the lottery."

"Where does she . . ."

"In the condo next door."

"You know you should try and improve . . ."

"Give me a break! At least I upped it to Cap'n Crunch one day. I just can't fix what isn't broken, Coop. If she didn't like Lucky Charms, I'm not sure I would still feel this way."

"Deacon," he goes into business mode, "let's get real. What's your timeline here? Because life is moving faster than you want it to right now."

"I know. She doesn't know anything yet. I keep trying to bring it up, but I just can't."

"Are you thinking about yourself when you say that or her? Because when Holly left . . ."

"It's not about me. Somehow I know she wouldn't react the same way. And you should see her with Lou and Amber. Pepper and Amber act like your sisters whenever they talk, and it hurts a little to admit, but I think she likes Lou more than she likes me."

That brings out Cooper's belly laugh. "I can tell I'm gonna like this one!"

We spend the next hour this way—him asking me everything about her and me not holding anything back.

"So, the great Deacon King has fallen." He lets out a sigh. "The last of the great ones."

"Not till you've fallen too, Coop."

"Don't hold your breath on that one. I haven't gone deeper than snorkeling for so long. Everyone I meet is so shallow." He laughs for a second. "That was an unintended pun, but it's sad how true it is. Yours sounds like the real deal."

"Mariana Trench, Coop. *Mariana Trench*."

The Mariana Trench is the deepest point of the ocean. Nothing goes deeper.

CHapTer 31

Samantha

SATURDAY MORNING, I'M WOKEN up by the customary knock on my back door.

It took me forever to get to sleep last night, because I kept replaying everything from the day before in my mind, so I'm still pretty tired.

Deke was great yesterday. After we got home, he made sure I came over for dinner because he thought being with everyone would be a good distraction. He was right. Being around those three helped me put things into perspective.

I wish Lou had given me another hour of sleep, but I would never turn that little girl away. I'm too tired, and too comfy, to get out of bed and answer the door, so I yell to Lou, "Walk in!" When I hear the back door open, I call out again. "Grab the blanket off the couch and bring it back to my bedroom."

I close my still sleepy eyes and wait for her to show up. When I hear her footsteps reach my bedroom door, I murmur, "Hey, Sweetie. Why don't you climb up here with me, and we can cuddle up and talk or whatever you want for a while. Is that okay?"

"If you insist."

My eyes fly open, and I bolt upright in bed. Deke is leaning against my doorway, holding the blanket from my couch.

"But I'd like some details on what *whatever* is, because that sounds interesting. And if we are working on pet names for each other, can mine be Macho Man instead of Sweetie? I feel it encompasses more of who I am."

"I'm-so-sorry-I-thought-you-were-Lou!!"

He starts slowly nodding his head. "I get that all the time." Then he pushes off the doorway and starts walking toward me. I suddenly remember that not only is there very little fabric to my pajamas, but they are also very sheer. And I'm not wearing a bra. I grab my blanket and hold it up to my neck.

"Why are you in my house? Why are you in my bedroom? Why are you walking toward me?" My words come out a little rushed, and—if I'm being honest—a little breathy because I find this slow walk very sexy. Is he really walking that slow? Or is my mind just processing it at this speed? Whichever it is, I'm absolutely okay with it.

"First off, because you told me to walk in. Then you told me to get a blanket so we could '*cuddle up and talk or whatever*' in your bed. Is that what the kids are calling it these days?"

Why do I feel so flustered? Why is my mouth suddenly dry? Why are my armpits sweating so badly?

I open my mouth to give a little retort, but nothing comes out. I'm speechless.

He must see my loss for words, and he gives a little laugh. "Don't worry Pepper, I'm just here for this." He holds up my phone. He would use that name right now, when my defenses are nowhere to be seen. "You left it at my place last night, and your friend Stephanie called a few minutes ago. I answered and told her that I would bring you the phone and that she should call back in a few minutes." Like magic, my phone starts ringing. He looks down at the screen. "Yep, Stephanie." He finishes walking over to my bed and hands me the phone. When I reach out for it, our hands brush and, once again, electricity shoots through my entire body. My eyes dart up to his. I would give anything to read his mind right now.

I force myself to look away from him so that I can get my bearings straight and talk to Steph, but when I answer my phone, my body is still zinging from the contact.

"Hey, what's up? I'm just lying in bed. Doing nothing. Just being here. Lying in bed." The zing has obviously short-circuited my brain.

"You left your phone at Sexy-Man's house?" Steph has never been a soft talker, and Deke is still standing right by my bed, so there is a ninety-nine-percent chance he heard that. His eyebrows raise slightly, and he smiles. Scratch that. It's a one-hundred-percent chance.

This is a nightmare. Steph talks too loud, Deke is standing too close, and I can't get out of bed because I'm in sheer pajamas with no bra in sight. And did I mention Deke is standing too close and Steph is a loud talker? So yeah, nightmare.

I try to act calm and casual. "Yeah. I guess I didn't realize that I left it over there last night. So what's up with you?"

"ARE YOU HAVING SLEEPOVERS NOW?"

He definitely heard that. I will kill her the next time I see her.

"Steph!! Calm down! We can chat about that later."

Deke loudly chimes in so that Steph can hear him. "It's fine, we can chat about it now if you'd like. Are we supposed to be having sleepovers? Because if so, I'm gonna need to leave a toothbrush here and have my own drawer." He's so full of it. He's trying to get a reaction out of me, and unfortunately, between him and Steph, I'm giving them quite the show. My body is feeling all sorts of reactions right now, so *mission accomplished. Tom Cruise would be very proud.*

"No! No sleepovers! I didn't stay over there—I was over there. Then I came here. To my own bed. By myself. In my bed." My voice has a definite panicked tone.

"Wait, but wasn't that just him? He's at your house? I thought you said you were lying in bed. IS HE IN YOUR BED?" The scream that follows is one that will go down in history as Steph's longest and loudest scream. It's like she can't be contained. And I can tell she's dancing. As soon as the scream ends, she starts yell-talking. "Let me talk to him!"

"No."

"Put him on the phone!"

"No."

"I wanna talk to Sexy-Man!" This time she sounds more like a whining child.

I hear Deke clear his throat. "Excuse me, I believe she wants to talk to me." He holds his hand out for the phone, and I want to die. Please, can a freak storm blow in and collapse my roof? Just the part over my bed? That would be super helpful!

"No." That is directed at Deke.

"But she said she wants to talk to Sexy-Man, and I can only assume she means me because . . . who else is it gonna be?" He holds his hands out in a gesture that says, *Look at me. I'm about as sexy as they come.*

Well, I can't disagree with that. He *is* about as sexy as they come. And kind and thoughtful and funny and perfect and easy to talk to and a million other things—and Steph knows them all. And I can tell she would love to throw me, and what are supposed to be other private conversations, under the bus right now and tell Deacon everything I've ever said about him! There is not a chance in you-know-where that I am letting them chat with each other.

"No." I say to both of them.

Deke then starts talking to Steph, but I have the phone, so he has to lean forward and talk loudly so that Steph can hear him. "Hi, Stephanie, this is Deacon, but some of my biggest fans call me Sexy-Man." He takes this opportunity to look me straight in the eyes with a look I can't even begin to decipher.

"This is not happening," I mumble to myself, since they've both stopped listening to me.

Deke calls out, "Stephanie, she's not going to let me talk to you on her phone, so call me on my phone." I know he's about to rattle off his phone number, and in a last ditch effort, I hold the phone as far away from him as I can, hoping Steph won't hear.

The problem is that I'm still in my very small and sheer pajamas and can't get out of bed. And I'm only about five foot five, so my arm length is nothing compared to the arm length of a man that is, say, six foot one. Deke places a knee on the bed, hovers his large body over mine, and lunges for the phone. When I keep it an inch from his reach, we start a kind of wrestling match for the phone—me, getting all tangled up in my sheets, and him, one knee up with a long arm reaching across me. The one thing I do have going for me is that Deke is (despite what is going on at this very moment) a gentleman. So while he could easily pin me and take the phone, I think he's trying to be a little careful, since—ya know—I'm still in my very small pajamas.

While we're fighting over the phone, we can hear Steph in the background. "Sometimes she can be such an unnecessary movie sequel. Okay, I've got a pencil now. Give me your number. You're going to be way more fun to talk to than *Samantha*." Her voice is positively giddy as she heavily emphasizes my name.

We continue our tug-of-war over the phone, and Deke yells out to Steph. "I don't call her Samantha. I call her Pepper."

"I know!" Steph is practically screaming with excitement. "She told me. And she said she pretends to hate it, but she actually *loves it*!" Her last few words are said in an overly loud, overly enthusiastic, and overly excited voice.

I. Will. Kill. Stephanie.

At Steph's declaration, the wrestling stops, and both Deke and I freeze in place and lock eyes. I am still holding the phone as far away from him as I can while trying to hold my covers up. He is leaning over my body, trying to reach the phone, but is still a few inches away from it. It takes a moment for any other reaction to happen—all the while, Steph is in the background blabbering on about something that neither of us is paying attention to—but slowly, a grin spreads across Deke's face.

I don't want to smile, but I'm about to, so I suck in my lips. The movement makes him look down at my mouth, and his eyes darken. All of a sudden, I can feel heat all over my body and energy pulsing in my veins. My heart rate picks up. Slowly his eyes come back up to mine, but he still has that grin. Then, in a hushed tone of victory and with absolute fireworks in his eyes, he simply says, "*Pepper.*"

Then we hear Steph. "You guys? Are you still there?"

I can't move—due to both the mortification of Steph telling Deacon that I secretly love the name Pepper and the fever coursing through my body. While I'm frozen, and without breaking eye contact, Deke leans two inches farther and gently removes the phone from my hand. I willingly let it go at this point.

He moves back to the side of the bed, stands up, and puts the phone to his ear—still never breaking eye contact with me. "Hey, Stephanie. This is Deacon. I think we should talk."

I can still hear her. "Why hellooooo, Deacon! She says your abs would put Hercules's to shame and you could be Chris Hemsworth's body double!"

"I DID NOT!" I yell from under my blanket—a much safer place to tell a lie. Goodbye world. I may not ever emerge from this very spot again.

"She has nothing but amaaaazing things to say about you." This is said in a perfect representation of Stephanie's carefully crafted persona: pop star plus stuffy art critic. Don't ask. Somehow she makes it work.

I peek out from under my blanket and see Deke still looking at me. He's eating up every single thing Steph is saying, and because Steph is talking so loudly, I can hear every syllable.

He slowly backs out of the room. I can't hear Steph anymore, but Deke points to me and mouths, "Breakfast. Ten minutes. Be there." Then he walks out of my room and out of my condo, with my phone, talking to the last person on earth I would ever want him to talk to.

That's it. I feel like packing everything up and moving to Madagascar! Or entering a convent and taking a vow of silence! Is it nuns that do that? Or monks? I can't remember.

After five minutes, I realize that it can't get much worse than it already has, so I start to get out of bed.

Then I remember some of the other things I've told Steph—that she may or may not be telling him right now—and throw my body back down on the bed, yanking the blanket over my head again.

Five minutes later, I decide to face the music and go eat breakfast. But I wait for twenty more minutes before I go.

"You're late," Lou blurts out when I arrive.

"Good morning, Samantha," Amber chimes in.

"Hey, Pepper. Here's your phone back. I won't need it again, since Stephanie and I exchanged numbers." Deke walks toward me with mischievous-looking eyes. When he reaches me, he takes my hand, opens it, puts my phone in it, and then closes my fingers around it. His hand holds mine a moment longer than necessary while standing closer than necessary. Then he lets go and goes back to making breakfast.

After that, the morning goes on like normal. Deke never makes it awkward for me. He calls me Pepper more—and exaggerates it a little more than usual—but he always does it with a fun glint in his eyes, like he's poking fun at the whole situation and not me.

There he goes again. Making me feel safe and like it's okay to have flaws, look stupid, or have silly-girl secrets.

It makes me finally want to share more of myself with him. Or at least, as much as I know how to share.

Deke doesn't go into work on Saturdays, so the post-breakfast conversation lasts a long time. Finally Amber announces to Lou that it's time for them to get dressed, and they go back to their rooms.

When I look up at Deke, I hear Steph's voice in my head, saying, *You are fierce and brave and strong. You are a woman warrior and can do anything.*

I decide to take a chance. A leap of faith.

CHAPTER 32

Deacon

I'M NOT SURE WHAT to make of the way Pepper is looking at me right now.

"Hi," she says with a twinkle in her eye and a small smile on her lips.

It's at this moment that Marco comes walking into the condo through the front door. "I've got Logan minding Sam's the rest of the day. I thought we could hit up the volleyball court and see if we can get anyone to play doubles with us." He strolls over and sits down at the table with us. "Hey, Samantha." He gives her the universal *what's up* nod.

I'm not normally a violent guy, but I want to punch him in the face. Visions of Marco unconscious on the floor with a black eye and a bloody nose swirl in my mind. I don't know what Pepper was going to say, but based on the look on her face, I really, really want to know.

I look over at her, and she seems curious. "Volleyball?"

Marco takes this opportunity to not throw his face against my very fisted hand and act like nothing's wrong here. "We play on the weekends sometimes. Do you play?"

"A little." She shrugs her shoulders.

The thing is—I'm a pretty good player. I mean, I'm not going to qualify for the Olympics or anything, but Marco and I play doubles a decent amount, and there aren't that many teams on the island who can beat us. We're scrappy, but our athleticism and height make up for what we lack in skill. It's not a normal reaction for me, but I like the idea of showing off a little bit in front of Pepper. And if I have to do it with my shirt off, then so be it. "You should come watch us. It will be fun."

As Amber and Lou walk back into the kitchen, Amber takes an unusual interest in the conversation.

"Can I play?" Pepper looks excited at the idea, but I don't know that she understands the level that Marco and I play at.

There is a hesitancy in my voice. "Marco and I play pretty hard, so," Amber gives a cough that demands I look at her. When I do, all I see are her eyes conveying a message from every feminist, living or dead: *ladies play hard, too.* "Yeah, that would be fun. Marco and I can . . . ," I was going to say *dial back our intensity*, but another cough from Amber has me putting away my caveman instincts, "call Cheryl to see if she's willing to be the fourth. She's actually a really good player."

"I'll go get ready!" Pepper jumps up and leaves to change her clothes.

The caveman inside of me comes back and begins picturing all the ways I can show her how to serve and wondering how much body contact I can create while doing it. Suddenly, I am hoping that she is really bad so I can give her a lot of help.

I call Cheryl and she agrees to be our fourth. She's short, but a fantastic player. She makes up for her lack of height with her speed and reflexes, and she's one of the best setters on the island.

When I hang up, I look over and see Marco clenching his jaw so hard that I think he's going to break it.

Then Amber starts chuckling. "I wouldn't miss this for the world." Her smile is like the Cheshire cat, giving me a sense of uneasiness. "Lou, Honey, grab your beach stuff. We're going to watch Dee-Dee and Marco play volleyball."

Marco and I take opposite sides of the court, assuming we will do co-ed teams—because of course we will do co-ed teams. Marco and

Cheryl used to play together all the time until they . . . didn't, but I bribed him to make sure Pepper and I would be on the same team. (It's going to cost him dearly to be on a team with Cheryl again. They don't exactly get along these days.)

The girls seem to have other ideas, because they both walk to my side of the court and signal with their eyes for me to join Marco.

Then, a completely nonverbal conversation happens between the four of us, and it goes something like this:

Girls: This is the girls' side. Go over there.

Boys: We can't play boys versus girls because we would destroy you.

Girls: We're a lot tougher than we look.

Boys: You can't possibly be serious!

Then both of the girls glare at us so intently that we give up, and I walk to what I guess I'll call the boys' side. The caveman inside me is not happy right now. "Fine. Ladies serve first."

On my way under the net, I slowly pull my shirt off and throw it on the sand by Amber and Lou. I have a smirk on my face when I turn around, only to find that Pepper has also stripped and is standing in an athletic bra and shorts. Heaven help me.

My show off shirtless plan just backfired. If someone asked me to recite the alphabet right now, I know I'd miss half the letters. She, on the other hand, doesn't seem fazed.

I'm still processing when Pepper throws the ball high into the air, steps forward to plant her feet, and then gracefully flies into the air with an insane vertical leap. Her right arm winds up and smashes the ball an inch off the net, and it lands in the deep back corner.

Neither Marco nor I even move the entire time.

The ladies stand waiting for one of us to get the ball, but I'm still in shock. I finally turn just my head to look at Marco, and he's glaring at

Cheryl like she's burned down his bar. I hear hysterical laughter to my right and turn to see Amber weeping because she's laughing so hard.

Through her tears, Amber yells, "Not gonna be as easy as you thought, is it, Big Brother?" She's hysterical.

Apparently, Marco and I are the only ones that didn't know about Pepper's volleyball skills. And from the looks of that serve, they aren't casual. My head rotates to look at Pepper, who is now standing only a few feet away from me.

"I'm not sure, but that's called a point? Right?" Then she smiles and winks.

Marco throws her the ball, and when she turns and walks away from me, I freeze—or I guess, remain frozen. Peeking out of her waistband is an intricate tattoo of a sleek jaguar. There is something incredibly strong, yet feminine, about it. Amber was right: it is a sexy tattoo. Both my knees and my resolve weaken. I'm going to end up staring at it every time she walks away from me today.

In the end, Marco and I pull off the win, but we have to fight for it. Pepper and Cheryl don't have the height for the hard hits, but their accuracy and placement had us diving and running the entire time. I have too much pride to ask, but I think we only won because the girls let up on us near the end.

"Where did you learn to play like that?"

Pepper's smile is pure devilish delight. "Wouldn't you like to know?" Then she turns away from me to grab a towel, and her tattoo is back in my line of sight. Yes, I would like to know, Pepper. I would like to know a lot of things.

We all have sand burns and sweat everywhere. So why do I look like a mop after cleaning up a junior-high lunchroom, while Pepper looks sexier than she ever has? My determination to keep my distance is uncoiling quickly, and now all I can think about is that almost-kiss at the end of her lesson yesterday. I need to cool off in the ocean and get some of this sand off, so I grab Lou and take her with me. Hopefully she can distract me from my racing thoughts.

CHapTer 33

Samantha

I SIT DOWN NEXT to Amber and watch Deke run into the water with Lou on his shoulders.

I'm not going to lie—the look on Deke's face after my first serve was very satisfying. We all played hard, but there were times I lost my concentration completely. A sandy, sweaty Deke is the sexiest thing I've ever seen. His golden hair was matted to the side of his tanned face, and his gorgeous chest and abs were glistening with sweat. And his legs . . . gah!

Deke has the best legs I've ever seen on a man. They are long and strong with muscle definition that belongs in a Marvel movie! I'm glad I was sweating so badly—it probably covered up the drool running down my chin. Why is it that I look like a wet dog and he looks like he belongs in the *Top Gun* volleyball scene?

My mind is whirling from the three encounters we've had in the last twenty-four hours.

First, he was incredibly sweet and tender with me at my lesson yesterday. He's always been like that. And I swear there was a moment when he was going to kiss me. It wouldn't have been the best timing because I was so emotionally frazzled—but let's just say, I wouldn't have turned him down if he'd have tried.

Then, there was our encounter in my bed this morning. Okay, that came out wrong! The encounter in my bedroom while I was in my bed under the covers and he was not under the covers with me but hovering above the covers directly above my body while trying to get my phone! *Fine.* I can try and spin that story any way I want to, but this morning, when his gaze fell down to my lips, I thought I was going to burst into flames. It was just *hot.* Even thinking about it now makes my heart rate and temperature soar. I feel a physical chemistry around him that I've never felt around any other man. But I also have an emotional chemistry with him—and all that does is amplify the physical.

Then this morning and . . . eye candy.

He's the whole package, and I didn't know men like him existed.

My thoughts must be projecting on my face, because Amber starts chuckling while watching me.

"Shut up." It's all I can say, because I have no defense.

"Penny for your thoughts?" I don't care how much she offers me, I will never share any of these thoughts with her.

"Nothing. Just really enjoying myself today." I try to keep my face neutral, but I'm pretty sure I fail. I look out at Deke and Lou again. "He's so incredible with her. Has he always been like this with kids?"

"Yeah. But it's different with Lou. He's the best father figure for Lou I could have ever hoped for."

"Can I ask you a really personal question?"

"Sure." She turns her body to face me.

"Is Lou's dad in the picture? I mean, if that's too personal . . ."

"It's fine." She's still smiling, but the smile shifts slightly. "Lou's dad, Mitch, was the love of my life. We were high-school sweethearts and got married the week he graduated college. Six months later, we learned we were expecting Lou. He was over the moon about it. Actually, he was quite ridiculous." Her smile grows, and she stares out toward the ocean as she talks, seemingly reliving amazing memories. "Every night he insisted on reading book after book after book to my belly. And not just reading but doing all the voices—even acting things out and singing songs. He insisted on doing the actions because he swore she could see him." Then her smile fades a little bit. "He was gonna be the best dad." She turns back and looks at me. "He was killed by a drunk driver two weeks before Lou was born."

The gut punch that hits me is as strong as the gasp I let out. I have no words. What do I say?

Amber reaches over and grabs my hand. "It's okay. It really is. I mean, I hate it, but it's not as hard as it used to be."

"How do you get through someone leaving you like that?"

She looks sad. "It helps the most when I remember that Lou has a guardian angel watching over her all the time." Some tears drift down her face as she says it. "And it helps that I am still surrounded by people I love. And you are one of those people." She squeezes my hand.

My heart swells. "I love you right back."

"So," she takes a big breath, "I've been sitting on these little beach chairs this whole time, and my butt has fallen asleep. We haven't had any ice cream yet, either. So let's get up and treat ourselves to something sweet," some shine and sparkle return to her eyes, "while we talk about the drool that was dripping off your chin every time you looked at my brother during that volleyball game." And just like that, Amber's grin turns positively wicked.

CHAPTER 34

Deacon

AFTER WE GET BACK to the condo, Amber and Lou lie down for a nap and Pepper sits outside. I grab two cold drinks for us, gathering my courage to finally have the hard talk, but when I join her outside, she beats me to it.

"Have dinner with me tonight on the beach. No noisy jukebox, no Lucky Charms, no five-year-olds, no sisters. Just you and me, having dinner. I'll pick up something from Sam's." She never breaks eye contact. "We can just talk and watch the sun go down."

I stare at her, my mouth hanging completely open. She has surprised me past my ability to speak.

We both wait for a moment, but still, I can't seem to respond.

Her eyebrows are raised, and I can tell that she's thrilled to have rendered me speechless.

I clear my throat, hoping it will help clear my mind. "I need to clarify first. You are asking me out on a date? A real date?"

"Yes."

"And when I pick you up, you won't be confused about why I'm there?"

"No."

"A real date? Where there is good food and good conversation?"

"Yes."

"And," a smile sweeps across my face and my eyebrows crawl up with my coming question, "at the end of the night . . . ?" I let my words trail off, suggesting that I want her to finish my sentence.

"At the end of the night . . . we will have finally had a decent meal together." Then she just smiles at me.

She's teasing me, and I'm drunk on the feeling. I don't know what has shifted in the last twenty-four hours, but it's something. And I feel like it's shifted in all the right ways—but Amber is right. I can't go on acting like everything is normal when I haven't told her everything.

"I'd love to go on a date with you." The look on my face hides nothing—my smile is large and genuine. My feelings have always been genuine with Pepper. I decide to wait until tonight to say anything. Maybe I can steer the conversation in a direction that will help me find the right words.

"Great." She stands up. "I'll pick you up at six."

And with that, she leaves me with what feels like an electric current bouncing around inside my body. I'm almost more charged than I was when I was wrestling her for the phone this morning.

I get the feeling this electricity isn't going away for the rest of the day.

CHAPTER 35

Samantha

I'M READY FOR THE date early, so I walk down to the beach to watch the incoming waves. Water like this doesn't bother me because I know I'm not getting in it. Ironically, the sounds soothe me. Nothing about that makes sense, but I stopped trying to figure it out a long time ago.

I've kept my look shockingly simple for a date. My hair is up in a very casual ponytail, and I have on a simple, pastel-pink T-shirt and navy shorts. I'm now realizing that I don't even think I put makeup on. I can't bring myself to care. Even though I've lived most of my life trying to live up to other people's standards, Deke makes me feel whole all on my own—without a powerful résumé, impeccable appearance, and worldly accolades.

I'm mulling over what to say to Deacon tonight. I've decided to talk to him about everything that brought me to the island. I'm not sure where to start, or what will come tumbling out of my mouth, but I'm trying to be brave.

The funny thing is, now that I've decided to talk to him, I don't feel the need to be brave anymore. I actually *want* to tell him. I should feel terrified at the prospect of sharing things that I've kept bottled up for so long, but I don't.

Steph doesn't even know everything—though she knows more than anyone else. But for some reason, I know I can trust Deacon with it all. I can't even bring myself to decipher what that means.

While I sort through my thoughts, I close my eyes, lift my face up toward the setting sun, and soak in this moment. I feel more vulnerable—yet stronger—than I ever have.

CHAPTER 36

Deacon

I'M STANDING IN MY back doorway watching her, and she's gorgeous. Her face is lifted toward the sun, and she's simply the most captivating woman I've ever met.

After today, I know she feels something too, but to what extent?

I only know I'm in a free fall, and I don't ever want it to stop. Only three weeks have passed since we met—turns out, I didn't need much time. I fell just like my dad.

I walk out the back door to join Pepper, wishing my heart rate would stop accelerating. "Hey, pretty lady," I call out to her, not caring anymore how flirtatious I might sound.

She turns to face me, and the smile on her face matches mine. "Hi back." She stays where she is. "Our date isn't supposed to start for another ten minutes."

"I saw you out here and thought I would join you." I walk down the few steps and join her on the beach. I'm wearing white linen pants and a dark-gray Henley shirt.

As I approach Pepper, I notice her eyes traveling from the bottom of my pants, up my legs, over my torso for a long second, past my shoulders, and then all the way up to my eyes. She has a look of approval. Her entire perusal wasn't very subtle, so she knows I've caught her checking me out. She's still smiling at me, though, so I guess she approves.

"This is quite a different look than our first date." She puts *date* in air quotes.

"Full disclosure?" She nods her approval. "I know how to dress for a date. Especially a date on which I'm hoping to impress a beautiful woman. I was completely aware that you never really asked me out, and I dressed like a slob on purpose—you seemed wound a little tight, and I thought it might rattle your cage." The shocked look on her face makes me feel so triumphant.

"You did not!" Her jaw is hanging hilariously open.

"I did. Not only that," the excitement in my voice grows, "I had the last-second idea to mess up my hair, so I ran my fingers through it just before you opened the door." She's still gaping at me, so I shrug my shoulders in a *what are you gonna do about it?* kind of way. "I figured I needed to do something to loosen you up."

"I guess it worked." She smiles and shakes her head at me. "You are obviously not to be trusted." Her cheeky tone of voice tells me she's full of it. We both stand there looking at each other for a few seconds.

"Where did you learn to play volleyball like that?" I blurt the question out without even thinking.

"Nope. A girl's gotta keep her secrets."

"I've gotta know." Is she gonna make me beg?

"Get used to disappointment." She gives one shoulder a slight shrug.

"Did you just *Princess Bride* me?"

"Maybe." When she chuckles, I just shake my head at her.

"Ouch."

We stand there smiling at each other, and the mood seems to shift a little, like maybe we're both a little lost in our own thoughts.

She starts with, "So . . . as long as . . ."

At the same time, I open with, "I wondered if we could . . ."

We both stop and laugh. I nod for her to go first.

"I was going to ask if you wanted to start our walk a little early, since you're already here? I promise we're actually going to eat good food—I gave Jimmy a big tip so he'd deliver it up the beach for me—but I wanted to talk to you first, if that's okay?"

I nod and we start walking, neither of us saying anything for a moment. I'm happy to stay silent until she feels like she's gathered her thoughts.

"Awhile back, on our first not-date," she looks over at me, gives me a small smile, and then turns her gaze back to the beach in front of us, "you said some things to me on the back deck, and I reacted in a way that might have surprised you and, quite frankly, that surprised me as well. I told you then that I didn't want to talk about it but that you were free to ask in the future." She looks back over at me for confirmation.

"Yes, I remember."

"I know you haven't asked, but I would like to tell you." She keeps looking at me, her eyes asking for permission. "If that's alright with you."

"You can tell me anything you want."

We pass a large tree trunk lying on the beach at the water's edge. "Can we sit?" She motions to the tree trunk. "What I'm about to tell you is hard for me, and I don't think I can walk and talk and process everything I need to at the same time." I start to talk, but she senses what I'm about to say. "It's okay. I really want to tell you. I want you to . . . understand me." She says the last two words like a question. Like she's not sure how to phrase the statement. But I think I understand, so I don't say anything and let her set the pace of the conversation.

"My parents hated each other. Honestly, I don't know how they ever got around to having me, because I never saw them share a tender look or word. They were both so absorbed in their own hatred that I was nothing more than an inconvenience to them—unless they wanted to use me as a weapon against each other."

She is looking straight out into the ocean while she's talking, the waves occasionally reaching up to the tree trunk we're sitting on. A light breeze gently moves the small hairs that have escaped her ponytail. She pulls her knees to her chest and wraps her arms around them. Her face is relaxed, but at the same time, she looks focused and intent, with a resolve to keep going. "One day we were at the lake with some of their friends. We had a boat, and they had dropped anchor a ways off the shore while they all drank and talked. I was the only kid there—I was always the only kid when we were with my parents' friends—and they let me splash in the water while they talked. I was watching something on the shore—I can't even remember now what it was—and when I was ready to get back in the boat, I turned around and the boat was gone. They had left me. Abandoned me."

It's like my lungs have forgotten how to breathe as my mind starts moving puzzle pieces into place.

She keeps looking ahead and continues, "When I looked up the shoreline, I could see their boat at the marina, so I started swimming. I had a life jacket on, but we had been pretty far out, and at my age, it looked like miles." I can't take my eyes off her, and the need to hold her in my arms and comfort her is overwhelming, but I use all my willpower to stay where I am while she finishes.

"It was almost sunset when I started swimming, and it was dark long before I got to the boat. I was . . . terrified." At this her voice cracks and tears begin freely streaming down her face. "It took another half hour or so to find them. They were all drinking at a beach-front bar. When my mother saw me, she said, 'You look like you swallowed a fish. Go back to the hotel and clean up.' I don't even think they knew they'd abandoned me. I was seven years old. And I've been terrified of water ever since."

I can't help myself anymore. I stand up and lift one leg over the tree trunk, straddling the log and sitting as close to her as I can. I wrap both my arms around her and pull her to my chest. She willingly complies, and I feel her mold into me.

"My parents divorced a few years later. My dad never visited or called. After a year or so, I asked my mom where he lived. She informed me that six months earlier he'd been skiing with one of his many girlfriends, had an accident, and died. Then she raised a glass, said, 'Thank goodness for that!' took a drink, and asked me to clear the dishes from the table. Years later, I tried to find out for myself if it was true, and I found the newspaper article about it. My mom had told me the truth."

With this, she sighs and molds into my chest even more.

Several minutes pass without either of us saying anything. I simply hold her, and she allows it. I want to say something, but I don't know what. I feel protective. I want to shield her from all of this—but these things happened over twenty years ago. There is nothing I can do to change it.

"From that moment on, I never felt like I was enough. I felt . . . very . . . forgettable." The sadness in her voice is agony. "I found validation in school through my grades and the extracurricular programs I forced myself into. I became very serious. They even called me *Samantha the Serious.*" She says that with a mock-serious tone of voice. "My teachers and advisors gave me the encouragement and support I always craved from my parents, but I never had any friends that I felt could love me just for me." At this point, she looks up at me for the first time. Then she moves out of my arms so that she can face me more fully.

"When I went to college, I wanted to shed Samantha the Serious and started to go by Sam. I met a lot of new people, and it was the first time I felt like I had friends that really had my back. They seemed to accept me for who I was, and it was the most amazing feeling. I started learning how to have fun and enjoy myself—it was so liberating. That lasted until my twenty-first birthday.

"Even though I'd loosened up, I was still a stickler for rules. In so many ways, my world was still black and white. That was how I lived and died. So, as a consequence, I was the only one of my friends that didn't drink before it was legal. Not a sip of wine or a swallow of beer. But on my twenty-first birthday, I was going to finally drink alcohol. I went out with my friends, and since they all had experience drinking, I had them order for me. I still don't know what they kept feeding me, but it was very . . . potent, and I reacted . . . strongly. The next morning, it was very apparent that I had gotten very, very drunk. What was not immediately apparent was the fact that they had taken a lot of videos of me while I was drunk. I guess I was very entertaining, and they wanted to capture it. Then they all uploaded these videos to social media, and I became quite the sensation on campus—but for all the wrong reasons. I'm glad TikTok hadn't been invented yet, or it could have been worse." She lets out a very burdened and sad sigh. "Then I saw less and less of my friends—until I didn't see them at all. They weren't real friends. After a while, I realized that they thought I was an oddity and kept me around to laugh at. Then, when I gave them something truly spectacular, they decided they didn't need me around anymore. That was the last time I had alcohol until a few weeks ago when we met." She tilts her head, and a sad little smile appears on her face.

"Anyway, I graduated from high school early and crammed four years of college into three, so I was already in law school at this time. After that birthday, I went back to finding validation through my accomplishments. I was top of my class at law school and then top in my field at the firm I've worked at for the last eight years.

"Everything I did was to prove my worth to the world—or to avoid screwing up and being ridiculed again. Or forgotten about completely . . . abandoned."

I remember her reaction during our private lesson when I had taken a few steps back to give her some space. *You were going to abandon me next to the water?* So many things make sense now.

"I also realized the pressure I'd been putting on myself, and I grew tired of it. Tired of the pressure. Tired of how much energy it took to keep those walls of protection up.

"I realized I needed to find a different way to live. A different way to find value in myself. A way to be okay if I was ever . . . ," she looks back out to the ocean with a little sigh, "abandoned again." Her tears have mostly dried by now, but her emotions are still so raw. "That first snorkel class I took from you was the first time I've submerged my face in water since I was seven. You don't know what that meant to me." She turns her face, and we lock eyes. "I've tried so many other times and never been able to do it. But then—thanks to you—I did. Somehow the words *thank you* seem to fall very short of expressing how I feel. I don't know how you got me to do it."

I'm still straddling the log and directly facing her. She stands up, and because of the slight dip in the sand, we are now eye to eye.

She stands looking at me, seemingly weighing her options. Then she slowly leans in and presses the softest kiss to my lips. She lingers long enough that there's time for her to bring her hand up and rest it on my cheek for a moment. Her touch is like a flame that spreads all over my body. It's not a flame of passion that will quickly burn out of control. This is something different. Something deeper.

I don't move to pull her closer or try to add to the heat of whatever this is. I soak up everything that is her. Her warmth. Her smell. Her taste. The softness of her lips on mine. The gentleness of her touch on my cheek. I want to memorize everything about this moment, because even though it's the most chaste kiss I've ever received, I feel everything in me shifting.

When she breaks the kiss, she takes a step back and looks at me with such gratitude.

"That was me saying thank you again."

"Pepper . . ." I had so many loud thoughts and feelings when she was recounting what had happened to her all those years ago. React! Defend! Comfort! Now, I can't hear any of those voices—they've been shocked into silence. "I didn't make you do anything at the pool. You did all of that by yourself."

She opens her mouth to say something, but I cut her off. "If you're going to try and change my mind, don't. I won't take any credit for anything you did that day. Did I physically force your face under water?" She doesn't speak or move, but her eyes tell me no. "Did I bribe you?" Her sigh of resignation also tells me no.

"Deke, please . . ."

I reach up and put a finger on her lips to stop her from speaking and instantly realize that this was both the best and worst thing to do, because my defenses crumble into dust.

As we stand there looking at each other, my finger on her lips, I can't help but lightly trace my thumb along her jawline. She leans into my touch, and I know she is feeling something. I just wish I knew exactly what it was.

CHAPTER 37

Samantha

Deacon's large hand moves across my skin so tenderly that a ripple of warmth cascades through my entire body, filling up places that have felt empty, withered, and cracked my entire life. My body has never reacted like this to such a simple touch.

But in equal measures, he is enraging my frustration! I want him to understand . . . gah! I don't know exactly what it is that I want him to understand. I don't know how to express it. How do I make him understand that for the first time in my life, I feel safe with someone? I know I have Steph, but this is different. I've never felt this kind of genuine *something*—from or for someone. I want him to understand, but I can tell he doesn't comprehend the gravity and depth of my gratitude. The depth of my feelings.

Yes—I. Was. Brave.

I will own that!

But what he has done for me is monumental. If I'm a kite, he is both the wind lifting me up and the string keeping me grounded. Yes, I'm flying—but I couldn't have done it without him.

I feel almost desperate for him to understand.

The second Deacon's thumb drags across my bottom lip, I come back to the moment and my eyes snap to his steel-blue ones, which are already locked on mine with an intensity that makes my body start to tremble.

His eyes fall to my lips and then slowly, almost reverently, start to travel all over my face. I know that tasting his lips again would be different this time. All of a sudden, new emotions are waiting to be expressed, and I see them all in his eyes. My heart thuds so loudly that I can hear it in my ears, and my breath catches as I feel the subtle changes in the way his thumb caresses my face. He is still gentle, but there is a longing and desire that wasn't there at first. It's palpable. Tangible. I reach up and grab hold of his shirt, steadying myself.

He takes my other hand in his, gliding his thumb over my knuckles for a long moment before letting go entirely to reach up to my cheek. My face is now cradled in both of his hands.

If he were the kind of man who asked permission before kissing a woman, he wouldn't need to, because the way my body is reacting to his every move and touch gives him all the answer he needs.

I know he's going to kiss me, and I already know it will be the best kiss of my life.

CHAPTER 38

Deacon

I'VE NEVER FELT THIS way about a woman. I've never wanted more from—or been willing to give more in—any other relationship. Can I even call this a relationship? My mind tells me no, since I haven't initiated a single kiss. But my heart tells me, in no uncertain terms, that *relationship* doesn't begin to capture what this is.

She has made no declarations of feelings or intentions, but I know we are on the same page. I can see it in her eyes and feel it in her body.

I take a deep breath, trying to gain control over my thoughts. Unfortunately, I know I can't kiss her—especially the way my body is telling me to—without giving her all the facts. I know she won't run when I tell her, but she still needs to know.

"Pepper, please know that I want to kiss you right now. The fact that I'm not is impressive, as I'm exercising an epic amount of self control that I didn't know I possessed. But once I start kissing you, I don't think I'm going to want to stop for a long time," I can't help but nuzzle my head against hers a little bit, "and some things need to be said first." She fists my shirt even tighter. Whether she's doing it to gather her own self control or make me lose some of mine, I can't tell, but it definitely has the latter effect.

I gently push her away and stand up, moving my leg up and over the log so that it sits between us. I can only hold off so much temptation. I tightly fold my arms against my body in a lame attempt to keep my hands to myself, even though she's more than an arm's length away now.

Her look is a combination of a little bit curious, a little bit confused, and a whole lot disappointed. *Me too, Pepper. Me too.*

I look down at the ground, close my eyes, and take a few deep breaths, trying to calm my heart rate. When I look back up at her, I give her a somewhat sheepish smile. "Give me a second to gather my thoughts. You've become a legendary distraction, and I need to have all my words straight for this." Her smile back at me is soft, sweet, and so, so tempting. "Stop it!!"

"Stop what?" Genuine confusion crosses her face.

"Stop that!!" I point at her in an accusatory way. "That. Stop doing that!" She looks around to see if there is something on the beach to help her understand. "Pepper, I need you to stop . . . distracting me."

I should have chosen different words, because by the look on her face, she takes this to be a challenge. It's a look I haven't seen from her before, and it instantly makes it that much harder for me to stay on my side of the log.

When she speaks, her voice has a singsong quality to it, and she knows exactly what she's doing. It's feigned innocence, womanly manipulation, and she knows it's complete torture to me. "Do you mean standing on this side of the log?" She opens her eyes as wide as she can so that she looks like an innocent little doe.

Innocent, this woman is not. "That was not entirely what I was talking about. No."

"I'm sorry, what did you say?" She raises her hand to her ear like she can't hear me. "Maybe I should come a little closer so that I can hear you." She starts to walk around the log. She's walking with so much fake innocence that she's even more tempting than she was a minute ago. I should have kissed her all night and had the conversation in the morning.

"Samantha." There is a warning tone in my voice as if I were a parent calling her out on bad behavior, but I'm sure she knows I'm feeling anything but parental toward her.

I start to back away, like she's some dangerous beast to be avoided. She looks so playful that I'm dying to grab her and be done with it. That's when I hear it.

"Dee-Dee! Where are you?" It's Lou. Her voice is not playful at all, and I can tell she's panicked. Pepper and I instantly sober up and run toward her.

When I get close enough to Lou, I throw my knees into the sand, grabbing her shoulders with my hands so I can see her face. "Lou, what is it?"

"Mommy couldn't stop throwing up in the toilet for a long time. Then she fell asleep right there, and I can't wake her up!" Lou's voice is quivering.

I don't even think—I run. I run as fast as I can into the condo, down the hall, and into the bathroom where I find Amber unconscious on the floor. I grab my phone to call 911 as a breathless Pepper runs in holding Lou.

The island is too small to have either an ambulance or a hospital, but dispatch is calling Marco, who has a van big enough to take Amber to the airstrip. From there, an island-hopper plane will fly her to the nearest hospital.

CHAPTER 39

Samantha

DEKE LOOKS WORRIED AND helpless. Amber is now awake and sitting on the couch. Her breathing is better—her heart isn't racing anymore—but she's very weak. It will be about five minutes before Marco gets here, so we're waiting.

Deke needs to go with Amber, but it's late, so Lou needs to stay here. "Lou, your mom is going to see a doctor, who's going to help her. Why don't we have a sleepover at my house? We can stay up too late and eat all the ice cream we want!" I smile big, trying to get her excited about it.

"Can I bring some of my things?"

"You bet. Why don't you go grab your pajamas, a toothbrush, and all the stuffed animals you want?"

She smiles a little and runs down the hall to gather her things.

Deke walks over to where I'm standing and throws his solid arms around me, pulling me into him in a fierce hold. He rests his cheek on the top of my head and takes deep breaths, while I do my best to hold him back just as fiercely. Then he suddenly pulls back and grabs hold of my upper arms like he's trying to steady me—but I think he might be doing it to steady himself. He still has a tortured look.

"Pepper, this isn't how I saw tonight going, and I didn't get to say a lot of things I wanted to say. Marco is going to be here any minute, and Lou will probably be back in the room before that . . ."

I reach up and place the palms of my hands on his cheeks, trying to calm and soothe him. "It's okay. Amber will be okay. I'll keep Lou as long as I need to. Do what you need to, and I'll be here when you get back."

He leans into my hand, and then all of a sudden he's kissing me. Or I'm kissing him. I don't know who leaned into whom, but his strong arms are enveloping my entire body, and his lips are searching mine, and everything feels like we only have a few moments to say with this kiss everything left unsaid on the beach—and we are packing as much into it as we can.

His hands are in my hair, then on my back, then pulling me into him even more. There is a desperation to everything, but in a way that says we both want the other to understand how we feel before he has to leave. He angles my head to deepen the kiss, and I willingly comply. My fingers tangle into the hair at the base of his neck, then into the longer waves on top, until my arms finally wrap completely around his neck, pulling him as close to me as I can.

We break apart when we hear Lou coming down the hall. Breaths heaving, lips swollen, hearts pounding. We simply stand facing each other as Lou walks into the room, oblivious of the fireworks that were just on display in her living room. I can't peel my eyes away from his—I can see so much in them.

Can he see the same thing in my eyes? I'm trying to tell him. But then I feel a stabbing remembrance of past relationships—or more specifically, my relationship with Trevor. Thanks to me, it crashed and burned in its own spectacular way, and now the doubts I've harbored for the last nine months about my ability to have a healthy relationship are slowly floating to the surface.

My thoughts must be written all over my face, because Deke squints his eyes as if he's trying to figure me out, then grabs my hand, and pulls me outside onto the back deck. He spins me around till my back is against the wall, and he pins me there by bracketing his hands on either side of my face, leaning in so close that his face is inches from mine.

"What was that look on your face just now?" His eyes are searching, but I don't know what to say. And even if I did, we don't have the time. Marco will be pulling up any minute, so I just shake my head.

"Listen," he closes his eyes for just a moment and takes a deep breath before looking back at me, "before I leave, you need to know a few things, and I have about sixty seconds to tell you before Marco shows up and I need to leave with Amber. First, we still need to have the conversation I just tried to have with you on the beach." His eyes become intense. "I'm serious about that. There are things you need to know. Second, I don't know what you were thinking in there, but your face looked like maybe you weren't sure where I stood, and I need you to know. I'm crazy about you." And with that he leans in for a short, but searing, kiss. The intensity of it almost makes my knees give out. When he pulls back, the blue in his eyes is dark and dangerous in a very alluring way. It makes me want to know what it would be like to be kissed by him when he had all the time in the world. "I wish I had more time to make that a better declaration of what I want, and to use different words, but I don't, and I don't want to rush it more than I already have." When I don't say anything, his brows crease. "Pepper, do you understand what I'm saying to you?"

"I think so." I do think I know what he's trying to say, and even though I feel the same way, I'm still trying to sort through the self-doubt screaming in my head.

"If you only think so, I need to do a better job of conveying exactly what I think of you." And with that, he leans down and kisses me as if we had all day. His body pushes into me, and my body instantly reacts. I feel as if we're the only two people on the island who have all the time in the world. It's like he's beginning to explore my lips and has a lifetime to finish the journey. But we don't have a lifetime. We have literal seconds.

He pulls back from the kiss at the sounds of Marco's arrival. Once again his hands are on my face, and he's looking at me as if his eyes could caress my skin. "When I get back, we will talk." After a brief second, a smile slides onto his lips—in direct contrast to the seriousness of the situation in the other room. "And then . . ." His words fade away as we hear Marco coming through the front door. He runs his thumb over my bottom lip, dips down to give me a simple and tender kiss, and then walks inside.

They quickly load Amber up and are gone, leaving my mind reeling for more than one reason.

Lou and I have ice cream before dinner, make cookies, play with her stuffed animals, sing silly songs at the top of our lungs, and watch *Moana*. Twice.

Lou is now getting her jammies on—she insisted she do it herself—and I'm thinking about how much my life has changed since coming to this island and how much Amber played a role in that. My stomach is in knots. I hate not knowing what's going on at the hospital. I've tried to call Deke several times, but I haven't been able to reach him.

And speaking of Deke, I don't even know where to begin. I remember my first lunch with Cheryl and wondering what it would be like to be kissed by someone who made me feel safe. Well, now I know. I can say it was nothing like I imagined. The feeling was indescribable. I didn't know it was possible to lose myself like that into someone else's energy and passion—and to feel so safe doing it. It was enough to overwhelm me. The kisses were rushed by the circumstances, but the intensity he packed into them completely consumed me. Even now, hours later, my lips are still buzzing and my body is still alive with the memory of his hands on my body and his arms wrapping me into him.

I'm lost in these thoughts as Lou runs into the room in her pajamas. "Can we watch *Moana* again?"

So Lou and I decide that, at 11:00 p.m., it's a great idea to have more ice cream and stay up even later.

CHAPTER 40

Deacon

THE HOSPITAL TRIP WAS long, hard, and draining. I stayed up all night as they ran tests and finally decided to admit Amber, so I came home sleep deprived, starving, and probably needing a shower.

I head straight to Pepper's condo, and as I walk into the family room, my heart stops at what I see. I'm really not prepared for this. Pepper is lying on the couch, sound asleep, with her dark-red hair messed up in a way that makes her look incredibly tempting. I want to see this sight every morning for the rest of my life. But the part that fillets my heart open is Lou lying right next to her, snuggled into her, while Pepper's arm is wrapped loosely around her. They look perfect together.

It's almost too much for me. Especially after last night. I can feel so many building emotions, but then I notice something else that evokes an entirely different feeling.

Pepper is wearing a man's shirt.

My shirt.

My brain tries again to process.

Pepper. Is. Wearing. My. Shirt.

It's one of my white, button-up dress shirts that I used to wear to the office—back when an office job was my life. The only way for her to have gotten this shirt would have been for her to go rummaging in the back of my closet. I love everything about this, and it's nice to smile after a long night.

She has the sleeves rolled up and it's hitting her mid-thigh, so her legs are almost in full view. She has great legs. I find myself taking a long look. After a moment, I start to wonder if this is a little creepy. I remember Amber loving the *Twilight* books when she was a teenager but thinking it was creepy when the vampire watched a girl while she slept. Now I'm that creepy guy.

I start to tear my eyes away from Pepper's legs when Lou shifts, which causes Pepper to shift, which causes Pepper's shirt to shift, and I get a glimpse of something bright red with a little bit of blue. Before I realize what I'm looking at, I lean in to get a better look, and—*I kid you not*—Pepper is wearing Superman underwear! There are little Superman logos all over it. I genuinely didn't mean to look at her underwear, but how could I not notice something bright red and blue—and then not wonder what it was? I stare for a moment out of sheer shock, and then I realize that now I'm *really* a creeper, so I tear my eyes away.

Lou's eyes open a little, and she smiles a sleepy smile when she sees me, but her eyes quickly become heavy sandbags again, and she falls back asleep. I lean down to carefully pick her up and smell something that instantly makes me smile. *Pepper has some explaining to do.*

I carry a sleeping Lou to her own bed back in my condo.

I take a quick shower, eat some Lucky Charms, and head back over to Pepper's condo to see if she's awake.

I already know I love this woman, but if I didn't, this morning would have sealed the deal. How can a woman be so sexy all while wearing Superman underwear and holding my sleeping Lou? She is a lethal combination for my heart.

When I see her still sleeping on the couch, I lay a blanket over her—and maybe take one more sniff. I'd like to think that the blanket was only to keep her warm, but it also allows me to string two words together in my brain, because have I mentioned she has great legs? And they are more than a little distracting. And the way she is lying on the couch accentuates her natural curves . . . yeah, I needed to cover her up.

I sit down in the chair next to her and try to mentally unpack everything that happened between the two of us last night. It's so much! So. Much. The talking on the beach. The not talking—which I'd be lying if I said I didn't want to do *that* again as soon as humanly possible. My rushed words before I left. Did I go too far? Did I scare her off? I don't know, and I won't know till she wakes up.

I close my eyes to get a few winks before she wakes up.

The next thing I know, I can smell waffles. I open my eyes and see Pepper in the kitchen with her back to me. She's making Eggo waffles in the toaster. Between my Lucky Charms and her toaster waffles, we make a killer team in the kitchen. Luckily she's put some little shorts on under my shirt, or I'd be a goner.

I walk over to her, and when I'm just a few feet away, she still hasn't noticed that I'm awake. I wrap my arms around her waist and lay my head on her shoulder.

She lets out a startled squeal and jumps around. When she realizes it's me, she throws her arms around me and holds me without saying a word. Her head nuzzles into my chest, and even though I'm a good seven inches taller than she is, she makes me feel completely enveloped in her embrace.

In this moment, I understand the difference between the words *hug* and *hold*. I've had a lot of hugs in my life, but this woman is holding me. I feel it down to my bones, and I melt into her, the stress slowly draining out of me.

After several seconds, she pulls back enough to look in my eyes. "How is Amber? When did you get back? How are you?" With the last question, she puts her hand on my chest.

"I got home at five. They're keeping her at least for today, but she should be back tomorrow." I close my eyes and relish in Pepper's nearness. "There is so much going on, and so much to talk about, but can I take a moment to say thanks? Thank you for staying here with Lou. It was one less thing to worry about."

She smiles up at me. "You know I didn't mind."

With that, I pick her up by her waist and set her on the kitchen counter as she lets out another little squeal. I then take hold of her shirt collar and give it a little tug. "Can I ask why you're wearing my shirt?"

The little vixen just smiles and shrugs. "I missed you, so I thought I would wear one of your shirts. When I went to your closet, I found all sorts of things I have questions about! Suits, ties, dress shoes, and white, button-up dress shirts." A little blush crosses over her cheeks. "I couldn't resist."

"And," I run my nose along her neck and take a nice long inhale, which causes her body to tremble a little, "why do you smell like my cologne?"

Her blush deepens. "When a man has suits, he usually has cologne, and I was curious, so I went snooping." She reaches up and traces a finger along my jawline. "The smell is perfect for you—a little bit of sweet with a bit of spice." When she says the last word, she has a coy look on her face and lifts a single eyebrow.

"So you think I'm sweet?"

"Maybe a little." I love how she's teasing me.

"And you think I'm spicy?"

"Well, a girl can hope." She looks at me with a smile of anticipation.

"You need to know that I'm definitely thinking some spicy thoughts, because this outfit is driving me crazy." I look down to appreciate her legs again. "I'm glad you finally put some shorts on!" I get a slap on the chest for my comment, but I reach up and trap her hand there with mine.

"I've had shorts on ever since I woke up."

I lean in a little closer and lower my voice. "While that may be true, I happened to see you on the couch earlier, and I thought the view was just . . . *super*." I know I've hit my intended target when her whole body freezes and she gives me a look of pure panic.

A crease forms in her brow and her voice is quiet and uncertain. "You saw those?" My smile tells her that I did, indeed, see them. "I was changing into your shirt and Lou needed help with something. I went to help her with every intention of going back and putting shorts on. Then . . . we just fell asleep before . . ."

I can tell she's embarrassed, and I think it's adorable. I give the hand that I'm holding captive a little squeeze. "Is it strange that they actually made you more attractive to me?"

Because Pepper is sitting on the counter, we are basically the same height. I start to lose myself in the field of her green eyes, but I know I need to dial it back for a moment. "Pepper, a lot of things happened last night. First, there was everything you said on the beach, and then we had some really rushed moments, and suddenly I was gone." I reach up and run my fingers through her delicious hair. "I want you to know that I have no regrets about anything I said or did last night. My only regret is that it was all too rushed—the words, the kisses, all of it. That's not how I intended anything to happen with you."

She shrugs as she looks at the hand that I'm still holding to my chest. "I think there were definitely some things out of our control." She looks back up at me. "Please tell me what's going on with Amber. You still haven't said anything, and it's making me more worried."

I wrap both of my arms around her and pull her into me. I bury my face into her hair while she wraps her arms up and around my neck. "I will tell you, but please, just let me enjoy this for a little longer. I should tell you everything about Amber first, but let me be selfish. Let me have right now with you, with Lou still sleeping and not yelling for me and no Marco on his way." I lift my head back up to look in her eyes. "Let me tell you again that I adore you. That I'm crazy about you. I'm not even going to tell you how long I've been crazy about you, because then you might think I'm insane." I give her a smile that she readily returns. "That I felt more in that thank-you kiss last night on the beach than I have in any kiss I've had with any other woman. I can't completely explain the effect you have on me, but you do affect me. Right here." I reach up and take her hand, moving it back to my chest.

Pepper looks down at our hands over my heart. "Deke . . ."

"Pepper, please. Just let me hold you." And with that, I release her hand and slowly pull her against me as I lean in and taste the corner of her mouth. Her body gives a small shiver as I move along her jawline.

While last night was rushed and fierce, this is the opposite. This is slow and savoring. This is me trying to show her how much I worship and adore her. My lips trace a line across her collarbone, and her breath catches.

One hand slides up her back and into her hair, while the other wraps around her waist.

I slowly bring my mouth up and place a soft and long kiss on her lips. She holds her breath as I do so, only letting it out when I'm done. She tastes like sweetness and forever. I kiss her again, and she wraps her arms back around my neck while pulling me in tighter and taking control of the kiss.

She deepens the kiss while her fingers rake up the back of my neck and into my hair. She then drags her lips across my skin to kiss my cheeks, jaw, and neck, sending lightning though my body. My need for her is fueled by my growing feelings and the heat of this moment. Everything intensifies with the taste and feel of each kiss and caress. My hands travel over her back and hips one moment and up to her face and into her hair the next.

We kiss for what seems like hours, but it's still not enough. At some point, we end up on the couch, her leaning against my chest while I hold her. We stay like this for a long time, holding each other. I relish the feel of her in my arms and know I never want to let her go.

CHAPTER 41

Samantha

LOU IS STILL ASLEEP, the toaster waffles are long forgotten, and we're lying on the couch. I'm leaning on Deke's chest with his arms wrapped around me, and I never want to leave. I know we need to talk, but I'm trying to figure out how to start.

"You're shaking, but it's not cold," Deacon says, breaking the silence.

I look up and he's smiling down at me, but then his brows pull together as he runs his finger over the crease in my brow. "What's this about?"

I close my eyes for a moment, trying to find a voice for my jumbled thoughts. "I don't know how to do this." My voice is a whisper.

"I would disagree wholeheartedly." Deke wears a devilish smile.

"No, not that," I lightly slap his chest, "... *this*." I point back and forth between the two of us, hoping he understands.

"Tell me what you think *this* is." His voice isn't worried, just curious.

I push off his chest to give myself some space. I'm not sure how clearly I can think while cradled against his body. "I want this to work. More than anything I've ever wanted. But you've had beautiful relationships surrounding you your whole life, and I've never had a successful long-term commitment." I stop when I realize what I've said. "I'm sorry. I don't know if that was the right thing to say. *Commitment* can be a big word, and maybe I shouldn't make presumptions when we've just . . .

barely . . ." I close my eyes, feeling so much uncertainty about how I'm going about this.

"Pepper, look at me." He puts his hand under my chin to lift my face toward him. Involuntary, my eyes open and look at him. "I told you last night how I felt about you. The word *commitment* is already tattooed on my heart when it comes to you, so you can't get me to run away that easily." His lips are turned up in an easy smile.

"Deke, I see what you have with your family, and as much as I want that, I've not only never had it—I'd never seen it until I met you and Amber and Lou. I have no idea if I'm even capable of being like that, and my track record makes me think . . . I'm not." My last words sound so achingly sad, because that's the way I feel. "I try to see what a future might look like—but I can't envision anything."

Deke sits up a little and looks at me. He still looks calm and relaxed. "Tell me what you're thinking, because I'm not sure you realize how hard I'm going to fight to never let you go. What is this really about?"

I'm not sure how to phrase everything so that Deke can understand, but I have to try. "Deke, have I ever mentioned someone named Trevor?"

His smile morphs into one of triumph. "If I remember correctly," he reaches out, unclasps my hands, and brings one of my palms up to rest on his left pec, "he is like a pillow, and I am . . . not. Sound about right?"

A small smile appears on my face despite my current mood. I take a deep sigh in mock-concern. "Poor Trevor. May he never meet you and learn of all the countless ways he is inferior to you."

I take back my hand and reign in my smile as I continue. "Trevor and I met through mutual acquaintances and knew each other for three years before we started seeing each other. Then, we dated for two years. It was very predictable. Very safe. We had dinner dates most weekends, and there were texts and phone calls that were, at times, flirtatious and fun."

This next part is not my proudest moment, so I give myself a moment to brace for what Deke's reaction might be. "One day he called to let me know he was back. My response was something like, 'Oh, where did you go?' I thought maybe he'd gotten groceries or run errands. He told me he'd gotten back from a work trip in LA, and I was surprised. I hadn't even known he'd been gone, and I commented that it must have been a quick trip." I squirm a little as the memory replays in my mind. "Then he told me that he'd been gone for the last three weeks doing work for a client." I instinctively close my eyes from embarrassment. "Deacon, I hadn't even realized he was gone!" I open my eyes, expecting to see his judgment.

I don't. He's just looking at me, waiting for some other revelation that is supposed to shock him.

"You don't get it!" As my emotions rise, so does the pitch of my voice. "I had a boyfriend and didn't know he was gone for three weeks! What kind of person doesn't notice the complete absence of their significant other? For obvious reasons, we broke up that night. I started wondering if, after witnessing my parents together, I was ever going to be capable of having a good relationship." I shift a little in my seat. "I started to realize that I needed to step back and figure a few things out. That was when I started making my plans to come here." I let out a deep breath. "What I did to Trevor feels a little like what my parents did to me—I'd forgotten about him! After what I did to him . . . ," my voice falters and I feel tears start to fall. "I'm trying to figure out how *this*," once again I point back and forth between the two of us, "can be what you deserve, when *this*," I point to myself, "is part of it."

The blank look on Deke's face confuses me, and I feel he must have misunderstood. He tenderly grabs the finger I'd used to point in his large hand. "What *you* did to him? Pepper, I think you're looking at this all wrong." Deke then slowly kisses the finger he's holding and moves to hold the next one. "Did he call you while he was gone?"

I shake my head a little. "No."

His lips part slightly as they skim the tip of the finger he's holding before moving on to hold the next one. "Did he text you while he was gone?"

A little shrug. "I don't remember."

Once again his lips press a kiss to the tip of my finger, and my eyes track the movement. "Did he send flowers while he was gone?"

I shutter a little at what his lips are doing to my fingers. "Trevor never brought me flowers. He knew I wouldn't like them." I try, and fail, to not react to his lips on my skin, while Deke's face is full of fake-shock.

"What? A woman who doesn't want flowers?" Deke kisses my fifth finger and then rotates my hand so that my palm is facing him.

"Deke, my life was the office. What good would flowers have done? I wouldn't have ever seen them. It would have been entirely impractical."

"Hmmm," Deke kisses my wrist, "I might have to change your mind." His words are talking about flowers, but his eyes are talking about something else entirely. "To me, the fault is all on him. He never gave you a reason to miss him. And he never called *you* either."

My eyes are focused on where he last kissed me, and Deke shakes my hand a little to grab my attention and make me look up. He then gives me a very pointed and serious look. "That was *not* you forgetting him the same way your parents forgot you. You were simply two people who didn't belong in a relationship together." When I open my mouth to protest, he stops me with just a look. "He obviously thought about you as much as you thought about him, which was clearly not an impressive amount. It's also a sign that he's the dumbest man on earth to not take every possible moment to tell you and show you how amazing you are.

How gorgeous you are. How compassionate you are. How funny and smart and brave and dead sexy you are."

His gaze sears into me, and he brings the palm of my hand up to his lips. "I can promise you this: I will give you a million reasons to miss me every"—he kisses my palm—"single"—another kiss—"day." Then he presses a longer kiss to my palm, his lips searing the skin of my hand while my bones turn to putty under the spell of his lips.

My mind is all over the place from not only his kisses but also his words. *You were simply two people who didn't belong in a relationship together*—not, *You are unfit for any relationship.* Somewhere deep inside, I think he's right. But a part of me still fights the idea, because I'd convinced myself for so long that any relationship might be trouble.

"Pepper, tell me truthfully. How invested were you in that relationship?"

I search my heart and probe my memories, and I come up with nothing. Not a single thing shows me that I was really invested in Trevor or that he was really invested in me—even a little bit. Not a blush or desire. Not a flicker of heat or passion. Not the comfort of friendship or trust.

I look up at Deke, and he must see the wheels in my head trying to make sense of everything. "Pepper," his voice soothes me, "I've been with you long enough to know that it's not that you can't do relationships, it's that you weren't in the *right* relationship."

Something in me shifts into a place that feels complete. It's a place where everything makes sense. It's subtle, but things feel different all of a sudden. Then I try to envision the future, and where once I couldn't see anything, I see happiness and fun and passion and something that could last. Something I could never forget. I don't even have to say anything. Deke can see it on my face.

His eyes start to dance. "Besides, Trevor dated *Samantha*. I'm not interested in her. She's not my type. I am, however," he pulls me closer to him, "very interested in dating . . . *Pepper.*" He says it softly. Like it's a promise. He leans in to kiss me again then stops short of my anxiously waiting lips. "Did you ever see him in his boxer briefs?" He's fishing for information and trying to throw me off guard with his seductive smile.

I take a moment to answer him, hoping to make him sweat a little before I slowly say, "No. I did not ever see him in jet-black boxer briefs." I emphasize the *jet black* a little to let Deke know that, yes, I did take a peek at him—once I knew I wasn't going to be eaten by Alex the man-eating lizard. I know I've hit my mark when the smile on his face deepens a little bit more. "I didn't see him in *any* boxers or briefs of any kind or color. At all. Ever."

Deke then gently kisses the corner of my jaw, and I feel like I've been hooked up to jumper cables as a shock runs through my body. "And tell me about his kissing skills." He moves his lips below my ear and kisses me again. "I need to know about my competition. Need to see if I have to up my game in that department." He pulls back a little, and I see one of his eyebrows raise enough to let me know that he's willing to do what is necessary. My skin happily sizzles under his gaze.

"Please don't." My voice is breathy and weak. "If you up your game any more, my entire body will spontaneously combust."

He completely ignores my request and wraps his arms around me so completely, and kisses me so deeply, that I feel like I'll soon cease to exist and simply become a part of him. I try to pull him closer as we continue to explore and taste and feel this new energy between us.

It feels consuming and powerful but, at the same time, gentle and perfect.

He is perfect.

Or at least, he feels perfect for me.

With my kisses, I try to tell him how much I love the way he holds me. I love the way he makes me laugh. I love the way he doesn't laugh at my fears but listens and makes me feel seen. I love the way he makes me feel safe in a way I never have before. I love the way he gives me wings to fly and make mistakes—but also a place to land and either lick my wounds or laugh at myself in a way I've never been able to. Right now, I love the way he is kissing me like I'm his only source of oxygen. I love . . . him.

I love Deke.

I dissolve a little bit more into his kisses as we spend not enough time getting swept away in each other.

CHAPTER 42

Deacon

WHEN THE HOSPITAL CALLED to say they were done with tests and we could bring Amber home, I took the first puddle jumper to the hospital (after giving Pepper a *very thorough* goodbye).

Lou and an anxious Pepper are waiting to greet us as we come through the front door. Lou runs to her mom with hugs and kisses and then pulls her down on the couch to excitedly explain how much ice cream she's eaten, how many hours of sleep she's missed, and what movies she's watched—including how many times she's watched them. I look over at Pepper, and she is outwardly cringing, like she feels certain that she's broken every parenting rule there is and will never be allowed to babysit again. When Lou finishes her monologue, she runs off to play in her room as if all is well with the world.

When Lou is gone, Amber looks over to Pepper, who then dissolves in tears and pulls Amber into a fierce embrace. "Amber, don't ever do that to me again! I've been so anxious for you to get home. Are you feeling better?"

Amber shrugs her shoulders as if she doesn't know what to say. "They ran some tests, but we won't hear anything back for a while. They told me the best thing I could do was rest."

"What can I do to help you?" Pepper is quickly scanning Amber with her eyes, trying to find something to help with. She grabs a blanket off the floor and starts tucking it around Amber's legs.

"Nothing!" Amber swats Pepper's hands away and takes the blanket off. "And I mean that. Cheryl is going to come by in a little bit and take Lou until tomorrow morning so that I can rest and you two don't have to worry. So you and Deke find somewhere else to be."

I voice my protest. "No way, little sister. I'm not leaving you the second you get home." I give her my best big-brother glare.

I open my mouth to say more, but Amber shuts me down. "I feel fine, and there is literally nothing you can do to help me. I saw the worry written all over Pepper's face when I walked in—you two are going to hover like mother hens over me, and I won't get a moment's sleep. So Deacon, take this woman somewhere—anywhere—that will get you both out of this house so I can rest."

Pepper and I stare at Amber like she's grown two heads. "Amber . . ."

"Stop it. Don't fuss over me. I mean it. Take Samantha to that water-fall you love, or anywhere else. It will get you out of my hair for hours, and that's what I need." And with that, she walks down the hall, ignoring our protests.

Pepper is the first to speak. "Deke, she can't be serious!"

"She is, but there's no way we're leaving."

"Get. Out. Of. This. House!" Amber's voice comes ripping down the hall. "I need sleep, not hovering worrywarts!"

Pepper and I stand completely still, not knowing what to do. Maybe if we don't move, she will think we've left. After about five minutes, Amber's footsteps echo down the hall and she comes around the corner and stops in front of us.

"Just so you know, your silent worrying is a lot louder than you think it is. Please, let me rest without worrying about you worrying about me."

She takes my hand in both of hers. "Deacon, give me three or four hours. That's all I ask. Please."

It was the way she said the last please. I realized that she really wouldn't get any rest if I stayed—so much for being quiet. I nod my head, letting her know that I understand.

Then Amber turns to Pepper and takes her hand. "Samantha, you're amazing. You're one of the brightest lights in my life." Then she pulls Samantha into her arms, and they hold each other, crying, until Amber pulls back. "You know I love you, right?"

Pepper's voice is just a whisper. "Yes."

"Great! Then will the two of you go anywhere but here for at least a few hours!?" Then she turns around and goes back to her room.

"If we don't leave, she really won't get any rest." I take a moment to gather my thoughts. "Looks like we're going to Bridge Falls." I sigh in resignation then look over at Pepper. "Hey," I find myself drifting to her without meaning to, "with all the attention on Amber since I've been back, I haven't had the chance to give you a proper hello." I wrap my arms around her and pull her into a kiss. Her hands crawl up my chest and around my neck, and she starts playing with the ends of my hair. I let out a little groan. All of my nerves go on high alert, and suddenly the kiss goes from a ten to a twenty in seconds. I can't get enough of her taste, of the feel of her, of her arms wrapped around me and her body pressed against mine. I finally break the kiss when I hear Lou coming down the hall. "Lou . . . coming." I'm more than a little out of breath.

"Yeah." Her short, breathy response validates my lack of ability to speak.

As Lou walks into the kitchen, I take a few more deep breaths to get my equilibrium back. "Why don't you go get ready while I make Lou a lunch before Cheryl gets here, and I'll pack a backpack with drinks and food for us. All you need is comfortable hiking clothes and shoes."

"Amber said something about a waterfall?" Her face is full of worry.

"It is, but you won't have to touch the water unless you want to. I promise. You can bring your swimsuit if you want to soak up some sun, but you don't need to touch it." I step closer to her so that Lou can't hear me and look down into her eyes with as much heat as I can muster up. "And, if you're lucky, I'll even take my shirt off for you, because I'm under the impression you're a fan." Then, after making sure Lou's not looking, I lean down to give her a quick, but fiery, kiss.

As she heads out the back door, she calls over her shoulder, "I am a *big* fan! President of the fan club. But I'm keeping the membership to one." Then she winks back at me with a coy smile and walks onto the back deck. This woman will be the death of me, but *what a way to go.*

A few minutes later, I've changed into my hiking clothes and gathered some food and drinks to take with us. I'm in the kitchen finishing up a lunch for Lou that she can take to Cheryl's.

"Dee-Dee." The way Lou says this makes me think that she's said it more than once. I guess I was still thinking about that last kiss—or maybe all of them. "Can Penelope be my new mom?"

My body goes completely still. I'm at the counter with my back to her, and I can't bring myself to turn around. Not this morning. Not after the last couple of days. "Lou, you need to remember that you already have a mom. Amber will never not be your mom."

"Okay." Lou keeps coloring without giving it a second thought.

This is a blow to my heart. Too much. Too many feelings that are in combat with each other. Too much . . . everything. I close my eyes and breathe in deeply, trying to find my mental equilibrium again.

Pepper chooses this moment to walk in the back door. She's wearing a white tank top over a royal-blue swimsuit, and her tan shorts are showing off way too much of her legs. That is not helpful right now. I needed a few more minutes.

CHAPTER 43

Samantha

I WALK INTO DEKE'S condo as Amber calls down the hallway, "Deacon, I'm trying to get a bottle of something open and can't do it!"

"Be right there!" Deke leaves to help her.

I turn to Lou, and she has the most serious face I've ever seen on such a little girl. "What's going on in that little head of yours?" I tap her forehead.

She keeps looking at the now-empty hallway. "I asked Dee-Dee if you could be my new mom, and he said no." Her shoulders droop a little, and she turns to look at me. "I think you would be a great mom." I'm stunned into silence, but she gains steam as she goes on. "You let me eat ice cream before dinner and before bed, and you're great at puzzles, and you listen to me when I talk, and I like you so much, and I can tell Dee-Dee likes you too, so that would make it easier."

Deke chooses that moment to reappear in the kitchen, obviously clueless to what Lou has just said. "Okay, Lou, we're headed out." He leans down and kisses the top of her head. "Here is your lunch to take with you once Cheryl gets here. See ya later." Then he takes my hand and ushers me out the back door.

The hike is gorgeous, but it's steep enough that we're not having a lot of conversation—there's just a lot of huffing and puffing. I'm okay with the silence, though, because I am still mulling over what Lou said to me in the kitchen.

After hiking for an hour or so, Deke stops and turns back to me with a smile. "Okay, we're here. I don't want to put any pressure on you, but this is my favorite place on the island, and if you don't immediately agree with me, I'll be crushed and go home crying." He thinks he's hilarious. He steps aside to allow me into the clearing first.

"Deke." My heart seems to stop, and I forget to breathe. This is the most gorgeous place I've ever seen. While the trees and growth had been dense during the climb up, this area opens to a breathtaking tropical oasis.

Most of it is entirely surrounded by tall tropical trees and large shrubs, which act like a protective wall keeping the world out. Colorful, flower-filled vines twist around the tree's branches, and their fragrance adds to the wonder.

The ground is covered in a layer of vibrant green moss, and it looks soft and inviting enough to take a nap on.

Filling up most of the clearing is a pond of the most crystal-clear water I've ever seen. Rocks and colorful shrubs create a picturesque border around most of the pond, but in several areas, someone could walk straight from the green moss into the clear water.

Across the water from where we stand is a rising hill of rock at least sixty-feet high. The rocks are in levels, creating a kind of nature-made retaining wall, and at the top is the crown jewel of it all: a gorgeous waterfall that cascades down and breaks into smaller waterfalls as the water hits different boulders and rocks. All of my senses are on overload—how does a place like this possibly exist?

Deke comes up from behind me and wraps his arms around my waist, pulling me flush against him. "What do you think? Worth the hike?"

"*Deke*," my voice comes out breathy, "this place is like the Garden of Eden." I turn in Deke's arms and look up at his face. "Is it? Because if you say yes, I will believe you." He leans down and gives me a too-short kiss before taking my hand and walking me around.

He doesn't say anything and lets me take it all in at my own speed. I start to notice all kinds of birds and their chirping sounds, something I missed during my first perusal of the area. "This place can't be real. Am I dreaming?"

Deke laughs a little. "That's what I thought the first time I stumbled upon it. I love coming up here. It's my little slice of heaven." He says it with a sigh. "I hadn't been on the island long and decided to go on a hike to clear my head. I literally stumbled upon it, and it's been a sanctuary to me ever since."

"Why isn't everyone on the island here? I mean, this is so incredible."

"I have no idea—I've never seen anyone else up here." Deke has been looking around and enjoying the scenery with me, but with his next words, he stops and turns to look at me, entangling our fingers together. "I've never *brought* anyone up here." I step into him, and he enfolds me in an embrace. I raise my face, resting my chin on his chest, and look up into his eyes. He looks down at me, and we stay this way for a few moments. It's perfect. He's perfect. I don't want to break this bubble we're in, but I need to.

"Deke?"

"Uh-huh?" His eyes roam over my face in a way that almost feels like a gentle kiss.

My brows pull together. "What's wrong with Amber?"

CHaPTer 44

Deacon

MY EYES CLOSE AS my heart sinks.

"I'm right, aren't I? Something's wrong with her."

I've gone over this speech a thousand times in my head, but right now, in my moment of need, I can't think of a single thing to say.

"Deke, why did Lou ask me to be her new mom this morning?"

Something breaks inside me, and I pull Pepper into such a fierce embrace that I'm afraid I might break her. She holds me back, and we simply stand there wrapped in an embrace. Then, slowly, I loosen my grip and pull back so we can see each other. It still takes a moment for words to finally fill my brain, and I don't know that they are the best words—but I can't put this off anymore.

I let out a heavy sigh. "Pepper, there have been so many times when I've tried to tell you but couldn't. The other night on the beach, I was finally going to do it, but you needed to talk first, and then everything spun out of control. I wasn't even planning on kissing you until we'd talked, because I thought that would be the right thing to do, and then . . . that night . . ." My words die off.

In an ironic turn of events, Pepper reaches up and gently wipes a tear from my cheek that I hadn't realized was there. "You're scaring me a little. Please just tell me."

I brace myself—not just for Pepper's reaction but also because it never gets easier to say out loud. "Pepper, Amber is dying." I didn't know how else to say it.

Pepper stares blankly at me for a moment, and I can tell she's processing what I've said. Emotions flow over her face: shock, confusion, disbelief. "Wait. I don't . . . why would you say that?"

I can't bring myself to reply.

"Why would you say that?"

"Because it's true. I wish it wasn't, but it is." Silence stretches between us. "I don't know what else to say."

"What's wrong with her?"

"She has stage four cancer."

"Wait, I'm so confused. She doesn't even have her test results back!"

I feel like I've aged a decade since standing here. "Those tests weren't to find out what's wrong. They ran tests to see if it's spread to other places that we don't know about yet."

"But . . . is there another opinion you can get? Isn't there some treatment that can make it better? Someone has to be able to fix her!" With each word, the panic in her eyes intensifies.

"We've already gotten second and third and fourth opinions, and she's been through all the treatments anyone can think of—nothing has worked. There's nothing we can do that we haven't already tried."

Sam's panic shifts, and anger builds behind the green of her eyes. I recognize it because that's how I reacted when I got the news from the doctor. Shock, disbelief, panic, then anger.

I lashed out at the doctor who told us, telling him he was incompetent and didn't know anything. Everything inside me went into crisis mode, and I reacted as if I were furious. Because I was.

Furious at life.

Furious for Amber.

Furious for Lou.

Furious for me.

Pepper lets out an angry, guttural scream.

She stops screaming, and her chest heaves. "Please," her voice is desperate, "they have to be wrong. There has to be something to fix her. She can't leave Lou like that! She can't . . . leave."

When I don't say anything, her tears start to fall and she dissolves, sobbing into my arms.

I've had years to adjust to this, but it's all new to Pepper, and I need to give her time to process the news however she needs to. She takes a shuddering breath. "I don't want her to leave me either."

"I know." I rub circles on her back. "But, Pepper, she doesn't want to go either. It's a reality none of us can control."

She alternates between feeling numb, furious, and devastated, and her tears continue to fall. We walk to a spot near the water where the moss is soft, and Pepper lies down, exhausted from emotions, and falls asleep in my arms.

She's still in my arms, my fingers running through her hair, when she wakes up and cuddles even deeper into my side.

"It hurts so much I can't breathe."

I kiss the top of her head. "I felt the same way at first. I've had a long time to process it, but even now, it's overwhelming sometimes. Not just because I'm losing my sister, but because I will be a single parent. Sometimes I get so afraid that I'll fail Amber by not doing a good enough job with Lou. It used to be almost paralyzing. When we found out, I was dating a woman named Holly. The second she learned that I was going to take care of Lou when Amber was gone, she bolted. It hurt in the moment, but it didn't take long for me to realize that I didn't want anyone in my life who didn't love Lou." I roll onto my side and prop myself up on an elbow to look down at her. "Holly was the reason I was avoiding kissing you on the beach the other night. I wanted to tell you first, so you'd know what kind of a situation you were getting into."

"Did you think I'd bolt too?"

I lean down and kiss her forehead. "No. I'm not dumb. I know Lou is probably the reason you haven't bolted already." Pepper shifts to look up into my face, pretending to think. "It really is true. You're not much fun, but she's adorable, so I stick around."

I grab the hem of my shirt and act like I might pull it up. "If I can't keep you around with my winning personality, I'm not above taking my shirt off."

She lets out a small chuckle and reaches up to play with a lock of my hair. After a few moments, she breaks the silence. "Deke, what do you do about it? I mean, how do you cope?"

"I didn't for a while. I ignored it, hoping it would go away. Holly left, I threw myself into my work, and then I realized that I was throwing away my last bit of time with Amber. So I talked to my business partner, and we sold our company. Then Amber, Lou, and I moved to the island, where life would be simpler for all three of us."

We sit in silence again while Pepper continues playing with the ends of my hair. "You owned a company?" I feel like Pepper is changing the subject, trying to put her heartache on the back burner for a moment. "I didn't know that. What did you do?"

"I owned an advertising and marketing company in LA with my friend Cooper."

"Marketing. That explains all your suits."

I nod. "When I approached Cooper about selling the company, he told me that he was more than ready to get out of LA, so it worked in both of our best interests. We made enough on the sale that neither of us need to work anymore, but I run the scuba and snorkel school because it gets me in the water more. That's where I find peace and solace when it's the hardest and I need to get in touch with my feelings. Which is why I go diving every morning. It helps."

"Why?"

"When I'm breathing under water, I can't hear the world. It's all blocked out: the noise, the distractions, the chaos. They all disappear. I can focus better on whatever I need to feel and what matters the most—Amber and Lou . . . and soon, just Lou."

"When you *breathe under water*." She repeats it to herself like she's trying to understand the concept. "Your snorkel school is named Breathing Under Water. Is that why?" I nod at her. She tilts her head in contemplation and thinks for a few minutes. "It's amazing to me that you can find peace in the same place that terrifies me." Her look is a little sad.

We lie there for a while, tracing lines along each other's hands and arms, each lost in our own thoughts.

"Okay." Pepper's voice breaks the silence, and she sounds tenuously resigned to something as she stands up. "Okay." Her voice is a little stronger this time. She grabs the bottom of her white tank top and pulls it over her head, revealing a royal-blue swimsuit top with a high neckline that reaches almost to her collarbone. The top ends a few inches above her tan shorts, revealing a wide strip of skin. She unbuttons her shorts and slides them off to show white swim bottoms with large, colorful flowers. The colors show off her olive skin perfectly, and I wish I could stare at her all day long. But then again, she could be in something far less flattering, and I'd still want to stare at her all day long.

I want to spend every day with her. I want to make her laugh. I want us to learn everything there is to know about each other. I want to know why she's so good at volleyball. I want to be the one to hold her when she's sad, hear her opinions about everything, and fight with her about stupid things. I want to adore her in the way I only can when she's truly mine and I'm truly hers. I want . . . her. Everything that is her. There are a million things about her, and I want them all.

She looks back at me and takes a few deep breaths.

In and out.

In and out.

Then she looks at the water and takes a few more deep breaths—though they are decidedly more shaky.

I slowly stand up as I realize what she's doing.

"Breathe." She says quietly to herself. Again, she looks at me and takes several deep breaths. "Look." She looks at the water again. "Relax." I can tell she's trying to relax, but her entire body is still shaking. "Touch." She walks up to the edge of the water, her breathing more shallow, and closes her eyes, trying to calm herself down. When she opens her eyes, she reaches her foot out and puts it in the water, immediately taking it back out.

Then she repeats the process. Breathe. Look. Relax. Touch. This time, she keeps her foot in the water for about five seconds.

I walk up and take her hand, and she flinches at the surprise contact. "You doing okay?"

"Trying to be." She nods, trying to convince herself. "You said the water helps you, so I thought I would try again." She looks at the water and then back at me. "That might be all I can do today."

"Pepper," I'm careful as I ask, "when someone is afraid of the water because of a trauma, creating new, positive memories around water is really helpful." I raise my eyebrows as I give her a questioning look. "Do you trust me?"

She nods again, and her grip on my hand tightens.

I reach down and gently pick her up in a bridal carry. "I'm going to walk into the water a little bit, but not very far. You won't even get wet. Is that okay?"

She nods her head, but her body tenses.

I wade in, then lean down and slowly kiss her. I feel the tension in her body, in her lips. It's in the grip she has around my neck. I keep the kiss sweet, but I linger a second, trying to help her relax. She's so tense that her lips don't respond. I pull back and look her in the eyes. "Hopefully that will be a good memory." Nothing about her look changes. "Is it okay if I go a little deeper into the water?"

She tightens her hold on my neck but still nods in approval. I take two small steps, then kiss her again.

I keep doing this—each time asking for her approval and each time kissing her a little more thoroughly. With each kiss, her lips become less tense and more pliable, until I'm not sure I'm the one in control anymore.

I'm deep enough now that the water comes up to the middle of my ribcage. She's shaking but also more relaxed than she was a few minutes ago.

"I know this doesn't change what your parents did to you. But I wanted to give you a memory in water that's *good*." I lean over and kiss her again. "And I need you to know that I will never abandon you. I will never forget you. And I will always be there for you."

She breaks her grip around my neck and reaches up to run her fingers through my hair. Her brows crease in concentration. "Deke, if I stand up in the water right here, do you promise you won't let me go?"

"I promise." Very carefully, I take my arm out from under her knees and let her body settle into the water and her feet touch the bottom of the pond. Now we are standing, facing each other, and I'm holding her as securely as I can. She is shaking all over, even though the water is warm.

"Deke, I want to say this while I'm in the water with you. Even though I'm still terrified." She takes a deep breath. "I think I always assumed I would end up alone. I didn't realize that there might be a man I would *want* to be with. Someone who could make me feel safe. Whom I could laugh with. Who could make me happy, and whom I could make happy in return. I didn't realize that there could be a man who might help me see how strong I was on my own— and that we could be even stronger together. I never realized I might meet a man who was so wonderful that I couldn't help but fall in love with him. But I did. I met you. And as hard as I tried not to," she smiles, "I fell completely in love with you. I love you, Deke. You're the best man I know." And then she laughs. Laughs! It's small, more like a chuckle, but I'm still so amazed at how brave this woman is.

"There," she says with a sense of finality. "I can't think of a better memory than telling the man of my dreams that I'm in love with him. And I will always remember that he was holding me in the water while I did it. That's a pretty good memory." And she smiles even bigger, as large tears start rolling down her face.

I've seen her mad tears. I've seen her embarrassed tears. Now I've seen her happy tears.

I lift her up so that I have better access to her lips, and I kiss her. I angle my face to deepen the kiss and pour as much into it as I can, while I fold her into me. She wraps her legs around me, still in the water, and we cling to each other even tighter. My hands are in her hair then exploring the skin of her back, arms, and legs.

I lose myself in her. In her confession and my still unspoken feelings. In my hopes for us going forward. In how she makes me know, somehow, that the future won't be as hard as I've feared. And when I'm done kissing her in the water, I carry her out, lay her down on the moss, and continue kissing her until the afternoon starts to fade and we know we need to go back home to Amber.

CHAPTER 45

Samantha

I KNOW IT TAKES more than passionately kissing the man of your dreams to cure someone of their fear of water, but Deke was right. Terror and abandonment are no longer the only things I think of when I picture being in the water.

And for the record—I am completely open to that kind of water therapy again in the future.

But for now, there are other hurdles to face.

On the way home, Deke suggested that I talk with Amber. I resisted at first. I thought it would be too hard. But he told me that talking to each other was how he and Amber were getting through it all. Which, I now realize, is what they were doing the first time I saw them out in the water together.

I agreed, but now that I'm standing on the back deck, getting ready to walk in the back door, I'm second guessing my decision.

Deke wraps me in his arms, his voice soft in my ear. "Go in and talk. Talk for one minute or one hour. It's up to you. Cheryl is keeping Lou overnight, so there is no one to interrupt you. I'll head back to my office, and you'll have all the privacy you need. Okay?"

"Okay." But I cling to him a little tighter.

"When you're done talking, you can come over to the office and let me know how it went." His hands gently rub up and down my back to soothe me. "Or, if you would rather, go home and go to sleep. That's okay too." He leans down and tenderly kisses the top of my head, my forehead, my cheek, and my lips. Then he walks back to his car and drives away.

As I pull the door open, Amber is walking into the kitchen, and she stops when she sees me. I dissolve into tears and crumble to the floor. Amber walks over, sits down on the floor with me, and wraps an arm around my shoulder, pulling me over to weep on her shoulder.

When my tears have somewhat subsided and I feel like talking, I sit up and turn to directly face her. "My heart is broken."

Amber looks at me with such understanding. "Mine too." She tilts her head like she's thinking about something. "I thought he might finally tell you today." She breaks eye contact and looks down at the floor, seemingly ashamed. "I'm so sorry I didn't tell you earlier. You quickly wormed your way into my heart in a way I wasn't expecting, so by the time I realized that you needed to know, I just . . . *couldn't*. For someone who has had cancer for as long as I have, I actually haven't had to tell that many people. So I don't have a perfect speech prepared that makes it less painful to say. Turns out, I'm a coward." She looks up with apologetic eyes. "I begged Deacon to do it for me. Bless his heart—he tried so many times. Turns out we're both *cowards*."

I pull her into a hug. "It's okay. I guess. I mean, it's not okay. But the last word I would use for you is coward." I grip her even tighter. When we finally release each other and sit back with wet cheeks, a heaviness hangs in the air. "Deke told me it was stage four cancer, but I was so upset that he never told me more than that."

"Breast cancer. I was diagnosed about seven months after Lou was born. I fought it as hard as I could, but my body didn't react to the treatments like the doctors hoped it would. The cancer ended up metastasizing to my lungs, liver, and brain. There isn't anything that can be done at this point. The treatments made it hard to even function, and since they made no difference, I decided to stop treatments and enjoy the time I have left with Lou. So Deke sold his firm, and we moved here to be together and live at a slow pace as long as we can."

"That day I watched Lou while you and Deke flew off the island—were you going to see a doctor?"

"Yeah. We fly over to a cancer clinic every once in a while. There's never good news, but it helps to know a little bit more about how much the cancer is growing or spreading."

I can't make my voice sound any louder than a whisper. "How much longer do they say?"

"No one can really tell you that. It's all guess work. But somewhere around four to ten months. Lou knows, and we talk about it openly—in ways that she can understand at her age. I'm so glad she'll have Deacon. He's incredible." At this, she smiles.

We sit in silence for a while. "How can you be so sick and not look so sick?"

She laughs with no mirth. "It's amazing how outside packaging doesn't always reflect what's going on inside. It will eventually become obvious, and there is medication I take that helps with the pain, but right now I'm mostly weak and tired. All the time."

All the times she slept in, took naps, went to bed early, needed help opening something, and looked pale take on new meanings in my head.

My voice comes out as a whisper. "I think you might have guessed that I struggle with . . . feeling abandoned." The words are hard to say. "I'm just wondering if that's how you felt when Mitch left you. And now, knowing . . . I mean, Lou will be left behind."

"Samantha, sometimes people abandon you for hurtful reasons. Other times, people don't have a choice. Mitch didn't have a choice. And

I'm not being given one either." Her shoulder lifts. "That's just how it is sometimes."

Her words strike a chord of truth in me. *Not all abandonment is neglectful.*

It's something I'd not considered before. Some people have a choice and make a bad one. But others, like Mitch and Amber, don't.

Silence rests between us for a few moments. "I guess . . . Lou will just have two guardian angels looking after her." It comes out more like a question.

Amber's smile is gentle. "That's right. And she'll still have Deacon." She reaches over and squeezes my hand. "And she'll have you too."

My eyes shoot up to hers, and I have no idea what to say.

"I have cancer, Samantha. I'm not blind."

And somehow she shifts the entire conversation and makes me talk about Deacon for the next hour.

CHaPTer 46

Samantha

AFTER TALKING TO AMBER, I realized there was only one place I wanted to be: with Deke. So now, I'm leaning on the front doorjamb at Breathing Under Water, watching Deke work at his desk. His back is to me, and I've been watching him for about twenty seconds undetected—although I don't know how, since both my car and opening the door made noise.

His desk faces a large window that looks out over the ocean. It's perfect for watching sunsets light up the sky with vibrant, Caribbean colors, but the sun set hours ago—right now, the sky is pitch black and no light is coming in. The only light is shining from Deke's computer screen in front of him, so he's mostly just a silhouette, but I can make out a few details.

His blonde hair is wet, making his natural waves a little tighter. His shirt is off and there is a towel around his waist, so he must have been in the pool recently. The light from his screen is casting shadows that perfectly show off some delicious muscle definition in his arms and shoulders, which I really don't hate studying for a moment.

A wave of calm washes over me. This gorgeous, wonderful, funny, charming, strong, loving, thoughtful, sexy, patient man has come into my life in—quite literally—the most unexpected way, and I feel so lucky. After growing up with my parents, I didn't know these kinds of feelings were even possible. I didn't know that loving someone could be so fulfilling.

I told him today that I loved him, and shockingly, I wasn't afraid. I have no regrets or embarrassment about it. He didn't say it back with words, but I'd like to think that the way he kissed me . . . many, many times . . . was his way of saying it back.

Deke stops typing on his computer and sits back in his chair for a moment. As he stands up, I start walking toward his desk, and when I reach him, I slowly snake my arms around his waist from behind. "Hi, there."

A full on scream—that sounds, seriously, half llama and half teenage girl in distress—escapes his lips! It's not the kind of sound I *ever* thought I'd hear from someone so decidedly masculine, and I freeze in shock. He quickly whips around to face me, but the room is dark, and he must not realize who it is because his arms start flailing around in a fight, flight, or freeze reaction—I'm not sure which. I instinctively tighten my grip around his waist and lay my head flat against his chest, hoping to keep away from his arms and fists!

He is still screaming.

"Deke! IT'S ME!" He finally stops screaming and goes completely still. Then four things happen, one right after another:

He finally sees that it's me.

His eyes slowly close and his shoulders and chin drop, like this is the most embarrassing thing he's ever done.

He reaches up and takes Airpods out of his ears—*no wonder he didn't hear me.*

And finally, with alarming speed and panic, he grabs me and pins me tightly to his chest. This is not a romantic embrace. This is a tense, vice-like grip.

His words are short, quick, and slightly terrified. "I had my Airpods in and didn't hear you come in, and . . . I scare very easily, and . . . unfortunately," his eyes are full of humiliation, "there is never anything manly about my reaction."

"Ya think?" I blurt out with a solid amount of laughter. "Mind letting up on your grip a little? Or I might think you're trying to break all my ribs."

"No." His eyes are so wide that I can see white all the way around his baby-blue irises, and he looks tense and flushed.

"No?" I wait for him to respond, but he simply closes his eyes and clenches his teeth—and his grip remains solid and unyielding. "I'm sorry I scared you, but genuinely, I think you're going to crush me." Okay, I'm not genuine about that. He isn't *crushing* me, but I will say that taking a very deep breath would not be an option right now.

"I went swimming, and now . . . ," his words die off. He does loosen his grip, but just slightly. He continues to hold me flush against him—no room to budge.

"I figured as much, since your hair is wet, but you do realize I've already seen you without a shirt on." My voice turns a little husky. "Remember, I'm president of the fan club." My fingers try crawling around to his abs as my look becomes saucy.

"STOP!" His eyebrows quickly crease, and his eyes beg me to understand what he is unwilling to say.

"Deke, I'm in the dark here." I look around the room. "Both literally and figuratively. What's got your undies in a bundle?"

His sigh of resignation is not small. It's like he's Napoleon unwillingly surrendering to the Duke of Wellington. Slowly and methodically, he speaks. "There is nothing to *get into a bundle.*"

Several beats of silence sit heavy between us while his meaning slowly sinks in.

"You mean . . ."

"Yes."

"So you have . . ."

"No."

"And right now you're . . ."

"That's correct."

"None?"

"None at all."

His face is stoic as, through our very brief conversation, I realize that he is not wearing any *undies* to be able to *get into a bundle*.

I have no idea how to react, so my body decides for me and bursts into laughter. Deke stares at me as my laughter only increases.

"Stop it." He looks ninety-five-percent serious, but the slight twitch at the corner of his mouth tells me that part of him wants to laugh as well.

"Why on earth are you sitting here, with nothing but a towel on, in a dark room while working at your computer?"

"I went swimming. No one else is here! Why would I put a swimsuit on?" His eyes are begging me to see reason, but I can barely contain my laughter. "I grabbed a towel to dry off, wrapped it around my waist, and sat down to do some work. Then you scared the ever living daylights out of me, and now . . ."

"So, what do we call this? Alex 2.0? Towelgate?" I can't stop laughing. "I love that you're the one with a towel flapping in the wind this time!"

"No, Pepper. My towel is not flapping in the wind." He looks me straight in the eyes with a look that is all business. "My towel is on the floor."

CHaPTeR 47

Deacon

THE LOOK ON PEPPER'S face is almost worth my own humiliation. *Almost*, but not quite. The woman I love startled me so badly that I screamed like a girl—I cannot express how embarrassed I am about that—and then I continued to behave in a less-than-manly way as my arms flailed about in surprise. I may have lost all my game in this woman's eyes. I have no recourse left other than to—once this current situation gets resolved—kiss her senseless and remind her how manly I can be. Now that I think about it, I'll admit, I look forward to doing that.

Pepper's body is completely still, but I see no less than twenty-five different reactions cross her face.

"Okay." I've been standing here, holding her prisoner against my body so that she can't back up and see . . . well, me . . . but I need to find a solution. "We can't stand here like this all night."

My words seem to break her out of her trance. "Why not? I'm all for it." Then she winks at me. *Winks*. The little vixen.

"Pepper." My voice is suddenly authoritative. She has the indecency to laugh. "Okay. This is what we're going to do: First, you will close your eyes. Then, we will both let go at the same time, and you will turn around, while I will walk back to the locker room. Then, I'll meet you outside, and we can go sit down on the beach. Agreed?"

"I'll agree, but can I say that I love how embarrassed you are? Also, I think I like this position better without the lobster." And she proceeds to kiss my left pec—right where the lobster was the first night we met—though she lingers a lot longer than she ever did when the lobster was there.

After extracting myself from the room and putting on some black joggers and a white T-shirt, I walk outside to find Pepper with a massive grin on her face. "You've got to admit that was funny."

I do my best to glare at her. "That was humiliating."

She's laughing as she sits down in a lounge chair. "Someone once taught me that it's better to relax and not take life so seriously."

I put a hand on each of her armrests and lean down to stare into her eyes. "I want to state one more time: I scare easily!" My eyes seek compassion—even though I'm laughing along with her—and she willingly gives it, pulling me to sit next to her and tangling her fingers around mine.

"I'll add it to the list of things I adore about you."

We sit like this for a long time—listening to the waves lap up on the beach and letting all the insanity of *Towelgate* melt away. When it feels right, I break the silence. "How was your conversation with Amber?"

Her smile turns a little sad. "It was good. Heartbreaking. A little of everything." The green eyes that were brimming with laughter now carry a sadness in them.

"Be sure to let yourself feel all of the things you need to. It's an important part of grieving." I reach up and run my fingers through her hair, holding onto one curl when I get to the end. "Amber and I got this news a long time ago, and I've had a lot of time to process and grieve. It's going to take time."

"Earlier today you talked about being in the water. You said it makes the world quiet and the distracting chaos and noise fall away. That you're able to better focus on the good things in life. I've never been able to do that. I've always either run away from my hard feelings or let them define me, but I don't want to do that anymore."

"No one can focus on *only* the good things. Life can be hard, and that can't be ignored. But I try to concentrate on the things that remind me life is still good. Look at me; I've lost both of my parents, I'm about to lose my only sister, and in the process, I will become a single parent. It's terrifying. I can't stop the hard things from happening, but I can't focus on them either. I find time to refocus and remember that life is still good, even when bad things are happening. It's about learning to breathe under water."

"Deke, you know I can't do that. Today is the first day I've ever felt the slightest bit okay in the water."

"*Breathing under water* can be your own way of doing exactly what you said you wanted: finding a way to focus on the good things in life." Her look tells me that she doesn't understand my meaning. "When life makes you feel like you're drowning and you don't know how you're even going to take your next breath, find what brings you peace—and that's your *water*. It's learning to breathe in the good despite the storms of life and how to not let those storms sweep you downstream." I pause to see if she understands.

CHAPTER 48

Samantha

BREATHING UNDER WATER . . .

My mind rolls over his explanation as I place my hand on his chest and feel his strong heart beating out a steady rhythm. I think back over all our interactions. He's never acted like he was a victim or to be pitied, even though his current circumstances are less than ideal. He makes joy and laughter thrive in his life, even when there is sadness hiding just under the surface. He's telling me that peace and happiness can be an intentional choice, but that I need to learn how to consistently choose them.

"Will you teach me to breathe under water?"

He cradles me into his chest and holds me. "Yes, and it can be whatever kind of water you need. It might take time, but we'll find it. Together."

We eventually go back into Deke's office, and I wait for him to collect some papers and his laptop. It's been a day of extreme emotions, and I'm trying to balance them out, but I'm failing. Am I supposed to be sad about Amber or happy about Deke? I don't know how two opposites can exist in the same space.

Somehow Deke reads my mind. "There were some amazing parts of today—try to remember those. Because at the end of the day, Amber wants us all to be happy."

I sigh a little. "It should be the happiest day of my life because I told the best man I know that I love him. Isn't it funny how the best days can also be the worst days?" I look up at him.

"It's the truth. And that's how we cope with everything. We take the good and the bad, even if they're both on the same day." He pulls me tight against his body and rests his chin on top of my head. "But I want you to know that you made me the happiest man on earth today. My Pepper loves me, and that's all I need." He starts rubbing his hands up and down my arms in slow, steady strokes. "And some day, my children will ask me when their mom fell in love with me, and I'll tell them that I don't know. I only know she told me when we were in the water."

"Deke . . ." I stare at him with wide eyes.

"Too much?" He tangles our fingers together. "I don't want to waste any more time hiding what I want. I've learned that you don't always have as much time with the people you love as you think you do." His hand moves up to my cheek, and I lean into it. "And when my children ask me when I began to fall in love with their mother, I'll tell them that it was the day I first called her . . . *Pepper*."

I take a step back and smile up at him because I don't believe him. "No. Deacon, that was maybe the third or fourth time you ever saw me! It was after the drunken night and my emotional meltdown in front of your office and . . ."

"It was the *second* time I saw you, and that's when it started for me. And it's been growing every day since then, and I plan on it growing a little more every day for the rest of my life."

"You can't be serious!"

"I am. I've never been so sure of anything as I am of you."

My body starts to tremble. "Deke, what exactly are you saying?"

He gives me a bemused smile. "I think you know what I'm saying. But do you really want me to say it out loud?"

All I can do is nod my head.

"Right now? In my office?"

I nod again.

"I'm saying that I have every intention of marrying you, if you'll have me." He moves his arms around me, and I feel his strong fingers gently press into my back. Heat spreads through my body like a wildfire out of control. "You're all I want, even though I don't deserve you." He leans down and kisses me with so much tenderness. So much feeling.

After a moment, I can't help but tease him just a little. "No flowers?"

He's stunned for a moment but recovers quickly. "You told me you don't like flowers." His eyes narrow.

"What about chocolates?"

"I've never seen you eat a single chocolate—and Amber keeps a box on the counter." He knows I'm playing some kind of game, and he's trying to figure out the rules.

My hands travel up his chest with intentional movements, taking their time and reveling in the feel of his body. "No keepsake for this moment? Like a ring?"

He picks me up so fast that I squeal and sets me on top of his desk, bracketing me in place with his hands on either side of me. Then he leans in, his mouth an inch away from my ear, and whispers, "I don't have a ring because I was planning on giving you at least a *little* more time, and I was hoping for a more romantic location than my office."

I let my shoulders droop dramatically to convey my message.

"Are you serious?" He lets out a small chuckle.

"Maybe I don't want to waste any more time either."

"But you'd like some kind of a keepsake? Even though this is turning into an incredibly spontaneous moment?" Now his eyebrows are raised and a little smirk plays on his lips.

"Maybe? I mean, a girl can dream, right?"

"How about a towel?" He bends down and picks up a towel from the floor.

"Is that the one you were wearing earlier?" He nods. "I will definitely dream about this."

"So, it works?"

I nod as I bite my lip, trying to stifle the grin wanting to take over my face.

His eyes dive into mine for a moment before he speaks. "Then, Samantha Turner, my Pepper-Girl, right now all I have is this ridiculous towel to give you, but I promise that I will give you the world if you would agree to be my wife, and . . ."

I pull his lips down onto mine—letting my kiss say YES—and he proceeds to thoroughly erase my memory of his less-than-manly scream.

In no time at all, there isn't a thing left on the desk. But I'm fairly certain Deke doesn't mind.

CHaPTer 49

Deacon

I STARE AT PEPPER'S phone in shock. "I didn't think you were serious."

"Now do you believe me?" Pepper speaks very matter of factly while we watch Steph, via Facetime, scream and jump around her room. "This is her go-to when she's really excited. Today she looks more like a prancing deer than usual." We're observing her in an almost clinical way.

"You've told me she does this, but I really thought it was more metaphorical and that she just fidgeted in her chair or something. I've got to give it to her," I nod my head in appreciation, "it's a really good prancing-deer impersonation." We Facetimed Steph to tell her we were engaged, and I've been completely mesmerized by her commitment to the prance.

Earlier this morning, Pepper called her law firm to let them know that she wouldn't be coming back. I told her that I would've loved to see the look on her boss's face as she got the news, but Pepper assured me that no part of Clarice's face would—or could—change.

Pepper wants to do some freelance work from the island, but not a lot. When Cooper and I sold our business, we made enough to never have to work again, so Pepper can be as picky as she wants with which clients she chooses.

After finishing up with Steph, we're planning to call Pepper's mom. Pepper has no idea what her mom will say or do, but she thought she should at least tell her.

My mind comes back to the present moment, and I see that Steph has collapsed on her bed and is holding her phone above her face, so it's looking down at her. "Dea-ntha. No, wait. What about Sam-eacon?" I have no idea what Steph is rambling on about. Is this girl code for something? She must see the look on my face and decides to put me out of my misery. "I'm trying out new couple names for you." She wags her eyebrows. "I could always use the name Samantha uses for you when we talk about you, but I don't think you want that said in public." The smile on her face is pure mischief.

"I'm aware, and approve, of Sexy-Man." I try to put a very masculine look on my face.

"No!" Steph is beside herself with joy. "She's been using a different one lately!"

"Wait." My gaze shoots to Pepper. "You have another name for me when you talk to Steph? How do I not know about this?" Pepper's face instantly reddens, and I must know. "Pepper," I fold my arms across my chest, all business, "if you don't tell me, I'll ask Steph, and it's a safe bet she's going to tell me."

"OKAY!" Pepper's blush seems to have spread over her entire body. When she leans over and whispers the name in my ear, a grin slowly covers my entire face. It's all I can do to not carry her to a secluded corner somewhere and show her exactly how I feel about it.

"Happy?" Pepper looks at me with a sense of fake exasperation.

"Quite frankly, I'm very happy about that. Feel free to use it at all times." I receive an elbow jab in the ribs.

Steph is simply observing us and loving it all. "My beautiful roomie is getting married. This is the furthest thing from an overdraft bank fee."

Steph has stopped all prancing and giggling and gives a sweet, sincere sigh. Right now, she is more stripped down than I've ever seen her. Her face shows a soft and sincere love for Pepper, and it makes me like her all the more. I know she was the only one there for Pepper for awhile, and I'll never be able to tell her how much that means to me—even though I didn't even know Pepper at the time.

Pepper and I share a look that carries an entire conversation, and I give her a small nod of agreement.

"Steph, I don't know what you're going to think about this, but the wedding's going to be in four weeks. Here on the island." We both wait, expecting some kind of dramatic reaction, but she's very calm and quiet. Pepper goes on, "Some people will think we're crazy because we haven't known each other that long, but we know we want this . . . and doing it sooner . . . well, we want to make sure we do it while Amber is still doing well." Pepper's voice gets quieter as she finishes.

Steph wipes a tear away. "That's perfect." Her voice is soft, and her love for both of us cascades through the phone like a waterfall and hits me square in the chest.

She's right; it really is perfect.

Steph wipes another tear before speaking. "Of course this needs to be done immediately. I'll book a flight today and be out next week to help with everything."

From Pepper's stories, I know enough about Steph to know that her zany, crazy side is only a small part of who she is. She is also a soft and tender woman with a heart of gold. She doesn't let many people see it, but I'm pretty sure I just did. No wonder Pepper trusted Steph so much these past few years.

While they keep chatting, I kiss Pepper on the cheek, give Steph a wave goodbye, and excuse myself to go into the kitchen.

Amber is there, looking out the window at the ocean. I step up beside her and wrap an arm around her shoulders. "Steph's the one that taught Pepper how to play volleyball."

"I know."

"She played Division I in college and started all four years and has been teaching Pepper to play the last two years."

"I know that too."

"Do you know more about my future wife than I do?" *Future wife*. I still can't believe how lucky I am.

"Maybe. I also know you don't deserve her." She smiles up at me and pokes me in the ribs.

"I know."

She's still smiling, but her face is clouded in sadness. "I don't want to go, but when the time comes," her voice breaks, "it won't be nearly as hard knowing that I'm leaving my little Lou to the two best people I know."

I pull my sister into an embrace, and we look out over the ocean for a long, long time.

THE END

EPILOGUE

Stephanie

Deke and Sam's wedding day

I'VE BEEN ON THE island the last few weeks to help with the wedding. Deke and Sam kept everything simple, but there are always things to take care of, so I jumped on a plane and have been staying with Sam in her condo. *Sidenote: I love that she's fine with everyone calling her Sam now.*

I thought that maybe Sam's mom—cow that she is—would step up and support her daughter, but true to form, she said she was too busy to come. That woman is the only blood family Sam has on earth, and she couldn't be bothered to show up! I want to punch her in the mouth till her teeth fall out! How someone as amazing as Sam came from that wretch of a human, I will never understand.

But I'm here because Sam is my girl, and I will protect her till my dying breath. She now has a found family who gives her love and support and all the things her mom should have. These people are incredible, and I'm thinking of asking them to adopt me too.

But now that the wedding day is here, everything is flying by, each moment passing so quickly that I barely have time to take it in. Early this morning we set everything up on the beach, which was basically twenty chairs—for their closest friends and the only family either of them have,

Amber and Lou—and a beautiful wooden arch dripping with cream, blush, and pink flowers. We were relying on Mother Nature to provide the rest of the backdrop. Looking outside, I can say that right now might be some of her best work! A gorgeously vibrant sunset is just beginning, with dazzling colors reaching across the horizon and into the sky. I can't think of a more picturesque setting.

Last week Sam asked me to walk her down the aisle, and I cried like a baby. Now here we are, only minutes from the wedding procession, and my tears haven't stopped. I'm just so happy that my Sam has someone like Deacon.

The wedding procession is only Lou, as the flower girl, and Sam and me. So it's just the three of us, standing in Sam's kitchen, when we hear the music begin.

Marco, a hulk of a man and one of Deacon's best friends, is playing an acoustic guitar. But the man is built to be an MMA fighter, not a wedding singer, so when the delicate sounds of his guitar first reach my ears, I could not be more shocked. I know a lot of musicians, and what he is doing isn't easy at all—yet he makes the music sound like it's floating on air. It's to his beautiful music that we send Lou out the door to begin marking Sam's path with rose petals.

Lou is dressed in a simple, cream-colored muslin dress with blush-colored flowers across the waist, and she has flowers twisted into her hair. She carries her basket of rose petals like it's made of glass, and when she gets to the beginning of the aisle, she starts individually handing the petals out instead of marking the path for the bride. It's so Lou that no one cares. Marco just keeps playing until Lou is done, at which time she flies into Deacon's waiting arms, gives him a big kiss, and then joins Amber where she is standing.

Now it's our turn. I look over at Sam, and she's absolutely breathtaking.

Her dress is an A-line silhouette that gently flares out from her natural waist, allowing the ivory-colored chiffon to flow effortlessly and Sam to have more ease of movement. The delicate shoulder straps highlight her neck and shoulders, while the deep, open back gives the dress an elegant sophistication. The dress has a small sweep train that will both glide perfectly on the sand and be easily bustled up for dancing later on. Her only accessories are simple pearl and diamond teardrop earrings—a gift from Deacon—and a crown of baby's breath woven into her gorgeous, red hair, which she wore down in her natural waves. Deacon's only request was that she be barefoot, so Sam has no shoes on, and her perfectly pedicured toes peek out when she walks. She looks so calm and stunning as we wait.

I can't help but ask, "How are you so calm, when I feel so nervous?"

She doesn't even look at me as we start walking out the door and onto the back deck. "You'll know some day, Steph. Someday there will be a man you love so much that walking toward him will feel like the safest and best thing you've ever done." She looks over at me, and the storm of hurt that has always raged somewhere in the back of her green eyes isn't there anymore. It's been replaced by something softer and calmer. I know she's still got that tiger inside that will take the world by storm, but now she won't be trying to prove anything to anyone while doing it.

As we move to the top of the stairs, Marco's guitar stops, everyone stands, and Marco starts a touchingly simple version of "Love" by John Lennon. When he starts to sing, my breath catches. How a man that looks like *that* can have a voice as smooth as John Legend, I will never know. It's the perfect song for this moment—Sam and I making our way down the stairs and walking barefoot across the sandy aisle.

My view is of the priest, Deacon, and Cooper, who is the best man. But all I can do is look at Deacon, standing there in his beige suit and white linen shirt with no tie. He can't take his eyes off Sam, and I don't think his look would be any different if she was wearing a flour sack. It's somehow the same look I've seen from him the last two weeks—because I don't think he's been able to take his eyes off Sam since I arrived—and also a new look I can't describe. This man loves my Sam so completely that it's almost overwhelming to watch sometimes.

The vows they exchange are simple, but flawless. With Amber and Lou standing by their sides, the ceremony is the single most beautiful thing I've ever seen.

I can only hope to find half of the love they have for each other—but with my track record, chances of even that are slim. Granted, I'm the one who keeps things shallow and uncommitted, but that's the way I need it. It's less complicated that way. So I'll continue to hide behind my crazy antics and enjoy life on my own.

The after party at Marco's is legendary. I've never seen a wedding reception like it. More food than could ever be consumed, an open bar with some of the best drinks I've ever tasted, really bad karaoke, and so much island dancing that I think my feet might fall off. And I don't know what the history is between Sam's friend Cheryl and the guitar-playing, bar-owning Marco, but *there's* a story that I would sell my favorite pair of Jimmy Choos to hear.

As much as Deacon couldn't take his eyes off Sam during the ceremony, he isn't taking his *hands* off her now. Wherever she is, he's standing right next to her, touching her. Her hands, her back, or her arms—he worships that woman, and she worships him right back.

Everyone on this island is fantastic. They're relaxed and fun and don't seem to take life too seriously. They don't seem jaded by . . . well . . . the things that people can get jaded by.

As I'm standing at the bar drinking something fruity and smooth, I look over to the dance floor and see the best man, Cooper, adorably dancing with Lou in his arms. The man is probably the most gorgeous person I've ever laid eyes on, but other than this one moment with Lou, I already can't stand him and his perfectly chiseled jaw and black, tailored suit. He almost missed the entire wedding—he showed up *three* hours before! Not what I would call best-man material. And there's something about his confident air that rubs me the wrong way. I've seen him dancing with almost every woman here, and they all seem to fall at his feet as soon as he flashes his brilliant smile. And those dimples should be categorized as weapons of mass destruction, because I'm sure they've destroyed their fair share of ladies' hearts. His smooth dance moves didn't repel any of the ladies, either, I'm sure. Whether the song is fast or slow, the man knows how to move on a dance floor. He has *player* written all over him, and nothing is worse than that. He's an expired coupon, and I'm not going to waste any more brain cells watching him.

After many hours of festivities, I'm back at Deacon and Amber's place—I guess it's now Deacon and Sam's place. Amber and Sam are just swapping condos. Amber and I will have finished moving everything around by the time Deacon and Sam get back from their honeymoon.

Turns out, Deacon is loaded and taking her on a no-expense-spared, ten-day honeymoon to a private island somewhere around Bora Bora. So I get to stick around and help Amber with Lou before I head back to Boston.

Right now I'm trying to unzip the dress I wore to the wedding. It's a strapless Prada that I saved for *way* too many months to buy, but this is the first event I've been able to wear it to. The dress is creamy silk with an ice-blue chiffon overlay, which does fantastic things for my skin tone. The silk hugs my curves in all the right places, while the chiffon gives the dress movement that makes me feel elegant—but also like a femme fatale.

Something on the dress is caught in one of my bra hooks, though, making it impossible to get the zipper down alone. I called loudly for

Amber, but she must not be back from the party because it's radio silence around here. I've been trying for at least ten minutes, but I can't see what is caught and don't want to risk tearing the dress. If I had an extra pair of eyes and hands, it would be easy—but I was not provided with either, so here I am.

I'm standing in the kitchen, looking out the back door at the moonlight reflecting off the ocean—all the while continuing to twist and contort my body.

How do I get out of this thing?

I hear the door open and let out a sigh of relief. "Thank heavens! I've been waiting for you and didn't know when you'd show up. Something is caught on one of my bra hooks, and I can't figure out how to get out of this dress. Can you undo my bra and free whatever is stuck?" Amber's warm fingers touch my back as she starts to examine the situation. My body gives a delighted reaction. "Hmmm. You have very warm hands. That feels nice." I fold an arm across the front of my dress, holding it up so that it won't fall to the floor when she frees the hook. Amber tugs a little more firmly on the back of my dress. "Be careful! This is my favorite bra—I think it's wicked sexy!"

The next moment, the fabric of my dress and hook of my bra are finally freed from their predicament—Hallelujah! I feel Amber leaning in toward my ear, and she whispers, "I can't disagree there. It really is wicked sexy." The warm baritone voice is not what I'm expecting.

I whip around to see *not* Amber but the best man! My hand immediately cocks back, and I land a solid slap across his face. "How dare you!"

He reaches up and touches his face, and I'm instantly annoyed at how little my slap seems to have affected him. "How dare I *what?*" His voice is casual and his smile dangerous. Like, *step away from the lit dynamite* kind of dangerous. When I'm too shocked to respond, his smile deepens and dimples pop out on each cheek. Dang. Triple that danger level. They are more lethal up close.

Slapping him was over the top, but he surprised me. It was a fight-or-flight impulse. I take a moment to compose myself, then spit out, "What kind of a man steps up to a complete stranger and unzips their dress?"

Nothing on his perfectly chiseled face changes except his eyes—which I wish weren't the color of a midnight sky. They spark with something. "Only a very chivalrous one." He gives the slightest shrug with his broad shoulder. "I came in, found you begging for assistance, and simply granted your wish."

Is it hot in here? Why is it so hot? And why is my heart rate elevated all of a sudden? I must be coming down with something. "I never asked you to undo my bra." I try to stand as straight and imposing as possible.

"Yes. You did."

I deflate slightly. "You're right." How could three little words completely disarm me like that? I'm furious with myself. "But I thought you were Amber."

"I thought that was probably the case." He takes a step closer while giving his head the slightest nod. "But what should I have done? Amber obviously wasn't coming anytime soon, and I could see that you were in distress. I thought it was the polite thing to do." He holds his hand out. "By the way, I'm Cooper. Cooper Mallory."

I let out an exaggerated guffaw. "*Cooper. Cooper Mallory?*" I repeat his name sarcastically. "Really? Who says their name like that? Do you think you're James Bond or something?"

He takes another step closer. So close that he easily places his hand on my forearm and leans in to whisper in my ear. "James Bond is a fictional character. I, on the other hand, am a very real man." He pulls back from my ear and drags his hand down my arm to take hold of my hand. Goosebumps erupt all over my skin like they're doing the wave at a sporting event. Without breaking eye contact, he lifts my hand, turns it over, and lays the softest, warmest kiss on my palm.

I am utterly speechless. This is the most arrogant man I've ever encountered. The most arrogant man—with the softest lips that have ever touched my skin.

He heads for the door but stops just before he leaves. "I almost forgot. I brought this by for Amber." He takes a small box out of his jacket pocket and puts it on the entryway table. Then he turns to face me again. "And please know that my very warm hands are at your disposal anytime." With that, he walks out of the condo.

I stand there, still speechless, holding up my dress with one arm as the other hangs limply by my side, while all the nerve endings in my palm are still celebrating like it's New Year's Eve. My jaw is gaping open, and I'm pretty sure my heart rate is over 175.

Amber chooses this moment to walk into the kitchen and look around. "Was that Cooper? I thought I heard his voice."

My head slowly rotates to her. "You've been home this whole time?" My voice is small, and I hate how affected it sounds.

"Sorry. Did you need me? I was in the bathtub listening to music with headphones on. Cheryl is keeping Lou overnight so that I can rest after a long day." She takes a good, long look at me. I don't know what's going through her mind, but I can tell I don't like it. "That *was* Cooper, wasn't it?" A grin slowly spreads across her face.

"Yes! Infuriating man!" I shuffle my feet a little and reach up to touch my hair for some unknown reason.

Amber starts chuckling, and it turns into a hardy laugh. As she turns to go back to her bedroom, she calls over her shoulder, "Oh, girl. You're in sooo much trouble.

Want to find out what's going on with Deacon, Sam, and Lou one year after the wedding and learn if Lou can keep a secret? Get the bonus epilogue when you sign up for my email list!

https://BookHip.com/JVRTLVZ

And stay tuned for Stephanie and Cooper's story:
Living on the Beach
Coming Spring 2024. You can preorder it now on Amazon:
https://a.co/d/gpi1PZi

Nicole loves to connect with her readers.

Feel free to message her on Instagram *(best way)* or to send her an email. And please consider following Nicole on Instagram or subscribing to her newsletter to be the first to find out about upcoming projects.

Email: authornjk@gmail.com

Newsletter: https://www.authornjk.com/newsletter

Website: https://authornjk.com

Interested in having your book club read *Breathing Under Water*?

Use the QR barcode to find book club questions.

(Warning: Questions contain spoilers. Please read after book is complete.)

Acknowledgements

First, I want to express gratitude for my Father in Heaven. He has blessed me with many things, including a love of being creative. He has continually carved out paths for me to use that love, and each has brought me so much joy.

Thanks to Boyfriend *(my husband)*, my real-life love story. His support, ideas, critiques, and everything else have meant the world to me during this process. I couldn't, and wouldn't, have done this without him.

Thanks to author Kortney Keisel for pushing me off the Cliff of Indecision and leading me to type those two magical words: *Chapter 1*. Kortney started out as an author I loved and has become a friend. Thanks for the invitation to join the *Author's Table*. (Now that I think about it, that is both figurative and literal.)

Thanks to author Dana "Leprechaun" LeCheminant for cheering me on at every moment of this journey. She was the second person to read the entire book, and her encouragement, support, and constructive feedback became essential to so much of this story. She's another author whom I'm so happy to call a friend.

Many other author-friends have been willing to answer all of the questions I've thrown at them. Their constant support and encouragement made this process so much easier than if I'd been navigating the waters on my own. So, additional thanks to Cindy Steel, Emma St Clair, Martha

Keyes, and Esther Hatch. Thank you so much! It's so fun to find out that authors you admire are also really nice, and super cool, people.

My beta readers' feedback and encouragement were *invaluable*. Thanks Kyle, Amber, Kaylee, Stephanie, Dana, Cindy, and Diane. Friendship is something I will never take for granted, and I'm blessed to have so many cheering me on.

Alyssa, you have been there from the very start. Every chapter. Every milestone. There have been hundreds of Marco Polo chats—*would it be an exaggeration to say thousands?*—centered around this book and this process. You're not just a book friend but a best friend.

You'll recognize the names of two of my other best friends: Stephanie and Cheryl. It's no coincidence that I have characters named after these two women. They have been there for me through thick and thin, and they mean the world to me. I will always love them. That being said, their fictional namesakes are nothing like the real things. For starters, I've never seen the real Cheryl pick up a volleyball or Stephanie prance like a deer.

There are other characters in this book, big and small, that are named after amazing people in my life: Amber, Lou, Mitch, Logan, Hunter, Eli, Heather West, King, Janet, and others. They say "it takes a village," and these are some of the amazing people in my village.

When writing a book, it's always nice when your daughter is an editor. She is brilliant at what she does! But even better, she's one of the best people I know. It's one of the coolest things on earth to have one of your children grow up to be one of your best friends. Thank you, Kaylee, for making my story *breathe*.

Last, but definitely not least, is *you*! Thank you for taking the time to add this story into your life. It means the world to me. If you know me, then you can probably see where I've written some of my soul's DNA into this story. You have a little piece of me with you now! Continue to read. Then spread your love of books everywhere you go.

ABOUT THE AUTHOR

NICOLE GREW UP IN the shadows of the Wasatch Mountains in Provo, Utah. Her young writing career began with plays, song lyrics, and variety shows, all of which her family and friends were happy to support (translation: forcibly persuaded to both pay money for and sit through).

After her young entrepreneurial days ended, she married her college sweetheart, *aka: Boyfriend*, who provides the inspiration for all her swoon-worthy leading men. They raised their two girls and two boys in Phoenix, Arizona, then St. George, Utah, where they still live.

She loves randomly breaking into show tunes, spontaneous Disney trips, sharing her faith and love of God, woodworking in her garage-turned-shop, and reading well-behaved books, and she is rarely seen without a Swig in hand. She's Marvel over DC, beach over mountains, Colin Firth over Matthew Macfadyen, and salty over sweet—but don't ask her to choose between *Harry Potter* and *Lord of the Rings*.

Nicole tries to infuse each of her stories with aspects from her own love story, including witty banter, laugh-out-loud moments, and sizzling chemistry. She'll always keep the kisses steamy and the bedroom door closed.

Made in the USA
Middletown, DE
14 October 2023

40536701R00156